the

SPOOKSHOW
HALF-BOYS AND GYPSY GIRLS

BOOK FIVE

TIM MCGREGOR

Perdido Pub
TORONTO

ISBN-13: 978-1522803171

ISBN-10: 1522803173

True love is like ghosts, which everybody talks about but few have seen.

– Francois de La Rochefoucauld

CHAPTER 1

BILLIE CULPEPPER DREAMT that she was being split apart like a wishbone. Pulled in opposite directions by warring forces until a tiny crack was heard and she ripped down the middle.

Another nightmare, the terrors now a constant part of her life that maligned her sleep each night, leaving her drained when the sun came up. The new normal. Duality exists in all things. Love and hate, life and death, and so on. Billie had begun to think of herself in the same way. There was life before the spookshow and there was life after. The dividing line was a muggy night in June when she had been knocked into the cold water of a Great Lake and nearly drowned.

Drowning was what she dreamt of this night, crashing under the inky waves and rolling about in the dark water. Disoriented, she couldn't tell which way was up and feared she was swimming in the wrong direction toward the muddy bottom. Gasping when she broke the surface, her hands clawed at the concrete embankment but its surface was slimy with algae and she could not latch on to anything.

"Take my hand."

A voice from above. A powerful grip locked onto her wrist. Looking up she saw Mockler reaching down from the steep embankment, straining to pull her out.

She lifted clean out of the cold water but something tugged on her ankle and down she went again. She didn't want to see what it was but instinct won out and when Billie looked down, she saw the dead shimmering under the lapping waves, their pale hands reaching out for her. A watery horde of the departed pulling her back down.

"Don't let go!" she cried, clinging to the man above.

Her fingers latched tighter to Mockler's arm but she felt herself slipping through his grip. The dead things in the water were legion and Mockler was outmatched in this grisly tug of war. The faces of the dead lifted from the waves and some she recognized. Evelyn Bourdain was there, her mouth twisted into raw fury, and there was the Undertaker Man with his empty sockets for eyes. Frank Riddel, her own father, clawing her down into the cold waves of the harbour. Bobbing to the surface last was John Gantry, the flesh of his pale face pockmarked and ravaged as if eaten away by small fish. She felt the Englishman's cold fingers latch onto her neck and pull her down below the surface. And then she heard nothing at all.

Another voice.

"Billie. Wake up, honey."

Her aunt, gently shaking her awake. She wasn't at the harbour, she was back in her old room in Aunt Maggie's house. Safe and sound.

"You're all right," her aunt cooed. "Just a bad dream."

Billie croaked up odd sounds until her vocal cords functioned. "Did I wake you?"

"You were making an awful racket," Maggie said, smoothing the hair from her niece's eyes.

"I'm sorry."

"Don't be. Was it about your mom again?"

"No." Billie sat up and rubbed her eyes. "It was just crazy stuff. You know what dreams are like. They never make any sense."

"You've had them every night since you've been here. That worries me."

"Dreams can't hurt you."

"It's the broken sleep that worries me. You can only go so far before that starts to affect you." Maggie patted her hand. "Do you want anything? Some warm milk?"

"Yuck. I'm fine. Go back to bed."

Maggie lingered a moment longer to ensure the young woman was fine before going back to her own room. Billie laid her head on the pillow feeling exhausted but alert. She had been at her aunt's house for three days now. Three days since the funeral. The time had passed quietly and without incident, something for which Billie was grateful after the mayhem that had preceded it. Details mattered here, the small everyday things like making a meal or raking leaves or taking a walk on the soggy beach as the November winds sought to push one over. The only down side was Mockler. They had texted and spoken on the phone every day since she'd been in Long Point but the communication paled to the real thing. She missed him and wished he was here.

Listening to the wind outside the window rattle the drybone branches of the tulip trees, Billie decided that it was time to go back. The grieving was still raw but it was settling into more of a constant strain rather than the acute pain of earlier. Life goes on whether one is ready for it or not. It was time to go home.

She closed her eyes and something small and fragile fluttered in her belly at the thought of seeing the detective again.

~

The ground shuddered as the bulldozer rumbled in like a tank, its blade plowing a load of earth and broken timbers before it. Detective Ray Mockler stepped out of the way of the grinding metal treads and watched the dozer push its load into an enormous furrow in the earth. Around him moved a small team of men in safety vests and hardhats, some with an arm propped on the spade they held and others warming their hands over a cup of coffee that he had provided. Earlier in the morning, he had phoned the foreman to tell him he would be on-site today to see the ground clearing and offered to pick up coffee on the way. He'd brought donuts too, which the crew were happy to see.

Over the roar of the bulldozer came the crack and pop of timbers breaking and the chalky snap of bricks tumbling together as debris was plowed into the crater. It was a burial of sorts, one that Mockler had wanted to witness with his own eyes.

"You ever work construction?" The foreman waved as he drew up alongside Mockler. A broad faced man with thick forearms, he smiled at the detective.

"One summer," Mockler said. "Back in college. Why?"

The foreman shrugged. "Just wondered what it was you wanted to see. We usually don't get much of an audience for moving earth around."

"It's a loose end in an investigation. I want to see it tied up." Mockler nodded at the vast trench before them. "When did the fire investigators finish up?"

"Late yesterday. He said they'd done all they could, given the unsafe conditions. Did they figure out how it started?"

"Not yet," Mockler replied. "Probably just kids messing about."

The foreman nodded his head in agreement. "I'm surprised it didn't happen sooner. Hell, I used to sneak up here as a kid."

"You did?"

"Back in high school. There were so many stories about this place. We came up on a dare, broke some windows. It was spooky even then."

Mockler's eyebrow went up. "What do you mean *spooky*?"

"It felt weird. I'm sure we had just psyched ourselves out with all the ghost stories the way kids do but, man, we didn't spend too long inside it. We smashed some windows, to say we did it, then took off."

"Everyone seems to have a story about this place."

"Well there won't be anymore new stories," the foreman said as they watched the dozer push more earth into the pit. "It's just rubble now."

"I hope so."

"I ought to get back." The foreman touched his hat and stepped away. "Thanks for the coffee, detective."

Mockler waved goodbye and leaned back against the fender of his car. He watched the crew work although there was little deviation to the routine, the bulldozer plowing the debris into the pit and covering it all with the sandy earth of the escarpment. He had needed to see this, to witness the burial of the awful Murder House and its terrible secrets. Although it was still a crime scene, the fire had gutted the house to the ground and the resulting ruins were unsafe to work in. Once the crew were done here, the former grand manor would be buried for good and, with time, the terrible legacy of Evelyn Bourdain would be forgotten.

~

Kaitlin startled when the plate hit the floor. It was perched on the edge of the counter when Kyle, clumsy and near-sighted in the morning, had knocked it over reaching for a cup. The piercing crack of china shattering against the floor almost stopped her heart.

Her reaction, while not typical, was gut-level. Shrieking, she had instantly dropped to the floor and covered her hands over her head.

"Whoops," grumbled Kyle.

Kaitlin peeked out from under the breakfast table. "What was that?"

"Dinner plate. One of the good ones too. Sorry." Kyle picked up the shards from the floor. "Jesus, you jumped a mile there."

"You gave me a heart attack!"

"Easy," he said. "It was just an accident."

"Why are you so clumsy?" Kaitlin fumed, crawling out. "God!"

"It was just a plate. No big deal."

Kaitlin straightened up but her nerves were fried and tingling. She held her hands out before her. "I'm shaking."

Kyle dumped the pieces in the trash and came around to her. "What is up with you? You've been so jumpy lately."

"How can I not be with you trashing the house every five minutes?"

He backed away. "Forget I asked."

She was still fuming when he went to fetch the broom. She

knew she had overreacted and should probably say something to mitigate the temper she'd unleashed on him but her anger was blowing too hot for that. He was right, she had been on edge for days now. Snapping and surly. She blamed it on the lack of sleep. Each night was a tortured churn of anxieties that kept her awake for hours. Was the stove turned off? The front door locked? If a fire broke out, did she know what to do? If an intruder broke in, could she call the police in time?

The crisis scenarios were endless, one fear tumbling into the next and each one upping her pulse until she saw the window brighten with dawn. She never used to be such a worry-wart. Now it was all she did, speculating over potential life-and-death disasters that lurked everywhere. Strange rituals had crept into her daily routine too, like triple-testing the lock before going to bed or checking the stove again and again to make sure the burner wasn't left on and leaking natural gas into the house. Asking Kyle to do it didn't help. He dismissed her fears as paranoia, which infuriated her.

Slowing her breathing to soothe her frayed nerves, Kaitlin resolved to apologize to Kyle for her outburst but the crack of another dish breaking against the floor fried her nerves all over again.

"Whoops."

CHAPTER 2

THE PHOTO ALBUM was old, its spine cracked and the corners frayed. It smelled faintly of mildew from being stored in her aunt's small garage for so long. She tried to remember the last time she had perused through its pages of old Polaroids. Not since her teens when she and Maggie and Uncle Larry had lived in Poole. The past had been weighing heavily on her since the funeral and when she rose early this morning, she remembered the photo album. Shivering in the cold garage, she had searched through the shelves of old ice-skates and chipped Christmas ornaments until she found it.

Nostalgia tugged hard revisiting these old photographs, grief rising to the surface again. Most were typical shots of holidays and birthdays but there were some she barely remembered. A picture of her first day of kindergarten, standing knee-high between her mom and aunt, both women beaming at the camera. The little girl with a gap between her bottom teeth. She studied the faces of both women. In picture after picture, there remained a telling contrast between the smiles of the sisters. Where Aunt Maggie's was big and full, her eyes squinted into arcs, her mother's was less by half. Never a full beam like her younger sister, her eyes open, as if she wouldn't commit to a full smile. There was a sense of wariness or reserve in every photograph of Mary Agnes Culpepper, no matter what the occasion. None of that surprised Billie. It was just startling to see the contrast laid so bare in this history told in pictures.

"Morning." Aunt Maggie chimed, stepping into the kitchen. She cinched her housecoat tight and yawned. "How long have you been up?"

"A while now," Billie replied. "Couldn't sleep. The coffee's made."

Maggie took a stool at the counter as Billie slid her a cup, its steam curling into the air. "That was quite the nightmare you had. Did you fall back to sleep?"

"Not really."

Maggie saw the photo album and pulled it closer. "Where did you find this?"

"In the garage. I wanted to see it again."

"Oh my God," Maggie sighed, pointing to a picture of Billie before a Christmas tree. "Look at that little face. Gosh, you were a cute kid."

"Stop." Billie turned the pages. "There's a picture I wanted to ask you about. Here. Who's this woman?"

Maggie reached for her glasses. The photograph Billie pointed to showed herself and Mary Agnes seated next to an old woman in a lawn chair. The two sisters, who looked to be in their twenties, were a stark contrast to the frail and wrinkled woman seated between them.

"That was Aunt Elsie. God, I haven't thought about her for ages."

"She looks like you and mom. Your dad's side of the family?"

"Yes, another Culpepper," Maggie said. "Our dad's older sister. She was a character, she was. Your mom was fond of Aunt Elsie, although we didn't see much of her. She died just before you were born."

"Did she live far away?"

"No. She and our dad quarreled. Aunt Elsie was different. I guess that's why she and your mother got along so well."

"Why didn't they get along?"

Maggie adjusted her glasses for a closer look at the photograph. "Dad said it was because she was a bad Catholic but there was more to it. Aunt Elsie had a bit of the spookiness in her. She used to do Tarot cards, hold seances and the like. That was the real reason we didn't see her. It annoyed our father to no end that Mary Agnes and his sister got along like thieves."

"She was a medium?" Billie uttered in surprise. "Just like mom."

"Mmm," Maggie confirmed. "A number of them were, on the

Culpepper side. It caused a lot of riffs between families. Needlessly, really. But those were different times."

"Why? Because it scared them?"

"Partly. But there was more to it. The Culpeppers were staunch Catholics. At least one of every generation were in the clergy. It was a much more significant thing in those days, the faith. The ones who dabbled in seances were considered a disgrace to the family."

Billie traced a finger over the image of her great aunt. "So it runs in the family. Like a hereditary disease? Beyond just me and mom. How come I never knew?"

"Because it was hushed up and hidden, I'm afraid. It tore families apart. That's just how it was dealt with back then."

"And that makes it okay?" Billie asked. She hadn't meant to frost her tone. It just came out that way.

"I'm not condoning it, honey. I'm just saying that that was how they dealt with it."

"But you never told me about it."

"I hoped you didn't have it. Especially with your mom gone." Maggie sighed and slipped the glasses from her nose. "You're still angry with me about that?"

"No," Billie said. "I didn't mean to snap at you."

Maggie slid from the stool and turned to the counter. "I'll start breakfast."

"I'll just have toast. I'm going to get on the road soon."

"You're leaving already?" A note of sadness in the older

woman's voice. "So soon?"

"It's time. You sit. I'll make breakfast this morning."

Her aunt protested but Billie made her sit and took down the pan from its hook. "Do you want the usual?"

"Please." Maggie watched her niece work, then she tilted her head as if a thought had just occurred to her. "Do you wonder if you'll pass it on?"

"Pass what on?"

"Your talent. To your own children."

The egg in Billie's hand slipped out and cracked against the counter. "Never thought about it. I haven't even thought about having kids. Let alone that."

"Of course. You're too young to think about kids but that might change."

The genie had slipped out of the bottle. Billie couldn't stop thinking about it now. "How weird is that idea? That I might pass it on to my own kid?"

"They'll be all right," Maggie said. "They'll have you to teach them."

Billie dismissed the notion as ludicrous as she wiped up the mess but, once flushed out in the open, the idea wouldn't stop flitting through her thoughts.

~

The apartment looked like a bomb had gone off.

Arriving home after the two hour drive from the northern shore of Lake Erie, Billie walked through the door to find a disaster waiting for her. During the hectic aftermath of the horrors at the Murder House and the hastily arranged funeral of her mother's remains, she hadn't paid much attention to the state of the tiny abode she called home. The sofa bore a nasty slash mark through it and the antique table that she never used tilted under one broken leg, both casualties of a brawl between Mockler and John Gantry.

The late John Gantry, she reminded herself.

Dropping her bag at the door, Billie sank onto the sofa and wondered if the wily Englishman was really gone. During the mayhem at the old house, Gantry had been arrested and locked up on a murder charge. While there, he had been stabbed in the back by another inmate and pronounced dead. It was hard to believe that a simple prison brawl could have taken the shifty Brit down, especially since his body vanished from the morgue the following day.

Billie sighed. How utterly messed-up was her world when someone she knew got stabbed in prison and then pulled a vanishing act? All occurring while she herself was being threatened by a ghostly woman who had wanted to possess her completely. Is this what her gift, her ability to speak to the dead, was doomed to provide? A macabre life of insane torments? Who in their right mind would pass this on to a child?

A child.

Billie sat up and cocked her ear to listen. The apartment was quiet, the only sound was a dull burr from her neighbour downstairs who kept his radio on day and night. There was no odd rattling from the next room, no scraping sounds overhead from something scuttling across the ceiling.

"I'm home," she called out to the destroyed flat. "Where are you?"

More silence. No legless figure crept out of the shadows, no mute phantom of a child sprang onto the arm of the sofa. Half-Boy wasn't home. Which was odd, since he had been an almost constant companion since Billie's latent psychic abilities had bloomed back during the humid swelter of summer.

She didn't realize how much she had missed him until he failed to materialize. Had she taken him for granted? Or had something happened? The last time she had seen him was in the cemetery, just after her mother's casket went into the ground. For a brief moment she thought she had glimpsed her mother there, far away among the tombstones, overseeing the internment of her mortal remains. And alongside the shimmering silhouette of her mother was the small form of the boy whose legs had been cruelly amputated. Had he moved on, crossing over to the other side for good? Was there some connection between her mother and Half-Boy or had the whole thing been a mirage brought on by grief?

She keyed Mockler's number but the call clicked over to his answering service. That meant he was on the job and couldn't pick up the phone. She hung up without leaving a message and sent him a text stating simply that she was home now. Uncertain if she should close the message with an XO, Billie omitted any sign-off. She still didn't know what to make of the whole situation with the detective. Was this the start of something serious or had they just tumbled together briefly during a harrowing time for both of them? They had spent one night together in a dingy motel in her hometown and remained in contact through the mayhem that followed and the subsequent funeral. Mockler had helped her arrange a burial plot and service. They continued to text when she retreated to Aunt Maggie's for some peace. Not the most romantic beginning to a new relationship but it had been unique.

The problem was, she thought as she propped her feet onto the battered coffee table, was that she was sick to death of unique, of weird. What she wanted most of all was a simple date with the man she'd crushed on for the last few months. Dinner, maybe a movie. Seeing a band play at one of the watering holes she and her friends frequented. Something almost boring. Or, at the very least, free of any hint of the macabre or the paranormal. Was that too much to ask?

Dropping her feet to the floor, Billie rose and scanned the mess around her. Dealing with the catastrophe seemed too daunting. What she wanted right now was to get on her bike and clear her head.

CHAPTER 3

THE VIDEO FOOTAGE from the security cameras was grainy, monotonous and, for the most part, utterly useless. Shot from two angles, the first camera captured the interior lobby of the city morgue while the second security camera covered the loading bay outside the building. There was just over six hours of footage to cover, from the time the last morgue attendant closed up for the night in question until 5:06 AM the next morning when the attendant arrived to unlock the doors. Six hours of static shots of an empty corridor and a quiet loading dock and nothing happened.

Mockler stretched his back, grumbled under his breath and set the footage back to the beginning and played them again, this time increasing the playback speed to half. There had to be something he missed the first time around. Dead men don't just rise up from the slab and saunter out of the morgue.

Do they?

In any other situation that would be true but the dead man in question was one John Herod Gantry, a murder suspect in one homicide here in Hamilton and another in London, England. He had been arrested by Mockler's partner and killed by another inmate during a fire inside the Hamilton-Wentworth Detention Centre. Before Mockler could identify the body, the remains had vanished while he and Billie were trapped in the Murder House. That, he knew, could not be a coincidence. So here he sat, going over the CCTV footage from the morgue. There was nothing to see, just the static, unchanging angles on an empty corridor and the roll-up door in the back where the meatwagon pulled up.

"Jesus Christ, Mock. Give it up already."

Mockler spun his chair at the voice behind him. "Give up? I can't even start on this."

Detective Odinbeck tossed his jacket onto the back of his chair and shook his computer awake. "You're starting to obsess over that footage, bud. There's nothing to see."

"True," Mockler said. "But it's what I don't see that's relevant."

"You wanna put that in English?"

"Take a look at this." Mockler turned to his screen and slid the counter forward on the playback bar. "Nothing changes all night until this part. At 4:23 AM."

Odinbeck leaned in to the screen as Mockler hit play at the designated time. The grainy feed displayed the corridor and the exterior bays then the footage scrambled, first the shot in the corridor and then the angle on the outside doors. It lasted no more than two minutes, all snowy static before the image resumed and everything appeared the same as before.

Mockler looked at his partner expectantly. Detective Odinbeck blinked his eyes. "What am I looking for?"

"Didn't you see it?"

"The static?"

"Yes," Mockler said. "First the corridor, then the exterior."

"It's static, buddy. Old cameras. That's all."

Mockler leaned back in his chair. "Something happened during those two snowy parts. It had to."

Odinbeck plunked a hand on the younger detective's shoulder. "You're seeing things that aren't there."

"I've been though the tapes twice. Nothing happens except for this."

Odinbeck sighed. "Okay. What do you think happened?"

"Somebody stole the corpse during the static. There's no other explanation."

The older detective tapped a finger against his lips in contemplation. Then he looked up, bright-eyed. "Or your friend Gantry got and walked out of the morgue on his own?"

"Thanks, Odin." Mockler tossed his pencil at him. "That's helpful."

Odinbeck grinned. One of his few true pleasures was winding up his younger partner. "Do you want some advice? Let it go, man. There's nothing more to be done until some new info pops up. Don't pull another Ahab."

"I'm not. I just need to know what happened."

"Mock, look at me. You obsessed over this guy when he was alive. Now you're doing it when he's dead. Let it go. Aren't you glad to be shed of all the spooky nonsense?"

Mockler chewed on the question. The camera footage kept playing on his monitor. "Like you wouldn't believe."

"Then turn it off and forget it. Focus on something you can actually do. Like the open files on our desks." Odinbeck picked over the paperwork crowding his desktop and pulled up a file. "Like this. The two fugitives on the loose."

Mockler killed the video, turning to peer at the file. "Which two?"

"The ones who attacked Billie's friend in the hospital. Tweedledee and Tweedledum."

"Justin Burroughs and Owen something-or-other."

Odinbeck checked the document. "Rinalto. They're still on the lam."

The two young men in question were part of the awful business at the house Mockler had watched bulldozed. They had tried to kill Kaitlin Grainger in her hospital room. Later they abducted Billie and took her back to the old house. Both were enthralled to something dark within the Murder House. "Okay," he ceded. "Let's focus on those two."

"Atta boy," Odinbeck grinned. "You should be grateful for this."

"Grateful?"

"For once we're not dealing with a murder file. Just plain old fugitives on the run." The older detective dug out the photographs they had of the two men in question. "Beavis and Butthead don't look like the brightest turnips in the patch. How hard is this gonna be?"

Mockler took the pictures from the other man and studied the faces of the two men. Odinbeck was right, neither of them looked particularly intelligent. Mouth-breathers with a dull glaze over their eyes as if they were high. The duo had been missing for almost two weeks now. They would turn up somewhere. If, the detective cautioned himself, they weren't already dead.

~

The man in the woods ran for his life. Crashing through the underbrush in the dark, his skin was flayed by spindly branches and cold thickets. His bare feet crunched over a carpet of pine needles, sharp twigs fallen from the trees. His foot snagged on the exposed root of a hemlock tree and he tumbled down hard, rolling through the deadfall of late autumn. He was cold and bleeding but he held his breath to listen.

He could hear them out there in the dark. Footfalls crunching through the woods, coming after him. The sounds were faint, fading off in the background under the sound of his own panting. How many were there? How close? It didn't matter. Keep moving.

Pitching forward, he pressed on, but the ground was uneven and in the darkness he fell again and didn't get up. Every square inch of his body was in pain. How much blood had he lost in the last few day? They had beaten him, his abductors in the hooded masks. They had cut his flesh with razors and pricked it with needles. They had shaved his head with dull shears and kept him starved and, thus, weak. It was hard to think straight.

What had happened to his friend? They had taken him too, hadn't they? Was he dead?

The noise of his pursuers filtered through the dark, stomping onward and getting closer. He tried to get up but his strength was gone. The ground was wet and it was cold but he lay down on his side and curled his legs into his chest. If he remained still, his abductors might pass right over him. The ground smelled of decaying vegetation and rich, loamy earth. Something crawled over his neck, making his flesh tingle but he made no move to brush it away.

Silence. He heard the wind in the branches overhead, but nothing more. Had he fallen asleep? Had his ruse worked, hiding in the leaves until the men passed over him and moved on?

"Little rabbit," whispered a voice in the dark.

The pain exploded him awake. A hard boot to the base of his spine. The running man looked up and went blind as the beam of a flashlight whited-out his vision. He tried to crawl away but another heavy boot stomped him down, flattening his belly to the wet ground.

"Fast little rabbit," said a voice.

"He wasn't starved enough," said another voice. Both male, both without pity. "He had enough strength to bolt."

The panting man felt himself hoisted from the ground by powerful hands. He tried to speak, to beg, but all that came out was a blubbery sob.

"We went too easy on him," came one of the voices. "We won't make that mistake again."

Dragged roughshod through the brush, the shivering man was hauled back through the woods like the prize carcass of some dead game animal. A five-point buck downed by hunters.

Antlers, the man thought as his legs were scratched raw by the thicket. He remembered seeing antlers in the place of his capture. Or were they horns?

CHAPTER 4

THE DAMAGE TO the shop on James Street wasn't as bad as Billie remembered. The glass in the front door had already been replaced and the shelving ripped from the walls was salvageable. The last time Billie had seen the Doll House, it looked like something out of a war zone. Aside from the visible damage done to her friend's shop, something else seemed off when she came through the newly-glazed door. The familiar ring overhead was missing. The antique bell over the door had been ripped down during the attack. It sat just inside the display window, bell and hanger, waiting to be put back up.

"Jen?" Billie called out. The shop appeared abandoned. With no bell over the door, there was no way to announce visitors to the shop.

Jen came out of the back room with a cordless drill in one hand. Her face lit up when she saw the visitor. "Billie. You're back!"

The hug was quick but warm. There had been some enmity between the two for the last month and Billie hadn't been sure what the reception would be like but Jen beamed her bubbly smile, genuinely glad to see her.

"How was your stay at Maggie's?" Jen asked.

"Quiet. Maggie took care of me, as always."

"You should have called to tell me you were coming back. I would have cleaned up instead of looking like this." Here, Jen took a step back to show off her attire. Loose jeans and her boyfriend's old sweater, both speckled white with primer paint. More of the paint dotted her hands, a smudge of it on her chin.

"You've been busy," Billie said.

"I wouldn't say busy. I couldn't bear to even look at it for a week. Dad finally forced me to face the damage and figure out how to repair it."

"That must have been heart-breaking, seeing it like this." Billie looked past her friend to the doorway of the back room. "Is your dad here?"

"No. He went back home yesterday."

"That's too bad. I like when your dad's here." Billie reached out and took her friend's hand. "Are you holding up okay? Since, you know, the attack?"

"I am now. I cried myself silly, thinking I was ruined." Jen shrugged and smiled. "But that wasn't doing me any good. So, here we are. It's almost like starting over."

Billie looked the space over. The long south wall was patched and primed, ready for colour. Shelves were piled on the floor, waiting to be put up again. The tables and racks were pushed against the north wall of exposed brick. The old church pew, salvaged from a flea market in Guelph, appeared unharmed. "How bad was the damage?"

"The fire wasn't too bad; only one rack of clothes was actually burned, but the stink of it got into everything. I had to chuck every garment that was on display, even the stuff that wasn't touched by the fire."

"Ouch. That's a lot of inventory to lose."

"It is," Jen agreed. She nodded at the bare wall. "I'm hoping the new paint will cover up the smoke smell."

"Are you going with a different colour for it?" The wall had been hot pink with accents of black. Billie loved the colour scheme.

"Nope. I want it exactly as it was before, the whole thing. When people walk back in here, I want it to look like nothing happened."

"Good. The pink and black rocks."

"You know what's really amazing? The people who've stopped in just to say hi or ask if I needed help. Customers, people who've shopped here. A few of them made me cry they were so sweet."

Smiling, Billie watched her friend's eyes become dewy. "I'm not surprised. People love your shop."

"Help me straighten this drop cloth, would you?" Jen nodded

at the sheet laid out to protect the floor from paint drops. "It keeps getting bunched up."

Pulling both ends, they stretched the cloth flat and weighted the corners with paint cans. Billie looked up. "Where's Adam?"

"He had to go to work, which is probably for the better. He just bitches a lot when I ask him to help out."

"I'm here," Billie said. "What do you want done?"

"Are you sure? I was going to put the colour on the wall, but you'll get your clothes messy."

Billie gave a wave of dismissal and reached for a paint can. "Hell, a touch of pink paint might spruce up my wardrobe." Prying the lid off, she breathed in the smell of wet paint. "Do you want to roll or do the trim?"

"I'll start the trim, you roll. We can swap out halfway." Jen tossed her a fresh roller pad and then looked for the small paintbrush. "We should go out tonight, now that you're back."

"I'd love that." Billie cautiously poured the bright pink paint into the roller tray. "Have you seen Tammy or Kaitlin?"

"They've both been by to help out. Even the messy stuff when we threw all the inventory out. You wouldn't believe how bad it reeked."

Billie dipped the roller into the thick paint. "Are they doing okay?"

"Kaitlin seems a little subdued."

"Subdued?"

"Quiet and a bit blue. Not herself, anyway." Jen dipped her

brush into the paint, scraped off the excess and went to work on the trim. "I think the hospital stay brought her down."

"Sure," Billie added, although she knew that Kaitlin had suffered much more than that. "I'm sure it's humbling to be stuck in one too long."

"So," Jen said. "What's the story with your boyfriend?"

"I don't have a boyfriend, remember?"

"You know who I mean," Jen teased. "Your detective friend. Mockler."

Billie tried to sound nonchalant. "Nothing. We talked on the phone when I was at Maggie's."

"Right. All very casual, huh?" Jen smirked at her friend. "You should invite him out with us tonight."

"I think I will," Billie said. If, she thought, she ever got a hold of him. The detective still hadn't returned her text. He's just busy, she told herself. Or he changed his mind completely and never wanted to hear from her again. The jury was still out.

~

They commandeered a table near the back, everyone squeezing in as people arrived. Jen and Tammy were already there, along with Jen's boyfriend Adam. Kaitlin and Kyle showed up just after Billie did. Hugs and well-wishes all around, everyone a little cautious around Billie as if she was made of glass. It wore off by the second round and the ladies shifted back into their usual demeanour. While Jen remained chatty and spirited, Tammy seemed subdued and distracted. Not her usual boisterous self, her conversation reduced to responses clipped and bored. Adam, aloof as always, barely spoke a word to Billie. She could only guess that he still blamed Billie for the damage done to Jen's shop. He had been hurt in the attack, she reminded herself, so perhaps he had good reason to be rude. So be it.

Kaitlin was happy to see her. Like Tammy, she seemed a bit muted. Her smile was still bright but the wattage in her eyes was dimmed, a certain lethargy to her movements. As the evening wore on and people circulated around the table, Kaitlin scooted to the empty chair beside Billie and slid her arm around hers.

"I'm glad you're back," Kaitlin said, leaning close to be heard above the noise of the bar. "Our little circle isn't quite the same when you're not here."

Billie looked at her. "Flatterer."

"Three just seems like an odd number. Jen acts like nothing happened and Tammy doesn't want to talk much."

Billie nodded. Kaitlin was referring to recent events. The fire at the old house. It was no surprise that Jen had rationalized it away and Tammy wanted to forget about it. Who could blame them? She herself didn't want to talk about it. "How are you healing up?"

"Better." Kaitlin's hand automatically covered the spot on her abdomen where she had been injured. "It'll be a while before I can hit the gym again, but it's almost back to normal."

"You hate the gym."

"Then, I'm not missing much, am I?" Kaitlin gave Billie's wrist a squeeze. "I thought you'd bring a date tonight."

"So did I," she said, trying to mask her disappointment. "He's busy."

"Have you seen him since you got back?"

"Not yet," Billie said.

"He couldn't spare a minute at least? That seems odd."

Billie smiled weakly. Kaitlin had articulated her own thoughts on the matter. Mockler had called earlier only to say that he couldn't get away. She offered to go to him, even if it was only a minute or two, but he had nixed the idea. Concealing her disappointment, she told him where she was meeting the ladies should he get away early. Mockler said he would drop by if he could, but didn't sound hopeful. Doubt crept in the moment she got off the phone, questioning the whole thing. Maybe it had just been a fluke, she and Mockler, both of them caught up in the chaos of the moment. Self-doubt, she reminded herself, was her Achilles' heel and Billie took a page from Jen's playbook to rationalize it out. This is what it is like dating a cop. A homicide detective no less. He was busy, that's all. Get used to it.

Changing subjects, Billie nodded to Kyle across the table. "What about you two? How are the wedding plans?"

"Kyle's being a dick," Kaitlin replied with a dismissive flourish.

"Did anything happen while I was gone?"

"No. It's not all him. My nerves are shot. No patience these days. So, we fight."

"You two always bicker." Billie looked at Kyle again. Like his girlfriend, he too seemed changed. Smaller somehow, as if he had lost a few inches of height. For as long as Billie had known Kaitlin, she and Kyle had been together. It was hard to imagine one without the other.

"I'm still not sleeping."

"The nightmares?"

Kaitlin nodded her head slowly. She shrugged, but her eyes were glassy. "I still dream about her."

There was no need to ask to whom she referred. Billie didn't want to speak her name or ever think about it again. She wanted it behind her. "It will go away," she comforted her friend. "It'll take time, but it will go away."

"There's still so much of it I don't understand." When Kaitlin looked up, there was pleading in her eyes. "I need to figure it out. Maybe we can sort it out together. You know? What happened to us."

"I can't," Billie said. "Not right now."

"Of course," Kaitlin hushed, remembering the funeral they all attended. "But later. I want to talk about it when you're ready."

Something shifted in the room, as subtle as a drop in the air pressure. Billie sat up straight and her eyes shot to the door. The fine hair on her arms was tingling and that could only mean one thing. One of the dead had found her, tracking her down like a bloodhound despite the fact that she kept herself closed to the other side. Some of the stronger ones still found her out. This one, she knew, would appear at the front entrance.

The door swung open and a man appeared, looking through the crowd of patrons for a familiar face. It was not a ghost.

Billie shot up, nearly knocking Kaitlin's drink over, and waved Mockler down. Her heart swelled when his face brightened upon seeing her.

The embrace was tight, but quick. Mockler leaned back to get a look at her. "Hi," he said.

"You made it!" she beamed back. "I didn't think I'd see you tonight."

"I double-timed it to wrap things up. How did everything go at your aunt's?"

"Kiss me."

He glanced around, wary of public displays, but Billie's eyes were closed and her lips were puckered comically. A peck but her lips were soft. She took his arm and led the way. "Come sit."

~

Tammy was the first to bail, claiming an early morning. Billie wondered if she felt like the odd man out, being the only person at the table not paired up. The mood wound down after that. Kaitlin and Kyle continued to snip at one another and Adam started yawning. Saying goodnight, Billie held onto Mockler's arm as they hit the chilly night air and walked to his car.

"I hope that wasn't too boring for you," Billie said. "Hanging out with my friends."

"Why would it be boring?"

"I dunno. I guess I was just worried you wouldn't get along with them."

"It was nice to see them under normal circumstances." He dug his keys out of a pocket. "They're nice. Except, what was up with Kaitlin and her boyfriend? Karl?"

"Kyle," Billie corrected. "They're hitting a rough patch, I guess. It happens."

"It does."

His tone was stone cold as he said it and she wondered what he was reflecting on. "You seem tired. Rough day?"

"Just busy. We're trying to tie off a couple of files before they go to court. Lot of details to iron out."

The wind picked up and blew her hair over her eyes. "Any word on Gantry?"

"Nothing. And I mean zip," he sighed. "I did want to talk to you about that."

"What about?"

"Most cases, there are friends and family to talk to, but with Gantry, I have nothing. The only friend he had was you."

"I know as much about him as you do," she said. "What about that rock musician guy? The one with the face paint?"

"He's dead. And his manager and crew have disappeared."

He raised the keys in his hand to unlock the car. "Is there anyone else who knew Gantry?"

Billie stopped. "Marta."

"Who?"

"Marta Ostensky. She's a psychic. She has a place on Roberts, near John."

"I've seen the sign," he said. "She knew Gantry?"

"I think they used to be lovers, actually." She pursed her lips, recalling the details. "There's that weirdo church too. The one with the blacked-out windows. Did you try there?"

"I did. The doors are padlocked. It looks abandoned." He stepped around to the driver's side. "Hop in."

Billie opened the door to find the passenger seat cluttered with paperwork. "Can I put this stuff in the back?"

"Damn. I forgot about that stuff. Let me put it in the trunk." He came around, scooped it up and unlatched the trunk. "I've been living out of the car for the past two days and I was in a rush to get here before you left." Dumping the files into an empty box, he shifted around a few items to make sure nothing would roll loose and then closed the trunk. He heard Billie say something, but her voice was low.

"What was that?" he asked.

Billie wasn't there. The passenger door stood open, the interior light casting down onto the sidewalk.

"Billie?"

She was to his right, standing at the entry to an alley. Her back to the street, she was speaking to someone in the darkened breezeway. He stepped up onto the sidewalk to see who it was, but the alley was empty.

"Billie? Who are you talking to?"

She didn't turn or react to his presence. Her voice was a whisper. "I can't help you," she said.

"Help me with what?" He came about to see her face and then stopped. Her eyes were glazed over, oblivious to his presence, and fixed on something before her. The trash strewn alleyway remained empty.

He felt useless, unsure of what to do. Shake her out of it, this spell she was in? Or was that dangerous, the way one wasn't supposed to wake a sleepwalker? When he moved closer, he saw a single tear glide down her cheek. He took her elbow gently and spoke her name.

She flinched, her eyes instantly alert and wheeling about as she got her bearings. Then, she leaned into him as her balance went sideways.

"What just happened?" he asked.

"Nothing. I'm sorry." Her hand locked around his arm until the dizziness faded.

The question was rhetorical. They both knew what had just happened. He led her back to the car. "Let's get out of here," he said.

Billie's movements were slow, as if unsure of her footing. She wiped her cheek and seemed surprised to find dampness there. "Was I crying?"

"Probably just the wind," he said and closed the car door after her.

CHAPTER 5

THERE WASN'T ANY question of them spending the night together. The question was where. Each party angled for home turf.

"We can go to my place," Mockler suggested as he pulled the car into traffic, the lights of King Street refracting off the windshield.

Billie settled into the passenger seat, dreading that very question. "Have you done anything with the house?"

"No," he said, somewhat confused by the question. "Haven't had the time. Why?"

"So it's still half empty?" She winced as soon as the words tumbled out. That had sounded bitchy.

"I like to think of it as uncluttered."

Billie reached out and took hold of his free hand. "Would you mind if we went back to my place? I know it's small and everything but, well…"

He squeezed her fingers together. "We can camp out in the park, if you want."

A wash of relief eased any misgivings she had. The last place she wanted to spend the night was his house. It was too haunted by the spectre of what had come before her. "Camper," she said.

"What?"

"Happy camper."

"That too," he agreed.

They rode on in silence for a time, Billie content as he steered the car past Gore Park and onto Hughson Street. No hurry, no crisis to race to. The sense of normalcy was comforting. "Do you ever get lonely out here?"

"Lonely?"

"In that house. All by yourself. It's a big place for one person."

"It is. Especially with it empty." He fell silent for a moment before speaking again. "The thought of refurnishing it makes me kind of ill."

She let slip a soft laugh. "You don't strike me as someone who likes to decorate much. I'm crap at that, too."

"You? Come on. I've seen Casa Culpepper. Eclectic. Is that the term I'm groping for?"

She rabbit-punched his shoulder. "Don't tease. I try. It just never turns out well."

A stray dog trotted across the road before them, heedless to the oncoming headlights. Mockler slowed and shot past her building before turning onto the side street where he parked behind a battered pickup truck.

"Wait," Billie said, squinting at the faded sign further down the block. "You need a permit to park here overnight."

"Don't sweat it," he said. Climbing out, he reached under the sun visor for a placard and threw it on the dashboard. The words POLICE VEHICLE in bold letters. "Let's go," he said.

Up two flights of worn stairwell, Billie hesitated before opening her door. "Don't mind the mess," she said. "The maid had the day off."

She led him inside, hit the light switch and realized how much of a hypocrite she was. Her flat still looked like an unkempt war zone.

"I like what you've done with the place," Mockler said, his eyes dropping to the stuffing bleeding from the rip in the sofa.

She had half expected Half-Boy to appear, ready to ruin her night or otherwise harass her date, but the legless ghost still wasn't home. Small mercies, she supposed. Billie turned on the old stand-up lamp that she adored and crossed back to the door where she killed the overhead light. The greenish light from the vintage lamp bathed the flat in a warm sargasso glow, concealing its flaws. Snatching up the collar of his jacket, she turned him round to face her. His face was lit up with a sly grin.

"Want to know something?" she asked. Lifting up onto her toes, she sought out his mouth. "I missed you."

He smiled back. "That's what I was gonna say."

~

The running man was back among the trees but this time it was not of his own volition. They had dragged him out here. His heart was rabbiting inside his chest, afraid of what they were going to do.

It was dark and it was cold. The trunks of the trees flared up in the light from the torches held aloft by his captors. His head dipped and lolled around on his neck, as if too heavy to keep upright. The meds were wearing off, the sedatives administered to dull the pain, while they prepped him. Alongside the pain came some small clarity to his thoughts. They had drilled something into his head, screws driven down right into his skull. The torment was awful and, had it not been for the drugs, he would have passed out. Something heavy had been attached directly to his skull and, each time he moved, he felt the weight of it lolling his head unnaturally.

He tried to beg, but his mouth didn't work properly, the words garbling into little more than animal grunts. His captors in their dark masks marched on without speaking at all, tramping down the underbrush as they dragged the injured man further into the dark woods.

They came to a stop and the man dropped to his knees on a bed of dry pine needles. They were in a clearing in the woods, an open expanse surrounded by a wall of forest on all sides. There was a lone tree in the centre, tall and old with spindly branches overhead. The torches they carried were fixed upright into the ground, the flames rippling up into the night sky. His captors moved around the small beacons of fire and he tried to count their number, but lost track as they passed in and out of the light. They pulled off their dark masks and began to disrobe, dropping their clothes to the ground. They were easier to see now, these men in their pale, naked flesh.

The running man was clad in only a tattered blanket with a hole cut out for his head, like a poncho. This was stripped from him, leaving him exposed to the elements. Thick callused hands snatched him up and leather twines were cinched over each wrist. Propelled forward, he was pushed against the tree and his arms wrapped around its trunk in an embrace. His wrists were lashed together to keep him upright. The things attached to his skull dragged their weight backward, forcing his gaze up, where he saw the thorny crown of the tree set against the night sky.

In his peripheral vision were snatches of the others, moving around him in the night. Some were making noises, low animal grunts in the dark. All were beating time with their feet, stomping a slow rhythm on the cold ground. They were calling something, entreating it to come near, and the running man knew that he was the bait. An image of a spring lamb tied to a post in the wilderness came to him, bleating in terror as the wolf circled it from the dark.

He wished they had given him more painkillers.

~

Her sleep was deep, fathoms down and content. Fulfilled even, with Mockler's warm body stretched out beside her, her head tucked against his shoulder. Knees crooked together. Afterwards she would wonder if the depth of her sleep was the reason she was awoken. Something about her contentment irked the thing that shared the cramped apartment with her.

Opening her eyes, she felt him in the room with her. With them, she corrected. Mockler remained asleep, his broad back to her, and she listened to his breathing for a moment before easing up onto one elbow. Her eye caught a trace of movement as the thing on the ceiling crawled over the lintel into the other room.

Padding into the living room, Billie cinched her robe tight and squinted into the dark. The room was cold, the window propped open from where she guessed he had crawled inside. Why he needed to physically open the window, she didn't know. With no corporeal boundaries, couldn't he slip through the tiniest crack in the brick? This habit of leaving the window open was going to be a problem with winter almost here.

She turned on the lamp. "Where are you?"

A scratching noise overhead. Half-Boy crouched in a corner of the ceiling, his dark eyes watching her.

"I thought you were gone for good." Shivering, she crossed the room and eased the window down. "Where have you been?"

The small ghost clambered down the wall like an enormous spider, propelling himself along on his hands. The bloodied stumps of his amputated legs left dark smear trails behind him. It was ghastly to see, but, then again, no one but herself could see him. The walls and ceiling of her small flat were covered in these phantom slime trails of black blood.

The boy sprang onto the arm of the sofa, lithe as a cat, and studied her. His threadbare cap sat off centre on his head, as if thrown on in haste. He stared at her for a moment, mute as a store window mannequin, and then his head rotated on his spindly neck as he turned to look at the bedroom door. The lines of his pale face were drawn and grim.

"You know who he is," Billie said. She folded her arms. "I don't have to explain him to you."

His expression didn't change. Disdained and disapproving.

"It's Gantry you don't like, remember?" She wagged her chin in the direction of the bedroom. "He's the nice one."

She studied him this time, this phantom child about whom she knew absolutely nothing. Outside of her own childhood, she hadn't had much experience with kids. No nieces or nephews to learn from. She tried to guess Half-Boy's age, pegging him around eight- or nine-years-old at the time of his death. No time to learn about the adult world or make sense of anything like love. Romantic love, that is. He didn't understand why the policeman was here so late, in her bed. How was she going to explain this to him?

"I like him. And he's going to be here a lot more." Billie sat down on the sofa, a few feet from the ghost. Even at that distance she felt the cold pouring off of him like a meat locker left open. "He's a good man. Honest. He's a policeman."

The scowl on his face deepened at her words. She was making it worse somehow. Billie leaned back into the cushion, blowing her cheeks out in frustration. Then she turned to look at him. "Can I ask you something?"

He didn't move.

"Did you know my mother?" she went on. "Her name was Mary Agnes. I thought I saw you with her at the cemetery, but I wasn't sure. Did she contact you somehow?"

Half-Boy dropped to the floor and scuttled across the room, like he hadn't heard a word she'd said.

Her frustration deepened and her tone became flinty. "You know, you could try to answer me sometimes. Nod your head or something."

The wooden floor creaked, but not in the direction the boy had scampered to. Mockler stood in the bedroom door, his hair disheveled in a way she liked. The look in his eyes was wary and alert, as if sensing trouble.

"What are you doing up?" he grumbled, his vocal cords still sleepy.

"Couldn't sleep." She tried not to sound startled.

Mockler cleared his throat. "Is everything okay?"

"Yeah. I have trouble sleeping sometimes."

He looked over the living room, the door to the kitchen. "Who were you talking to?"

The look in his eyes was troublesome. Did he think she was crazy, talking to herself or did he sense something else was going on? How could she explain the Half-Boy to him? He'd hoof it out the door and never come back. He might insist they spend their nights at his house after that and that was something she couldn't do. "No one," she answered.

A white lie and they both knew it, but he let it ride. Not the best way to start a relationship, she scolded herself. Billie rose to her feet and came to him. "Let's go back to bed."

"What time is it?" he asked, eyes searching the room for a clock.

Billie took a step back to where she could see the microwave in the kitchen. "Almost five."

"I should go," he said.

"Now?" She couldn't mask her disappointment.

"Early start today. I gotta get home first and change."

Billie leaned into him, her palm flattening against his chest. "Do you want some coffee?"

"I'll grab some on the way. You go back to bed."

"I will if you come with me." Her smile was hopeful. A tad mischievous.

"Next time," he said, kissing her.

A scraping noise near the window interrupted them. The sash in the window slid up all on its own, letting in the cold air.

Seated on the sill was a wine bottle topped with a candle. It toppled over, banged against the floor and rolled into a corner.

Mockler blinked at it for a moment and then turned to go back into the bedroom. "I'm gonna get dressed," was all he said.

~

Standing under the hot shower, Mockler tried a thousand different ways to explain away or dismiss the sight of the window opening under its own volition. The wind had caught it at some strange angle. It was old, operating on a rope and pulley system like the windows of his childhood home. A squirrel in the wall scampered up the sash cord, tripping the pulley upward. The logic became increasingly more complicated as the steam fogged the glass in the mirror. Shutting off the water, he smacked his hands against his cheeks to dispel the crazy thoughts altogether.

You know what it was. You just don't want to admit it.

Fine, he concluded. That's what it was. He knew Billie was different. He knew the things she could do. It was the disappointment that was clawing at his nerves. He hoped it was over. With the Murder House razed, and Billie's mother found and laid to rest, he had hoped the spooky stuff would end. He'd have to reassess that conclusion. But later, when he had time.

Dressing took less than five minutes, the tie cinching straight the first time. He loosened the collar just a little, hating anything that chafed against his Adam's apple, and boomed down the stairs to the kitchen.

The house was unchanged, still in its pathetic vacant look of being half-emptied. He hadn't even bought groceries, let alone furniture. The thought of shopping for all that stuff was flat-out repugnant. Was it any wonder Billie didn't want to come back to this sad-looking house? The idea of selling it had flitted across his mind twice already. It was too big for one person, especially someone who was routinely called away. Renting it might be more lucrative though. While not a huge house, it was big enough to be split into two apartments and let the tenants cover the mortgage with a little leftover. The renovations would take time though. Would he live in the house during the reno or rent somewhere else for the time being? Too many questions, not enough time.

Locking the front door behind him, he heard a sharp tapping sound ring out from the next yard over. He looked up to see a smartly dressed woman struggling to wield a sledgehammer. Barely able to lift the blunt tool, she tried to hammer a post into the ground but missed and cursed.

"Morning," he hollered to her. "Do you want a hand with that?"

The woman looked up, relief blooming over her face. "Would you mind?"

Mockler crossed into his neighbour's yard and took up the sledgehammer. The woman held a realtor's sign fixed to the post. "I didn't know Ivo had listed his house," he said.

"Yesterday," the woman said. "It took a lot of hand-holding to do it. He's still not sure."

"He's been here a long time." Mockler looked at the photograph of the realtor on the sign. It matched the woman before him. "And you're Cynthia?"

"Cynthia Trucillo." She shook his hand. "Thanks for helping. I normally have someone else do this but Ivo wanted the sign up today."

"No problem." He saw that a small hole had already been dug in the grass. He slotted the post in, tapped it until it stood on its own and drove it down with two hard knocks. "There you go," he said.

"Thanks." The realtor nodded at his own house across the hedgerow. "Is that your house there?"

"Yup."

Cynthia Trucillo already had her card out and offered to him. "It's got charm. If you ever think about selling, give me a call. I promise you won't have to hammer anymore signs."

Mockler looked at the card, an exact replica of the shingle on the post. "Thanks, Cynthia," he said as he walked to his car. "I just might do that."

CHAPTER 6

THE PRINTED TYPE on the page blurred in Mockler's vision. A transcript of an interview with a witness that was as gripping as a telephone directory. Yawning, he dropped the document onto his desk and massaged his eyes with both hands to stave off the fatigue. He couldn't take anymore coffee, his guts queasy from the overload, and it wasn't even noon.

"Late night, chief?"

Mockler raised his head to see his partner, Detective Odinbeck, return to his desk with an oversized muffin in his mitt. "Yup," Mockler replied, and then he nodded at the pastry. "I thought you'd sworn off that stuff."

"Fell off the wagon," Odinbeck shrugged. "So, what's the story? Did you go out last night?"

"Billie's back in town."

Odinbeck smirked and winked. "I guess she was glad to see you, huh?"

"Stop."

"Killjoy. So, what's the deal? You two an item now?"

Mockler just shrugged. Discussing his love life with Odinbeck was not something he was keen to do. Despite the older detective's gruff demeanour, Odinbeck was oddly open to it, often prodding his partner with questions about his relationship. Mockler couldn't tell if the detective was truly interested or if he just got a vicarious thrill out of it. Either way, he never felt comfortable discussing it.

"Don't be such a prig, Mock. Spill. I want to know the details."

"Why? So you can mock me?"

"You're too young to be an uptight schoolmarm. Sometimes it's good to talk about these things."

The desk phone rang. *Thank God.* Mockler sighed as he reached for it. "Mockler," he answered.

"Someone here to see you, detective," came the voice from the lobby reception.

Mockler sat up, wondering if Billie was downstairs. "Who is it?"

"His name's Jameson. Says he needs to talk to you."

The name wasn't familiar. "I'll be right down. Did he say what it's about?"

"No, sir. Just that he needs to talk to only you."

Mockler hung up and slung his jacket from the back of his chair. He prayed that it wasn't another chatty nutjob looking to waste his time with UFO conspiracies and Bigfoot sightings. He had fielded three of those calls last week alone.

The man in the lobby surprised Mockler by his well groomed appearance and tasteful attire. Casual but expensive. His eyes clear and intelligent, his handshake firm but the hands soft. White collar all the way. "I'm Detective Mockler. Have we met?"

"Richard Jameson. Thanks for meeting me, detective."

"What can I do for you, Mr. Jameson?" Mockler studied the man, the way his eyes darted around the lobby of Division One.

"Is there somewhere we can talk?"

Tucked behind the lobby was a large boardroom that was often used for press conferences. It was empty now. Mockler led the man inside and closed the door behind them. "Have a seat," he said.

Richard Jameson remained standing. "I won't take much of your time, detective. You are the lead investigator in the John Gantry case, correct?"

This was getting interesting. "Yes sir. Do you have any information on John Gantry?"

"I need to know something." Here, Jameson took a breath. He had the odd look of someone making a wish before blowing out birthday candles. "Is he really dead?"

"Yes," Mockler said. He paused long enough to see the fact register on the man's face. Immediate relief, the tension slacking out of his shoulders so quickly that he seemed to be deflating. "Did you know Gantry personally?"

"How did it happen? Did someone kill him? I'd heard he had been arrested."

"That's true. He was assaulted by another inmate in jail."

"I think I'll take that seat after all." He wheeled the nearest chair over and sunk into it.

Mockler sat down and spoke softly to the man. "You seemed relieved. Tell me how you knew Gantry."

"He'd often call me for help. Favours."

The detective fought the urge to dig out his notepad. "What kind of favours?"

"Ridiculous ones. He often needed a lift somewhere. I think it amused him to treat me like a chauffeur. Sometimes, he needed to be stitched up."

"Stitched up?" The other man nodded and Mockler went on. "You're a doctor?"

"I was. A surgeon, actually."

"You don't practise anymore?"

"No. Mostly consulting work these days." Jameson's eyes narrowed, wary all of a sudden. "Detective, this is an informal meeting, yes?"

"We're just chatting as far as I'm concerned. Don't worry." Mockler smiled to put the man at ease. "Were you and Gantry friends? Or did you know him from work?"

"I hated him."

"But you drove him around and stitched his cuts when he didn't want to show his face in a hospital?"

"I haven't done anything wrong," Jameson shot back.

Mockler softened his tone. He didn't want to scare Jameson off. "Forget all that. Gantry's dead and the file is closed as far as I'm concerned. I'm just trying to understand the man. His motivations, his actions."

Jameson eased back down. He seemed tired all of a sudden. "I once made a mistake. No, two mistakes. The second was asking Gantry for help with the first. Gantry operated like the mob. Once you owed him, you just keep paying. The man was a bastard of a manipulator."

"So I've heard." Mockler scratched his chin. "Can I ask what he helped you with?"

"Do you need to know, detective? If Gantry's dead, I mean. It was…personal."

The conversation was winding down of its own accord. Mockler stood up. "No. I don't think I need to know. I might want to know more about Gantry himself. Just details, anything. Can I call you if I think of something?"

"Of course." Jameson retrieved a business card and laid it on the table. "I still find it hard to believe he's dead. Did you see him when it happened? Was it ghastly?"

"I missed the whole thing," Mockler admitted. He walked the visitor to the door. "I never got a look at him."

"That's odd. Didn't you examine the body? I thought that was procedure."

"It is. The body went missing from the morgue."

The blood ran out of Jameson's face. "Oh God," was all he said before marching briskly for the front doors.

Mockler was about to go after him when he felt a hand on his elbow. His partner, huffing it down the corridor. "Heads up, chief. We got a call."

"What is it?"

"Body found in the woods, out by Crooks Hollow." Odinbeck took a left to the elevators that would take them down to the motor pool. "Nasty one by the sounds of it."

"Who took the call?"

"Hoffmann and Latimer. They're already on site. We're assisting."

The two men loaded onto the elevator and Mockler jabbed the button down. "What's so nasty about it?"

"Latimer wouldn't elaborate. He said we gotta see it to believe it."

~

Crooks Hollow was a 25 minute drive from Division One. Across the bay to a forested glen that had once been the site of a mill operation in the late Victorian period. The limestone ruins of the mill still stood and the place was reputed to be haunted. That fact didn't sit well with Mockler as he drove past the limestone pylons of the bridge.

Subdivisions gave way to farmland and then forest. A canopy of naked branches arced over the paved road, sunlight dappling the cracked asphalt. Mockler pulled up behind the forensic truck and a uniformed officer led the way through the damp brush. Odinbeck cursed when he emerged from the tangles with spiky burrs clinging to his pant leg. Stepping out of the trees, the two detectives entered a clearing.

"Christ," muttered Odin.

Another uniformed officer stood nearby, waving them through. Behind him were detectives Hoffmann and Latimer. Sozen, the lead on the forensic team, was kneeling on the ground going over his equipment. Still waiting for the signal to go in.

"Is that the sergeant?" Odinbeck asked. "What's she doing here?"

Mockler saw their superior standing further away, pacing slowly through the weeds. Nodding to the other detectives, he strode in and saw what had brought the sergeant out to the field.

The dead body was a male Caucasian, naked. The age looked to be between 20 and 30 years. Adult, but not by much. The victim's arms were wrapped tight around the trunk of a black oak, bound at the wrist and cinched tight. The strain on the arms kept the body upright, the torso pressed tight against the bark of the tree. The skin was almost blue, the legs and hands dark with smeared dirt stains like he had crawled through the mud before being tied to the tree. Blood and dirt stained the victim's face, obscuring his features. The eyes were open and wide, staring like cold marbles up at the branches overhead. There was something wrong with the victim's head.

At first glance, Mockler thought that the body was wearing some kind of headdress or strange hat but he could see now that they were horns. Antlers, to be more precise. Like those of a deer. He counted the points on the antler. Ten in all. A large deer. What he couldn't figure out was how the antlers stayed on the victim's head. He saw no strings or wires.

"That's the craziest shit I ever saw," blurted Odinbeck.

Latimer came up alongside them, looking out at the body. "You should have seen it in the dawn. Scared the hell out of me."

"Are those real?" Mockler asked. "The antlers."

"Yep. Ten point buck. Big animal."

"How are the antlers staying on? I can't see the strings."

"That's the really fun part. Fucking things are screwed on."

Odinbeck blanched. "To what? His skull?"

"Straight into the bone." Latimer shook his head. "We think it was done while he was still alive, too."

Mockler pointed at three lengths of wood standing upright in the ground. "What are those? They looked burnt."

"Torches. Old school too, fueled by pitch. We're guessing that they were used to light the scene at night."

"This guy didn't have a flashlight?" Odinbeck huffed. "What's that stuff on his back? Did they draw on him?"

"Weirdo symbols," Latimer said. "Carved in with a knife."

Mockler looked away from the grisly sight to the wall of trees at the edge of the clearing. Then, he forced his eyes back to the body. The whole tableau was a shock. The position of the body and the horns, the torches. Like something he'd seen in a medieval woodcut or a horror movie. He was grateful that he and Odinbeck had been at the bottom of the rotation when this particular call came in. "Is Hoffmann all right?" he asked Latimer. "He's pacing a lot."

"He's keeping it together, but this kind of shit doesn't sit well with him."

"Where do you want us?" Odinbeck asked.

"Could you sweep the perimeter and work your way in. Just in case we missed something. Later, we can hit the woods around the clearing."

Odinbeck agreed and he walked with Mockler to the edge of the clearing. Here, they tread slowly, side-by-side, eyes glued to the ground for anything. Mockler heard his name being called and looked up to see their sergeant approaching them.

"Sarge," he said. "Nice to see you out of the office."

"I wish it was for a better reason." Sergeant Gibson stood a little over five feet, but the respect she commanded gave her the stature of LeBron James. She nodded at the scene behind them. "Did you take a close look at the victim?"

"Not yet," Mockler said. "Hoffmann hasn't closed in yet. His case."

"Of course." Sergeant Gibson watched the lead investigator as he lingered outside the focal point. Her eyes stitched in concern, as if she didn't like what she was seeing. "What do you make of it?"

"Hard to say without looking closer. It's a nasty mess, I'll tell you that."

"Ballpark it for me," she said. "From here."

"It's ritualistic. More of this stupid occult stuff we've been seeing."

Odinbeck piped up, watching his colleague. "Why is Hoffmann taking so long? He's dithering around like an old man."

"He hates this stuff," said the Sergeant.

"Since when does that matter?" Odinbeck spat. "He needs to get in there before it gets any colder."

Sergeant Gibson turned back, looking to Mockler and then Odinbeck. "Would you consider swapping out on this one? Taking the lead on it?"

Both detectives bristled, exchanging glances. "Why?" Odinbeck sputtered. "Hoff and Latimer caught this one. It's their case."

The Sergeant fixed her eyes on Mockler, and Mockler alone. "You've had experience with this kind of thing. This spooky occult stuff. Hoffmann's clearly uncomfortable with it."

The younger detective's jaw clenched at the term she'd used, the muscle in his cheek flashing. Spooky. Hating what he had been asked, he grasped for a way to be diplomatic. "I don't have anything special to bring to this. Hoffmann and Latimer will do just as good a job."

"You sure?" she asked, looking him in the eye.

"Sorry, Sarge. I can't."

"Understood. Stay close with them on this one. This is going to become a shit-show once the press gets wind of it." Sergeant Gibson nodded a farewell and trudged through the weeds toward the pathway leading out of the clearing.

Odinbeck shook his head, watching their superior leave. "What the hell was that all about?"

Mockler wouldn't speculate. "Come on. Let's get back to the sweep."

The two men resumed the ground search, but Odinbeck wouldn't let it go. "Since when are you the spooky expert?"

The younger detective remained quiet. There were times when he wished his partner would learn to shut his trap.

CHAPTER 7

THE AFTERNOON SHIFT at the Gunner's Daughter was all that was available and Billie was glad to get it. She had barely worked in the last few weeks and her bank account was looking frighteningly anemic. The evening shifts were better but Mario, the bar owner, could only offer her the afternoon one on such short notice. She jumped at it and showed up early.

Settled in behind the bar with its familiar smell of lime trays and draft spillage, Billie was grateful for the quiet predictability of work. The chaotic events of the last few weeks had left her rattled to the core and she craved routine, even if her boss had become wary of her since she'd been outed as a psychic. Mario was a gruff bear of a man, born and raised on the rougher side of town, and unafraid of anyone...except when it came to Billie. The man was leery of her now, uneasy to be alone with her in the same room, but he was a decent man and had accommodated Billie's absence over the last while. Another boss would have simply fired her.

Mockler showed up at the end of her shift during the changeover hour when she worked alongside the evening shift bartender. Surprised, Billie lit up when she saw him walk through the door. "Hey," she beamed. "I didn't think I'd see you today."

"We punched the clock 10 minutes ago." Mockler dropped onto the barstool like he'd been carrying weights all day. "I thought I'd stop in before heading home."

Billie could see the exhaustion in his eyes. She poured him a pint without asking and set it down before him. "Tough day?"

"Yeah. New job."

Billie nodded. A new job meant a new homicide. She didn't want to pry, but it was hard not to wonder about it. "A bad one?"

Mockler sipped his pint, reflecting on the grisly scene that had scalded his eyes earlier in the day. His sergeant's words kept nagging at him, about being the expert in the spooky stuff. That was the last thing Billie needed to hear now. She'd been through enough already. "They're all bad."

A patron further down the bar waved at her for service. Billie excused herself, got the orders in and came back to the detective sitting rumpled on the barstool. She reached out and smoothed the hair that had fallen across his eyes. "You look pooped."

"I am. I just wanted to say hi before heading home."

That made her happy. Small things often did. "I'm just finishing up here. Do you want some company?"

"Aren't you here till closing?" he asked, checking his watch.

"Nah. I'm done." She tried to gauge his mood, the lethargy in his eyes. "But if you want to just go home and crash, that's cool."

"I'd love some company. Finish up. I'll wait."

They stopped in at the Owl on Main for a late dinner. With its stark fluorescent lighting and blaring TV in the corner, the place was neither romantic nor intimate, but Billie didn't care. He was sitting across the table and that's all that mattered. Mockler swore that the short ribs here were the best meal in town. She had never had Korean before but she was happy to try something new with him, a spot off of her beaten path that could be theirs. She couldn't get enough of the kimchi and that made him smile.

His place was a five minute drive away but she asked if she could be selfish and go to hers instead. Stepping into her apartment on the third floor, he saw that the place had been cleaned and scrubbed. There was still a hole in the plaster where he had driven in Gantry's skull, but contrasting that was a vase of fresh flowers on the table. "I like the daisies," he said.

"I like things simple," she said, heading into the kitchen. "Have a seat."

She came back with beer for both of them and they talked quietly for a while. Nothing important, just idle chit chat while their meals settled in their bellies. Billie rose to her feet. "I got you something."

"Me?" he said.

She held out her hand for him to take. "It's nothing big. Come here."

Leading him by the hand into the narrow bathroom, Billie opened the cabinet and took out a few items and laid them out on the edge of the sink. A new toothbrush and a tube of toothpaste, disposable razors and a can of shaving cream.

"It's not much," she said, looking at him with a spark in her eyes. "Just morning stuff, so you don't always have to rush home before going to work."

"You got that for me?"

Her eyeteeth clamped over her bottom lip. "Is that okay? Too presumptuous?"

"No. It's sweet." He picked up the tube of toothpaste. "You got the kind I use, too."

"I peeked last time I was at your place."

He also appreciated small gestures. "Thank you."

A quick kiss, interrupted by a noise from the other room. Billie looked out the door to see what it was.

"Is that your mysterious cat?" Mockler said, referring to the inexplicable sounds that always occurred when he had his back turned. What happened next confirmed forever the absence of any cat.

The toothbrush Billie had bought for him lifted vertically from the sink and spun in the air like a twirling baton. Mockler couldn't even blink, eyes glued to the thing floating in the air. It levitated three feet to his right and then dropped as if released from an invisible grip. A small splash as it went into the toilet.

Billie turned at the sound, just in time to witness the toothpaste and razors rise into the air, spin about and follow the same trajectory into the bowl.

The look on his face was almost comical. Billie offered a sheepish smile. "We need to talk."

~

"Who is he?"

"I don't have a clue," Billie said. Trying to explain Half-Boy was difficult. She kept it brief. "But he's saved my behind more than once. Kaitlin's too, when she was attacked in the hospital."

They had withdrawn to the sofa. Mockler stared at the bathroom door, while she told him about the boy. His jaw muscles flexed as he listened. "He won't tell you his name? Or what he wants?"

"He can't speak," Billie said, realizing how much detail she had omitted. "His tongue was cut out. I'm not even sure if he speaks English."

"And he what, lives here? With you? How long has he been here?"

Billie shrugged. "He's been here since it started. When I came home from the hospital and began seeing the, you know, the dead. It was like he'd always been here. Waiting for me."

Mockler scratched the stubble on his chin. A scrim of

annoyance was clouding his thoughts. Couldn't they just get shed of this spooky business once and for all? "What does he want with you?"

"Again, I don't know. He's protective of me. He hated Gantry with a passion."

"Good call on his part."

"I'm surprised he's turned on you," Billie said. "Gantry I could see how he'd think he was a threat. I thought he was fine with you. Until now."

"Now that Gantry's gone?" He looked at her.

"Or," she mused, "since you've been around more."

His brow arced in disbelief. "He wants you all to himself?"

She folded and unfolded her hands, unable to answer the question. The playful mood of earlier had evaporated entirely.

Mockler glanced around the room. "Is he still here?"

She didn't want to tell him that the little ghost was watching them. "Yes."

"I see." He turned to her, as if about to say something, but hesitated. Starting over, he asked "Aren't ghosts supposed to cross over? Or move into the light or something? Isn't that the goal?"

"I don't know if there's a goal. Or a point to anything. Are you asking me if there's a heaven?"

"No. Maybe." Another hesitation, another shifting of restless hands. "Have you ever seen a light?"

"Once. I didn't see any light, I just felt this pull toward

something. I saw the dead move into it. I almost wanted to go to it, too." She left out the rest of the story, how it had happened shortly after the ability had surfaced in her. How she had encountered a malignant ghost with flies in his mouth and how it had attached itself to Mockler. How she had pulled free the souls of other ghosts it had devoured.

"So," he went on, "how come this one hasn't moved into the light, this half-thing?"

"Half-Boy," she corrected him. "I don't know why he hasn't crossed over."

Both of them fell silent. The only sound was that of the leaky faucet in the kitchen tapping the sink. The ghost on the ceiling remained still, his small eyes ever watchful.

Mockler stirred. "Do you ever watch scary movies?"

"I hate scary movies."

"I used to love them when I was a kid," he said. "There was one that always gave me the willies. It was about this widow who was being haunted by her dead husband. He died in a car accident; she was driving. The guilt was driving her crazy. She thought he was out for revenge but the story flipped at the end. She was keeping him around, trapping him here as a ghost because she couldn't let go."

His recollection made her bristle. "What are you saying? I'm keeping him here? I can't let him go?"

"I don't know. This is out of my depth." He hadn't meant to offend her. He took her hand in his. "Maybe he just needs help to move on. That's all."

"I tried," Billie said. "I don't know what else to do."

The monotonous tapping of the faucet returned and he felt her slump beside him in defeat. He pulled her close and words were whispered into each others ears, punctuated with tiny kisses until, after a while, they rose and moved into the other room. Billie glanced back quickly as she closed the bedroom door, but Half-Boy was gone, fled from his roost on the ceiling.

Later, long after Billie had turned off the bedside lamp, Mockler couldn't sleep. His slumber was disrupted three times by the eerie sensation of tiny hands pressing down on his chest, as if trying to collapse his lungs in his sleep. He related none of this experience to Billie the next morning. With his new toothbrush and shaving kit ruined, he left in a hurry to get home to change for work.

CHAPTER 8

MOST OF THE day was spent assisting Hoffmann and Latimer in their new case, doing the grunt work of secondary area searches and canvassing the surrounding area, while the primary investigators focused on the body. The ruins at Crooks Hollow were fairly remote with few residences nearby, so the chances that anyone had seen or heard anything was nil, but the process had to be exercised. Mockler and Odinbeck rapped on doors until their knuckles were raw.

It was a washout. No one had seen anything, no one had heard anything, but all were curious about the police presence in the area and speculation ran wild. Surprisingly, the media had barely picked up on the story. Human remains found in the woods. That was the extent of the coverage. The details would be leaked sooner or later and, once they got wind of the gruesome circumstances, the press would descend on them like wolves. It allowed them some leeway, so the two detectives pressed on with canvassing before the locals would be tainted by the news coverage.

Five hours later, they drove back across the bay and into the city. The days were getting shorter as November crept on and the lights of the ambitious city were already twinkling at full capacity. Odinbeck grumbled a weary goodbye when he got out and Mockler drove home to his empty house on Bristol Street. Climbing out of the car, he discovered a mass of old furniture laid out on his neighbour's lawn. He came around the hedge as two young men carried a sideboard from the house and placed it on the grass.

"Hi," he said. One of them he recognized as his neighbour's son, but the young man's name escaped him. "Danny, isn't it?"

"Darko," the man corrected. They shook hands. "How are you?"

"Good. How's your dad? I haven't seen him in a while."

"He's living with our sister now, over in Ancaster," said the man named Darko. "He had a fall couple weeks back, broke his wrist. He's been staying with her ever since."

"I'm sorry to hear that," Mockler said. "I saw the realtor's sign go up. I thought the worst since I hadn't seen Ivo for so long."

"The house is just too big for him now that mom is gone. Too many stairs."

"Must have been tough for him to let go," Mockler nodded. "Your dad was pretty proud of his home."

"It took a lot of convincing," Darko agreed. "Pop hates change."

Mockler looked over the furniture tilted onto the grass. "So, you guys get the job of clearing the place out? You having a yard sale?"

"Most of it's going to the Sally Ann. They're coming by with a truck."

The other young man hollered at his brother to get his butt in gear and Darko went back into the house. Mockler walked around the pieces on the lawn. The stuff from the dining room and kitchen was ugly or damaged, but the living room suite caught his eye. Old Ivo and his wife had a proper sitting room in the front of the house that was kept pristine because it was never used. Plastic covers on the sofa and armchair, a runner over the carpet. The family used the den in the basement as a living room. He remembered Ivo joking about his wife's insistence on keeping the sitting room in such a pristine condition, in case the Pope ever dropped in for coffee. The pieces were all from the fifties, the mid-century modern stuff that some people loved. In fact, it was the kind of furniture that Billie decorated her apartment with. She'd go crazy for this stuff, he thought.

The two came back outside, placing a battered hutch onto the grass. Mockler waved at them. "Darko, how much do you want for this stuff? The sitting room pieces?"

"You want it?" Darko asked, surprised.

His brother jabbed him in the ribs. "See? I told you it was

worth something."

"I have a friend who loves this kind of furniture," Mockler said. "What will you take for the whole suite?"

Darko looked over the sofa, sealed under its plastic shroud. "Gee. I dunno."

"Two hundred," said the brother.

"Sold," Mockler said, "if you help me haul it into my place."

The brothers agreed and Mockler ran to his house to prop the door open. He hoped there was some beer in the fridge to offer them for their help.

~

Bicycling season was coming to an end. The days were getting colder and the wind froze Billie's hands on the bars so bad they would ache. Gloves did little to keep her fingers warm and mittens were impossible to bike with. Snow was on its way. There were some hardcore cyclists, mostly couriers, who biked through the deep winter, but Billie didn't know how they did it. A higher pain tolerance, she guessed. Another week and she'd have to hang up the bike until spring and walk everywhere. Or worse, take the bus. Buying a car seemed impossible, given her finances.

Gliding to a stop on Wilson Street, she braced herself against the curb and blew into her hands to warm them. Her fingers were already stinging and it wouldn't be much longer before they went numb. She clenched and unclenched her fists to get the blood pumping in them.

"Wake up!"

The voice rang out off to the right. Billie looked over to see a man staggering out of a building to the sidewalk. He was slapping his cheeks as if to rouse himself from a bad dream. His sallow complexion identified him as one of the newly dead. Billie glanced up at the building the man had run out of and she frowned. A funeral home. A black limousine parked outside the front doors.

Brilliant move, she thought. You just had to stop outside a funeral home.

The dead man, who looked no older than herself, caught Billie looking at him and stumbled toward her. Panic lit up his eyes. "Hey! Can you see me?"

She thought about pushing off from the curb and riding away, but her hands hurt too much to grip the bars again. "I see you," she said. "You need to calm down."

He swayed down the last few steps, coming closer. "Please, help me. Something awful has happened. Nobody can see me. I scream at them, but they look right through me. I thought I was having a nightmare."

Billie looked out at the cars whooshing past in the street. The newly dead were difficult to deal with, the ones who had yet to realize what had happened to them. She avoided passing near funeral homes for this very reason. "You're not having a nightmare," she said.

"Well, I'm not high, I know that much." The man patted down his pockets, looking for something. "Where the hell is my phone? And why am I wearing this stupid suit? I hate this suit."

Billie reached out and took hold of the man's arm. "Take a breath and calm down," she said. "You know what's happening. Let it sink in."

"I don't have a clue what the hell is going on."

"Turn around. Take a look at that building you came out of."

The man spun about. "What? What is that supposed to mean?"

She sighed. This one wasn't going to go easy. She dismounted and locked the bike to a post before coming alongside the man. Together, they looked over the funeral home with its faux-Tudor facade and leaded glass windows. "I'm sorry," she said as softly as she could.

His arms fell to his sides and he grew still. His head dipped and the sobs came tumbling out. "Why?"

"I don't know why," Billie said. "I don't think there's answer to that one."

"But I can't die now! I'm not even finished my degree. And my parents? God, this is gonna kill them."

Billie took the man's hand and pulled him along. "Come with me."

"Are you crazy?" He dug his heels in. "I'm not going back in there!"

"There's something you need to see. Just come and take a look. If you don't like it, you can leave."

It took a moment's coaxing, but he followed her up the stairs. There were a few odd looks from the mourners as Billie stepped into the foyer. The man clung to her side, afraid to go any further.

"Can we leave now?" he whined.

Billie didn't want to appear to be talking to herself, but there was no way around it. "Not yet."

They lingered in the lobby a moment longer and, then, there it was. She whispered to him. "Do you feel that?"

He looked at her as if she was crazy, but then the apprehension fell from his face. "What is it?"

It was coming from down the hall, from the room where the mourners were gathered for the viewing. A warmth, as if a blazing fire roared in a hearth. Not the light, as was the common notion. "Go see," she urged.

"Come with me."

Billie shook her head. "I can't. It's not meant for me."

The pull toward the warmth was undeniable, its appeal almost magnetic. Not for the first time, Billie wondered what would happen if someone living approached that candescent heat.

The man dithered, drawn to the warmth, but afraid of it at the same time. She reassured him that it wouldn't hurt and he ventured further into the corridor. "I'm just going to take a peek," he said. "Hang on."

"I'm not waiting here," Billie said. "You either go to it or you remain behind. Your choice."

He tiptoed on toward the room where the casket lay. He didn't look back.

Stepping back into the chill wind, Billie was unlocking her bike when her phone rang. Mockler's number appeared on the display. "Hey," she answered. "I was just thinking about you."

"Did you know I was going to call?"

"I don't need to be psychic to guess that one. Where are you?"

"Just got home," he said. "Do you want to meet up later?"

"I have to work the evening shift. I don't supposed you'd want some company at four in the morning?"

"Damn. I gotta be up before sunrise tomorrow."

The scheduling conflict irked her. She knew it shouldn't, but it did. "You can crash at my place," she suggested. It was a long shot. "I promise I won't wake you when I come home."

She wondered if that sounded desperate. When there was a pause, she concluded that it had. Or Mockler was reluctant to stay at her apartment alone since she revealed the truth about the secret roommate she had.

"That's okay," he said. "What time do you go into work?"

"Seven. Why?"

"I'm gonna come pick you up. There's something here I want you to see."

He refused to give her a hint, the big tease. Billie mounted the bike and cruised back onto Cannon Street wondering what the detective was being so cagey about.

~

"Can you at least give me a hint?"

Mockler slowed the car before turning into his driveway. "No. That would ruin it. Don't you like surprises?"

"I hate surprises," Billie said.

"Oh." That was news to him. Who hated surprises? Mockler suddenly doubted his plan, wondering if it was about to blow up in his face. Climbing out of the car, he clicked his teeth. "Well, too late to back out now. Come on."

They clomped up the wooden steps and Billie followed him into the house, her mind racing ahead to what he had in store. It wasn't her birthday and they didn't have an anniversary. She doubted he even knew when her birthday was. A ball of ice was forming in her guts as she watched him turn on the lights.

"Well?" she said impatiently.

"This way." He took her hand and led her into the living room. Hitting the light switch, he flourished a hand over the room. "Ta-dah!"

The last time she had seen the room, it had been bare. A box near the wall and an open expanse of hardwood floor, that was all. Now there was furniture. Nice stuff, too. All of it from the fifties, the kind she drooled over and spent hours at flea markets to decorate her own home with. There was a long sofa in green baize, flanked by two matching armchairs. The coffee table was a kidney shape of burled walnut. Behind the sofa was a pole lamp with green shades, a heavy stand-up ashtray near one armchair.

"Wow," Billie uttered. "How did you find this stuff?"

"Do you like it?" His smile was skewed.

"I love this kind of stuff. It's like a swinging bachelor pad now."

"You haven't seen the best part yet. Check it out." He turned her around and pointed to a low cabinet against the south wall. It was an old Hi-Fi cabinet with big speakers inlaid in both ends. Mockler tilted the top panel back on its hinges and exposed the record player, a platter already on the turntable. Hitting the switch, the dials lit up and the disk spun. He dropped the needle and the warm buzz of high fidelity swooned from the cabinet speakers.

She clapped her hands. "It works!"

"Pretty groovy, huh?"

Billie listened to the song, trying to place the singer. "Who is that?"

He lifted the record sleeve from the slot in the deck and read the cover. "Lee Hazelwood?"

Her smile widened. "Ray Mockler, you're such a hipster now!"

"It came with the cabinet." He slipped the sleeve back down. "I thought you'd like it?"

Billie dropped onto the sofa and laid her arms across the backrest. "Like it? I love it. Where'd you get it?"

"My neighbour. They were throwing it out."

"Throwing it out? Don't they know how much they could get for it?"

He dug out some of the other records that were stored in the deck pocket. "They got two hundred bucks for it."

"That was a steal." She smoothed her hands over the upholstery. "Usually this stuff is worn out. This feels brand new."

"That's because it was kept under plastic for the last 60 years or so," he said. "In fact, you might just be the first person to actually sit on it."

Billie laughed. "Old school, huh? Were they Italian, your neighbours?"

"Croatian."

"You really scored with this stuff." She got up and tried one of the chairs.

"Better than Ikea."

"A million times better," she said, taking a closer look at the stand-up ashtray with its heavy dish of black glass. "And you don't even smoke."

The music thrummed through the room with the echo-chamber voice of Hazelwood. Mockler dropped onto the sofa and looked at her. "I'm glad you like it."

"I didn't know you were into this retro stuff," she said.

"I'm not."

Her nose wrinkled in surprise. "Then, why did you get it?"

"Because I knew you'd like it."

She couldn't swallow. The knock to her heart sent everything sideways. There had never been a lot of good luck for Billie when it came to men. Not a lot of door-stopper moments where a gesture of kindness or love had made her swallow her tongue. It was just furniture, for Pete's sake. Unable to speak, all Billie could do was blink at him with a peculiar look until even that became too much and she looked away.

Mockler flinched when he saw her tear up. He took her hand. "Is it too much?" he said softly. "Maybe I went overboard."

"No, no." She squeezed his hand. "It's sweet of you. I'm just not used to it."

"I want you to like it here."

"I do," she said without thinking. A tiny fib. She hoped it would become true. "I mean, I will. In time."

Mockler sat up straight, his features flattening. "I'm no good at decorating or getting the right kind of furniture. I thought you could help me with it. If you want to."

"Of course, I'll help you." She nudged her knee against his. "I'd do anything for you."

"Think about that first," he cautioned. "It's a big job, doing the whole house, but there's more to it."

"What?"

"I'm not saying right now. It's too soon, I know. But I want you to come live with me. To share the house with me. Make it your home."

In a proper world, this moment would have put a lump in Billie's throat. Instead it, made her skin crawl. Not him, the house itself, the memories it harboured, the ghost it reeked of.

Mockler's brow furrowed when she didn't respond. Billie felt her mouth go dry. She asked him for some water, just to get a moment to breathe.

CHAPTER 9

IT COULDN'T HAVE gone worse if she had tried. The awkward moment as she realized what he was asking; Billie stalled for time to think. She repeated that she wasn't fond of surprises, which came out harsh and he withdrew a little. The mood soured. She tried to explain herself. Moving in was a huge step, one she'd never taken before. They had just started dating for pity's sake.

He nodded, suggesting that maybe he hadn't thought it through. He stressed that he didn't mean right away, but further down the calendar. Maybe a month, maybe six. He said he just wanted her to think about it but he seemed crestfallen at her reaction. Hurt even. They danced around one another's feelings for a minute longer, each fumbling their attempts to be understood. And then she had to go to work.

Small talk on the drive over. Pulling up before the Gunner's Daughter, he got out and took her by the arms. "Listen, I didn't mean to knock you for a loop with that idea. No more surprises, I promise."

"It's okay. I just need time to think about it." She kissed him quick. "So, don't go and take it the wrong way."

"Deal."

Another kiss and then she went inside. She stole a last glance at him through the dirty window of the bar. Mockler stood on the sidewalk for a moment, lost in thought as dry leaves tumbled over his shoes. Then, he climbed into the car and drove away.

Getting busy behind the bar, she tried not to fret over it. The simple truth was that she didn't want to spend a single night in that house, let alone live in it. He had lived there with his ex-girlfriend for two years and no matter how hard he tried to make her feel comfortable, it would never be her home. The irony of it stung. Mockler was uneasy in her home because it was haunted by a ghost and she was reluctant to be in his because it was haunted by his former lover. It was like a cruel joke.

Self-doubt and second guessing were twin companions in Billie's life, always there, always ready to rattle her resolve and cajole her into bad decisions. She had to guard against those twin gremlins and she could feel them now, perched on each shoulder, nagging her with troubling questions. Why would Mockler want to be with her? How long before he saw her for what she was and fled? He had just ended a serious relationship and this liaison was no more than a rebound fling for him. Did she really expect this relationship to last, this bond founded on ghosts and death and misery?

"Stop."

Two patrons sitting at the bar looked up at her, wondering who she was talking to. Flustered, Billie turned her back on them to clear away the dirty glassware. Talking to herself out loud was embarrassing but it had at least silenced the nagging voice in her head. Finishing the task, she turned back to see a new patron approaching the bar. A young woman in a cocktail mini-dress and go-go boots. Taken aback by the groovy attire, it took a moment before Billie realized that no one else in the bar could see the woman. Her skin was pale and the whites of her eyes were blistered red in burst capillaries. When she looked at Billie, something dark foamed from the corner of her mouth.

"God," the dead woman said, blood dribbling down her chin. "I'd kill for a drink right now."

Billie flinched. In her fretting over Mockler, she must have absentmindedly let her guard down and opened up to the other side. This phantom had picked up on it and wandered inside. She'd have to be more careful in the future. The dead were quick when they sensed a beacon. She took a breath and said "I'm afraid your money's no good here."

"That's a shame." The dead woman's eyes lingered over the drink of the man next to her. A whiskey sour, garnished with a curly lemon rind. "Just something to wash this wretched taste from my mouth."

Billie studied the women. Her big hair was pulled under a

white patent headband, her eyes framed with false lashes. She would be stunning if not for the foamy drool and bloodshot eyes. Billie couldn't help but guess at how the young woman had exited this world. Poison? Some awful stomach disease?

The dead that Billie saw were the tormented ones, the souls still caught in a web of their own rage or anguish or terror. The intensity of their tragedies kept them tethered to this world like an anchor. Others had simply lost their wits and drifted aimlessly, eternally wandering with no purpose or reason. The cruel irony was that Billie could not help these souls. The best she could do was hear them out, let them tell their tale of tragedy, allowing them a moment's respite from the endless torment. She leaned on the bar and spoke quietly to the dead woman. "What happened to you?"

"I was a fool in love," the woman said, batting her eyes. One of her lashes had come loose, flapping like a loose thread. "Or just a fool, depending how you look at it."

"What was his name?" asked Billie.

"Her." The dead woman placed her finger over a dribble of water on the bar and spelt a name on the countertop. "Clarice."

Intrigued, Billie leaned in. "What was Clarice like?"

"She was unlike anyone I had ever known." The loose lash continued to flap, but the woman paid it no attention, her eyes cast in a long gaze to another era. "Brash and bold, but tender, too. With me anyway."

"She broke your heart?"

"No. The others did." The woman shook her head. "No one knew about Clarice and I. Not at first anyway. We had to hide it. We both pretended to have boyfriends, just to fit in with the others. We got careless one night at the Flamingo Lounge. Do you remember that place?"

"No," Billie said. "Before my time."

"I loved it. We saw The Yardbirds play there once. Anyway, Clarice and I snuck into one of the rooms upstairs. Our friends caught us. And that was the end." The woman's heavy mascara ran, trailing a black tear. She dabbed at it and the loose eyelash came away, clinging to her index finger. "Look at me. I'm falling apart."

"Let me see that," Billie said, taking the lash from her. One aspect of her gift was the ability to make the ethereal corporeal. The false eyelash was solid in her fingers. "Go on."

"We were tormented after that. Shunned from the group. They told everyone about us. Such a juicy scandal, they couldn't help themselves. We both lost our jobs. And then Clarice died."

"How did she die?"

"She was beaten to death," the woman said. "The boyfriends of our former friends. They waited outside Clarice's building one night and attacked her. They beat her so badly I didn't recognize her in the hospital. She had beautiful lips. Clarice passed the next day."

Billie watched the woman's eyes glaze over as she spoke. "Did they attack you, too?"

"No. I just didn't want to be alone anymore. Clarice was gone and everyone I knew treated me like a leper. My family disowned me. So, I went home and mixed myself a drink. I used to try my hand at making new cocktails. This one was special. I ground an entire bottle of pills with a mortar and pestle and jazzed it up with a quart of gin and some lime. It did the trick."

The woman wiped the bloody foam from her mouth and grimaced at the foul red it left on her fingertips. She looked up at Billie. "I keep hoping to find Clarice out there. Wandering the streets of this city the way I do, but she's not here. I guess she moved on. Without me."

"I'm sorry for your loss," Billie replied. She handed back the lash. "Can I ask you something?"

"Shoot."

"Why don't you move on?"

The woman lowered her eyes. "I'm not sure anymore. I guess I'm afraid."

"There's nothing to be afraid of."

"How would you know?" The dead woman reapplied the false lash. "I'm afraid of what happens to suicides on the other side. I'm afraid Clarice won't be there to meet me."

With no answer to the question, Billie remained quiet. Useless. She took a metal shaker and filled it with ice, lemon mash, syrup and whiskey and shook it vigorously. Pouring it into a heavy rock glass, she topped it with lemon rind. "Take my hand," she said.

A quizzical look came over the dead woman's face, the false lashes fluttering. She reached out and took Billie's hand.

"This one's on me," Billie said. She pushed the glass forward. "Go on."

The woman laughed it off at first, but saw the level gaze of the bartender. She reached for the glass and her eyes lit with surprise that it was solid in her hand. Raising it to her lips, she tasted it and her eyes closed in relief as the tart bite of lemon flushed the awful taste from her mouth. She drained it dry, the ice clinking in the glass. Her voice was brittle when she spoke. "Thank you."

Her cold hand slipped out of Billie's and the rock glass fell to the bar, rolling over the lip to the floor.

~

It was almost 4 AM when Billie trudged up the two flights of stairs to her small apartment on Barton East. The climb murdered her lats after being on her feet all night and the only thing pushing her on was the thought of collapsing into bed. Even if the bed was empty. Curling up beside a warm body would have been ideal, but beggars can't be choosers, as her aunt was fond of saying.

Pushing through the door, she saw that her flatmate was up. Half-Boy squatted on the floor near the window.

"Are you waiting up for me?" she said, dropping her bag at

the door.

The legless ghost turned and dragged himself away on his hands into the other room, leaving a fresh trail of dark blood on the floor.

Someone was in a bad mood, she thought. Her flatmate could be oddly temperamental sometimes. Brushing it off, Billie crossed the room to fetch a glass of water before heading to bed, but stopped at the doorway to the kitchen. A glass lay broken on the tiled floor, shards of it scattered everywhere. That's why the little ghost had skulked off like a guilty dog.

"Another glass?" she fumed. "I barely have any left."

For a phantom that could scale walls like a spider, the Half-Boy was oddly clumsy in the kitchen, often knocking things from the counter as he scuttled through the room. Sweeping up the splintered glass, she dumped the mess into the waste bin, wondering how much glassware she had left. Opening a cupboard, she saw that she was down to three water glasses, all mismatched. Maybe it was time to buy the plastic kind that wouldn't shatter when knocked aside by a clumsy spirit.

Glancing over the narrow kitchen sparked an ember of disgust. She lived like a college student. None of her dishes or glasses matched, everything gleaned from flea markets and second-hand shops. The place was a constant mess and it was haunted. She thought again about Mockler's offer to move in together and halfway reconsidered. If it was some other house, she'd agree in a heartbeat. The thought of starting fresh in a new place seemed like complete fantasy as she lingered in the cramped confines of this worn down kitchen.

Falling into bed, she pulled the duvet up to her chin to get warm after the cold bike ride home. A shadow moved across the ceiling. Half-Boy scuttled down the wall to the chair opposite the bed. He perched there and watched her like a housecat. Blood from his amputated thighs dribbled from the edge of the chair and spattered to the floor in a slow drip.

Billie watched the blood pool under him. By morning it would be gone. "Will you try to be more careful? Or at least clean up if you break something."

The boy didn't move, his small eyes narrowing under the brim of his cap.

Watching him, Billie thought back to the woman in the go-go boots at the bar and how she was afraid to move on, stuck here on this side and doomed to haunt the streets of the city looking for a lover who would never return. She thought back to the spirit of the newly dead man outside his own funeral. He, too, had been afraid to move on. Like the woman in the kicky boots, he would have been left behind to haunt the streets if she hadn't guided him back to the light. Studying this child across the room with his shorn limbs and tongue cut out, she wondered if he, too, had been afraid to move on and, thus, became trapped on this side of the veil. Judging by his garments, he had haunted the streets of Hamilton for a long time. A hundred years, maybe more?

He'd had a chance once to cross over. Back in the summer when she was still learning to deal with her abilities. Half-Boy had been swallowed whole by a monstrous phantom she had nicknamed the Undertaker. In a hidden mortuary room, Billie had pulled the Half-Boy out of the monster, along with a hundred other souls that the Undertaker had devoured. A light had appeared from above and the lost souls made their way to it. She had felt its pull and would have wandered into it had it not been for the boy stopping her, but, in doing so, he had missed his own chance to go with the others. The warmth had receded, leaving Half-Boy behind.

Something clicked together in her scattered thoughts and stray puzzle pieces linked together. Billie slid her hand out from under the covers and she patted the bed next to her. "Come here."

The boy dropped to the floor and sprang onto the bed. She patted his cold hand. "We're going to sort it out. You and me."

The small ghost looked at her, but the woman was already asleep.

CHAPTER 10

NO ONE LIKED the morgue, least of all Mockler. Arriving late for the viewing, he hurried through the doors into the examining room. Detectives Hoffmann and Latimer were there, lingering by the door, well away from the wheeled gurney holding centre stage in the middle of the room. Both men nodded a hello.

He didn't have to be here. As primaries on the case, Hoffmann and Latimer were obligated to examine the deceased. As secondary, Mockler could have skipped the procedure altogether, settling for a quick update by the primary investigator afterward. Odinbeck was absent, having the good judgment to stay away.

The door swung open and a woman in a lab coat swept into the room. Marla Tran was the deputy coroner. Her cheery smile was a marked contrast to the grim features of the assembled officers. "Morning, gentlemen. Sorry I'm late."

"No worries," said Hoffmann. "I just want to get this over

with."

"Of course," Marla said. She nodded to Mockler. "How are you, Ray?"

"Good," Mockler replied. "You look tanned. Did you go away?"

"Conference in Key West. The weather was gorgeous." The coroner lifted away the sheet to reveal the body on the table. "Shall we get started?"

"Please," said Hoffmann, a slight impatience to his tone.

Mockler held back a little and let the other detectives take charge. Hoffmann was a good detective, but he was a little territorial for Mockler's liking, especially when he was primary on an investigation.

"As you can see," Marla began, "we have a white male, approximately 20 to 30-years-old. Five eleven, 173 pounds. Brown hair and eyes. The fingerprints and dental shots are complete so you can start running for matches there. Physical characteristics, a scar over the thorax, about six centimetres long. Possibly from surgery at a younger age."

Hoffmann nodded. "That's the details. What's the cause of death?"

"It's a bit of a toss up at the moment, between blood loss and hypothermia."

"You don't know?" asked Latimer.

"Not precisely." Marla pointed to a long wound along the abdomen. "We have major trauma here. The wound was caused by a blade, penetrating seven centimetres down where it punctured the liver. At the same time we have signs of hypothermia. Both would have caused death; it's just a matter of figuring out which one got to him first."

Hoffmann moved around the table. "What about the horns?"

Marla wheeled in a small cart. Atop the stainless steel tray lay a set of antlers. "A ten point rack of your common cervidae. A white-tailed deer."

"Jesus," Hoffmann uttered. "These things were growing out of the victims head."

Mockler leaned in for a better look. Up close, the rack was big and lethal looking. "How were they attached, Marla?"

Hoffmann fired a dirty look at him and Mockler backed off. Leave the questions to the primary, he reminded himself.

Marla tilted one of the racks to show the root. "The base of the antler was fixed to a band of crimp metal. The metal band was attached to the victim with six millimetre surgical screws."

Latimer winced. "They drilled it into his skull? Wouldn't that kill him?"

"No," the coroner answered. "The screws went into the bone without piercing the meningeal layer. They didn't hit the brain."

"That must have hurt."

"It would have," Marla said, "but we found a number of narcotics in the tox screen. He may not have felt it too much."

Latimer sighed. "Why the hell would they do that?"

The million dollar question. No one present had an answer

and the question lingered over the room.

Hoffmann pointed at the victim's left arm. "What about all these scrapes and cuts to his limbs?"

"Some of these may have occurred at the scene if the victim was dragged through the brush." Marla indicated a spot on the chest where the skin was scarred with tiny markings. "Some are intentional. Here, it appears that the skin was lacerated with a sharp instrument, like a razor blade, into a pattern or figure."

The detectives bent over the body for a closer look. Obscured by the scrape marks, there was a pattern to the hairline cuts that formed a strange design.

"I can barely make that out," Latimer said. "You sure it was intentional?"

"It's too precise to be random. The flesh has been cleaned up, but, at the time it was done, it would have been more noticeable. There are seven occurrences of these on the body. Here on the throat, the lower abdomen and the right knee. The remaining four are on the back."

"This one looks like a triangle." Latimer squinted at the hatching marks on the stomach and then looked up at his partner. "What do you make of it?"

"It's like they doodled on the guy with a knife," Hoffmann said. "God knows what these figures are. You sure that's a triangle? Maybe it's a letter."

"Like the perp cut his initials into him?" Latimer asked.

"It's a sigil," Mockler said.

Hoffmann and Latimer straightened up. "A what?"

"It's like a signature, but with a design. It's an occult thing." Mockler pointed out the cuts on the throat and chest. "This one means the devil. The one over the heart means life. Or birth."

"Devil?" Latimer scoffed. "Are you shitting me?"

Detective Hoffmann's eyes hardened on the younger detective. "How do you know that?"

From Gantry, Mockler recalled. The symbols painted over the cellar of the Murder House, more of them scrawled in the notes of a dead pulp writer who had mysteriously vanished. Gantry had explained what some of the glyphs signified. It had seemed like malarkey to Mockler at the time, but seeing the same marks on the victim here brought it all back. "I've seen these before. The last case Odin and I worked."

Hoffmann raised an eyebrow. "You sure these are the same?"

"They look the same. Given the nature of the crime, the way the victim was bound, I'd say it's the same weird occult stuff."

Latimer shook his head in disgust. "I hate spooky shit."

"That makes two of us," Hoffmann replied. "Good thing we got the spooky expert on our side."

Mockler gritted his teeth at the nickname, but let it go. He turned to the medical examiner. "Marla, have you photographed all of these marks yet?"

"All done. They're attached to the report."

"I'll forward them," Hoffmann said as he turned for the door. "Mock, can you take a look at them? Tell me what you think?"

He should have kept his mouth shut. Now, he was going to have to delve back into the creepy stuff just when he'd thought it was all behind him. Mockler nodded. "Sure."

~

Seated at the kitchen table in her pajamas, Billie warmed her hands around a mug of coffee. With the laptop opened before her, she scrolled through a list of funeral homes downtown and began calling each one. It was past noon and she'd already missed one service, but there was another this afternoon at Dunwich Funeral Chapel on Cannon. Seven blocks away. That just might work.

The real question was whether or not the boy would come.

They had a routine, these two odd roomies. The Half-Boy emerged after the sun went down, creeping out from the shadows in the room. They would spend their evenings together or a shorter time when Billie came home from work. The boy would often return to the shadows when the sun rose on the new day. Occasionally, he would spend the day with her, typically if she was ill. The recent experience at the house on Laguna Road had left her weak as a foal. The ghost child had watched over her.

Billie slid the phone onto the table and crossed to the other room. It appeared empty. "Where are you?"

A book fell from the shelf, but the living room still appeared to be unoccupied. It was too bright in here, too much sunlight from the windows. She drew the blinds, dimming the room. Half-Boy materialized on the floor, leafing through the pages of the fallen book.

"What is that?" She came around and knelt at his side. The book was a pictorial history of old Hamilton, something she'd found at a church sale last spring. Black and white photographs from a time before the automobile. The unpaved streets of mud crowded with shanty stalls and horse-drawn wagons. Stern-faced men in waistcoats and derbies, the women lifting the hems of their long skirts out of the mud of the streets.

"I like these old pictures," Billie said, entranced by the images. "It's hard to imagine what life must have been like back then."

The boy turned another page. He didn't react, as if unaware of her presence. With most spirits that Billie encountered, manipulating objects in the physical world took a great deal of effort. Many were unable to move so much as a feather. The boy was different. He could move things with ease, often with great force. She had once witnessed him hurl John Gantry across the room. The boy seemed unaware of his own strength.

She watched him turn the pages. The women in their hobble skirts, the boys in short pants. "What do you see in those pictures? Is there something you recognize?"

The lad came to the last page and closed the book. He pushed it away.

"Look at me," Billie said.

He turned his head partway. His pale face was dirty, smeared with soot and dried blood. With her ability to make the ethereal real, physical contact could make a ghost as solid as she was. Billie had once tried to wash the grime from his cheeks but the stains would not come clean.

She reached out and took his hand. Cold as stone in winter. "I want you to come with me today. There's something I want to show you."

He didn't meet her gaze. He never did this close, but he nodded slowly.

"Okay," she smiled. "Let me get dressed, then we'll go."

She didn't have a lot in the way of proper attire, but Billie cobbled together an outfit that was basic, respectful and black. The shoes were nice, but they pinched, her feet unused to walking in heels. Mercifully, the Dunwich Funeral Chapel wasn't that far away. The wind chilled her bare legs.

"We're almost there," she said.

The Half-Boy hobbled along on his hands, keeping pace with his peculiar trot. His eyes darted around nervously, as if wary of danger. She wondered if the boy saw the same streets that she did or if he perceived the city differently, from his era. Everything about the little ghost was a mystery.

The covered portico of the Dunwich Funeral Chapel rose up before her. The boy stopped in his tracks when Billie climbed the front steps.

"It's all right," Billie said. She didn't think he'd balk so soon. She hadn't even gotten him inside yet. "Come on. I want you to see this."

He looked up at the building and then scratched his head, tipping his cap askew. He reminded Billie of a reluctant child on the first day of school, curious, but scared. She held out her hand and he scuttled up the concrete steps to take it.

There was a signboard in the lobby, indicating that the wake for Lucretia DiNotta was in the east wing. Billie led the way down the corridor to a spacious room filled with flowers, some real and fragrant, the others false and odourless. Less than a dozen mourners present, standing or seated on folding chairs about the room. A small table to her left held a guest book and a few framed photographs of the deceased. One was a recent shot of a frail woman with white hair and a thin smile. The other was greyscale from another era. The deceased as a young woman in saddle-shoes and a pleated skirt. The woman's smile remained thin in both photographs, as if afraid to show her teeth.

The open casket rested at the far end of the room, flanked by wreaths on both sides.

Billie took an empty seat near the door, staying out of the way of the mourning party. She glanced at the coffin again, but all she could see were two thin hands clasped together. Half-Boy sprang onto the empty chair next to her. His head twitched about at every movement in the room like a pigeon alert to danger. She smoothed her hand down his back to calm him.

She had prepared an excuse for being here if any of the mourners should ask if she was family or friend to the deceased woman, but no one approached her. A few minutes passed and then the room seemed to dim by a degree. What she was waiting for began to unfold. The boy sensed it, too, craning his neck to see over the people in the room.

Lucretia DiNotta entered the room, invisible to anyone, but the psychic and the crippled boy next to her. Her appearance resembled the one in the black and white photograph. A young woman in her early 20s but without the smile. Her hand dabbed away tears as she looked through the faces of those who had come to mourn her. She glanced once at the casket and then turned away.

The boy at Billie's side had begun to fidget in his seat, tensing up as if ready to bolt from the room. She wondered if he disliked being around other ghosts or if something else was making him uncomfortable. She kept quiet and waited for the next moment, the reason she had brought the boy to this place.

A crest of warmth flushed over her, coming from outside the room. There was a stillness to it that immediately lowered her pulse, a silence that baffled her ears against all other sound. She turned to see if the boy was feeling it too, but her heart sank when she saw him cower at it. He gripped her arm and hunkered behind her as if to hide from it.

"It's okay," she cooed to him. "There's nothing to be scared of."

Lucretia's DiNotta's face brightened as the warmth fell over her. She smiled and Billie could see her teeth now. The woman was bucktoothed, but she no longer bothered to hide them. She stepped away from the mourners and their grief toward the beacon coming from the hallway.

Then, she stopped and looked directly at Billie and the child hiding behind her. "Is he coming too?" she asked.

The boy shrank away at the dead woman's voice. Billie took his hand and squeezed it. "I think you should go with her."

The boy shook his head.

"Listen to me. You saved my life twice now." Her voice was already cracking and she struggled to keep it calm. "I don't know how to thank you for that, but I can't keep you here. You deserve better."

His tears cracked into ice as they fell onto her arm. His grip on her hand clamped tighter.

"Go with her," Billie pleaded. "She'll show you the way."

The dead woman held her hand out to the boy.

Billie watched him swipe his forearm over his eyes, as if shamed by his tears. She touched his cheek, her voice breaking. "I love you, but I don't even know your name. You deserve to be at peace."

He jerked his hand away. His face darkened, in anger or pain or both. The boy dropped to the floor and scuttled up the wall to the window. The glass broke as he smashed through it and then he was gone. Everyone in the room startled at the noise, their heads snapping toward Billie.

Lucretia DiNotta let her hand fall to her side. "I suppose he's not ready. What will happen to him?"

"I don't know," Billie answered.

The dead woman left the room and the warmth dissipated shortly thereafter. An older man in a dark suit approached Billie and asked if she was a friend or family to the deceased.

"Neither," Billie said as she hurried from the room.

CHAPTER 11

"I QUIT," BILLIE declared.

Kaitlin sat across the table in the busy cafe. "What do you mean, you quit? Quit what?"

"The spookshow," Billie replied. "Talking to ghosts, being a psychic. I'm done with it."

Kaitlin leaned back with a puzzled expression, as if she hadn't heard her friend correctly. Patrons swept past their table toward the counter, the cafe filling up quickly.

Billie hadn't been in the mood for company when her friend had called. Left shattered at the boy's refusal to cross over, she had circled the block outside the funeral chapel for him, but Half-Boy was gone. Walking home, she kept glancing back to see if he was following, but the street remained empty. Instead, other phantoms had sought her out, slithering from the shadows or rising up out of the earth before her. Her guard had slipped and the dead swarmed in, drawn to her. She pushed them out of her way, deaf to their tales of tragedy and rage. There was only one ghost she wanted to see, but every time she looked back, he wasn't there.

The dead followed her home, crowding into the narrow stairwell as she climbed the steps to her apartment. A few continued to weep, but some had become angry at being denied, shouting after her and tugging at her coattails like persistent children.

Reaching the top of the stairs, Billie spun around and roared at them to go away. More than just a scream, some other force swept out of her and pushed the dead away. They tumbled and scattered down the steps like daisies in a windstorm.

That had been the moment of decision, to quit the dead and get her life back.

Salt had been poured over the threshold of her front door, more of it spilled into the window sills. The only tangible line of defence to keep the dead out of her home. Billie still didn't understand how it sealed them out, all she knew was that it worked. There was one window left to secure, but she wavered, the tin of sea salt in her hand. This window was faulty, the pane never slipping properly into its casement, making it drafty in the winter. It was also the one the Half-Boy used to crawl in and out of her home like a burglar in the night. She didn't know why he insisted on physically opening the window. As spirit he could simply pass through solid brick and glass, but, for some reason the boy chose to raise the window pane. Maybe, she wondered, it was his own skewed sense of etiquette.

Billie turned away and returned the salt tin to the kitchen counter, leaving his window unsealed. Her phone rang five minutes later. Kaitlin wanted to meet for coffee.

"How can you just quit?" Kaitlin asked. "Is that even possible?"

"Why not?"

Kaitlin fired back a look of suspicion, expecting a joke. "I don't know if it works that way, Billie."

"There's no need for it anymore." Billie tucked her hair behind her ear. "It's served its purpose. Now, it's over. I never wanted this ability in the first place."

"What purpose are you talking about?"

"I found my mother's remains and now she's laid to rest," Billie shrugged. "The Bourdain woman is gone and you're out of danger. There's no need to talk to dead people anymore. I just want to put it all behind me. Especially now."

"Oh." The look of disappointment in Kaitlin's eyes was sharp.

"What is it?"

"I don't know about that last part. About being out of danger."

Billie sat up. "Did something happen? Is she back?"

"No," Kaitlin said. "But I keep thinking about it. She's always there in my dreams. I'm always tense, like something awful is going to jump out and hurt me."

"I'm sorry. You look a little exhausted."

Kaitlin rubbed her eyes. "I haven't slept properly in ages. My nerves are shot and I'm just...angry all the time."

"Is Kyle looking after you?"

"No. He just tells me to get over it. All we do is snap at one another now." Kaitlin's eyes fell to the mug in her hand. "Jen doesn't want to talk about any of this stuff. Same with Tammy."

That sounded familiar. Billie had experienced the same thing when her abilities first disrupted her life. She remembered how isolating it had been. "It's a bit of a conversation killer, isn't it?"

"That's just it though. I think that if I could talk through it, then I could deal with it. If I could understand what happened to me, to all of us, then I could deal with it better."

"I don't think there is a way to understand it," Billie said. "I don't understand any of it. How it works or why it happens. There's no logic that applies to it."

Kaitlin looked up in surprise. "How can that be? You live with this stuff all the time. You must understand something of what it all means. The ghosts and the hereafter and all the weirdo paranormal stuff."

Billie looked up at the younger woman's eyes, eager for help, pleading for some scrap of understanding. "I wish I did, but the truth is, I don't have a clue. I don't know why some people move on after death and others don't. I don't know why I have this ability to see the souls that are lost and trapped here. I don't even know if there's a heaven or hell. All I know is that I'm tired of looking for meaning in something that appears meaningless. I just want to put it all behind me. I want my life back. That's all."

Kaitlin's face drained, the hope dying in her eyes.

"I wish I had answers for you, Kaitlin," Billie added. "I honestly do, but all I have are questions. And I'm sick of asking."

Their table jostled from a passerby, the cafe filling up with the after-work rush. Billie reached for her things. "Let's get out of here."

Back on the street, Kaitlin said little, withdrawing into herself. Billie linked her arm around her friend's elbow as they walked down John Street. "You've been through an awful experience. Like any trauma, it takes time to get over it. Do you still see that therapist?"

"Not anymore. I thought I didn't need her." She laughed. "It's kind of funny now."

"Call her," Billie suggested. "Maybe you could talk through it with her."

"And tell her about this? She'll think I'm crazy."

Billie pulled her along. "You *are* crazy, Kaitlin. You're seeing ghosts."

~

"Bingo!" Detective Odinbeck exclaimed, hanging up the phone. "We got a match!"

Mockler looked up from his monitor. "Who was that?"

"Hoffmann," Odinbeck said, rising out of his chair. "He said we got a hit on the fingerprints of the antler man. Victim identified."

"Who is it?"

"He wants to show us in person, the big drama queen. Let's go."

Mockler rose and followed his partner through the cubicles to the other side of the homicide bullpen. Detective Hoffmann sat behind his desk with a grim expression. Latimer leaned against the wall. Both men looked up when the secondaries entered.

"So the gods have cut us a break?" Odinbeck said. "What do we got?"

Hoffmann reached into the printer and handed up the sheet. Mockler drew alongside his partner to scan the photograph on the page. A standard driver's license photo, the man pictured meant nothing.

"Justin Burroughs," stated Hoffmann. "Lately of 1240 Hastings Avenue."

The name bit hard. Mockler scrambled his brain to dredge up where he knew it from. "I know that name," he uttered.

"You should," Hoffmann said. "He's your case."

Odinbeck lowered the page in his hand. "Our case?"

"He's wanted on an assault charge on Kaitlin Granger three weeks ago."

Justin. The details came screaming back to Mockler instantly.

Justin Burroughs and another man named Owen had tried to kill Kaitlin when she was in the hospital. Both men were part of some ghost-hunting team that Kaitlin had gotten mixed up with. They were also under the control of something evil that lurked within the hated Murder House. Less than a week later, these two men had abducted Billie and taken her to the house. Something terrible had happened there and Mockler felt a chill recalling it all.

"I remember now." Odinbeck turned to his partner. "He went after Billie's friend when she was in Hamilton General. Part of that awful shit that went down at the Murder House. Remember?"

Mockler would never forget it, no matter how long he lived. "I don't believe this," he said, scanning the details on the page again. Justin and his accomplice had fled from the Murder House minutes before he and Billie had burned it to the ground.

"That makes antler-boy your case now," Hoffmann said. He gathered up the murder book, a binder that held the pertinent paperwork, and placed it in Mockler's hands. "To be honest, I'm kinda grateful. I hate spooky cases like this."

Odinbeck winced, as if he'd swallowed something bitter. "You gotta be kidding me. This shit case?"

"Prior investigation means you two are primaries now," Hoffman declared. "But don't worry, we got your back."

Odinbeck stayed to rib the other investigators about passing the bloody buck. Mockler went back to his desk. The murder book felt like an iron anchor in his hands.

Laying the book down, he leafed through the reports, trying to recall a name. Justin had an accomplice with him, another amateur ghost-hunter type. The two of them had website where they posted their adventures. Tapping at the keyboard, he called up the report on the assault on Kaitlin and found the man's name. Owen Rinalto. The two men had vanished together. If Justin had ended up dying in some bizarre ritual, then where the hell was Owen?

~

Why hadn't he been rescued yet?

The man in the darkness sat on the cold floor and pulled his knees to his chest. He had been trying to keep track of the passing days, but the number got mixed up. The cell he was in had no window. There was no way to see sunlight or nighttime, no way to mark the days. It was always night.

His friend had escaped. He had promised that he would get help and return to rescue him. Had it been three days ago or four?

Don't cry, he scolded himself. Justin will come back. He wouldn't leave you here.

The man in the darkness hugged his knees tighter to stay warm. He tried to remember how the two of them had come to be in this foul dungeon. Everything was a blur. He remembered the big house on the hill. He remembered the woman who had promised them so many things. They had tried to help her, but something went wrong. Something had ruined the plans and the last thing he remembered was running through the woods with Justin, tripping over the branches and scrambling up to keep going. The old house was on fire and the inferno lit up the night behind them.

Then, everything went dark and they woke up in this cold room where there was no light and no window. There was a door. It opened once a day and someone with a flashlight would blind them, toss in a bowl of cold meat and take out the slop bucket. Sometimes they were questioned about the woman in the house.

Justin had decided that he'd had enough. He sat next to the door for hours, waiting for it to open. When it did, he rushed their unseen jailer, smashing his head into the wall. The two of them ran, headlong into a dark corridor. Their captors chased after them. He couldn't keep up with Justin and the raw hands of their jailers pulled him down. Justin ran on, hollering that he would get help and come back to rescue him.

Three days or four? The man in the darkness could not remember. He shivered against the cold and tried ignore the scuttling sound of the rats sharing the darkness with him.

CHAPTER 12

WITH THE VICTIM identified, the next task was the toughest of the lot. Informing the family. Mockler climbed out of the car before a two-story Craftsman on Leland Avenue and steeled his gut for the duty before him. The irony wasn't missed, how the case had shifted to his desk just before this wretched task had to be accomplished.

Detective Odinbeck closed the car door and looked up at the house. "You ready, chief?"

"Nope," Mockler replied. He took a deep breath and exhaled slowly, a method he used to shut down internally, to close off his emotions to avoid being swept along in the grief he was about to dump on this poor family. "Let's go," he said.

Mockler had met Justin Burroughs's parents before, shortly after the assault on Kaitlin Grainger. Dennis and Anita were nice people. He was a mechanic, she a bank manager. There was nothing unusual about either of them, nothing to hint at their son's near obsession with the paranormal. Dennis and Anita were lifelong Ti-Cats fans. They liked to go to Mexico for two weeks every winter.

Dennis Burroughs answered the door and his face went ashen when the detectives introduced themselves. He seemed to sense what was coming next. Anita was the opposite, her eyes brightening with hope that the two police officers at her door were here with good news about their missing son. Odinbeck asked if they could all sit first. He knew immediately that the mother would collapse once she heard the news. Better to have her on the sofa first.

Mockler cleared his throat and informed the parents that their son was dead. The next 20 minutes played out exactly as he knew it would. The shock, the denial, the confused questions before the awful truth came down and crushed both of them. Anita went down, Dennis struggled to stay upright. The two detectives split the task, knowing what to do without even a glance at one another. Odinbeck took Anita, Mockler asked Dennis for a glass of water.

They sat in the kitchen, Dennis looking at the floor with a shell-shocked wash on his face. Mockler stayed quiet for a few minutes. He had already asked all of the pertinent questions in his previous interview with Dennis Burroughs about his son. How Justin spent most of his time chasing ghosts with these strange devices that read electromagnetic waves. How he and his friend Owen had a website that documented their investigations into the paranormal. How Justin had gone missing just before the assault on the young woman in the hospital.

"Is there anyone you'd like me to call?" Mockler asked. "A family member, a friend?"

Dennis shook his head. "There's a hundred people I have to call now, but at the moment I can't think of a single name."

"The names will come back. When they do, I can make some calls. Get someone over here to help."

The father nodded and went back to staring at a patch of the kitchen floor.

Mockler gave it another minute. "Dennis, did you see or hear from Justin after I was here last? Did he come home or call?"

"No," Dennis said. His eyes glanced once at the detective and quickly looked away.

Mockler noted the furtive look and scrutinized the grieving man's movements. The restless hands, the jittery knee. "I know you want to protect him, his memory, but I need to know everything. You saw him again?"

The father exhaled. Little fight was left in him after the weight of the bad news. "He called. Anita answered."

"When was this?"

"A few days before Halloween? I don't remember the exact date."

"Do you know what Justin told his mother?"

"Anita said he didn't sound right. Not himself. He told her everything was going to be okay. He'd met someone. A woman.

They were going to be happy together."

Mockler opened his notepad and began scribbling bullet points. "Did he mention who this woman was? A name?"

"Evelyn, I think. He said she was sick or something. He was going to help her so they could be together."

The name still put a chill into Mockler's spine. "Did he say anything about where he was staying? Or who he was with?"

"No. He told his mother not to worry and then hung up. He didn't ask to speak to me."

Those last words turned the father's eyes red again and he clenched his teeth to push his grief back down. Mockler closed the notepad and stayed quiet. The man's grief was almost physical, pushing down the air pressure in the room.

"Sheryl," said the father.

"Sheryl?" Mockler sat up. "Is that someone I can call for you? Family?"

"No. Owen's mother. You should tell her about this. She'll want to know."

"We're going to see her next."

"Have you found any trace of Owen?"

"Not yet," said Mockler.

Dennis Burroughs looked out the window. The sky was dark, the clouds like smoke. "Those two were inseparable. Have been since college. Maybe he got away."

"I hope so."

~

Ancaster was a 20 minute drive outside the city, a small town of pretty homes that served as a bedroom community. Yawning in the passenger seat of Jen's car, Billie still wasn't awake yet.

"Do you need another coffee?" Jen asked. "We can stop at the Timmy Ho's in town."

"Please," Billie answered. "I'm so tired that I feel hungover."

"You didn't have to come this morning."

"I wanted to," Billie mumbled. "I miss our flea market runs."

The flea market trips used to be a regular outing that Billie did with her oldest friend, something they'd done since high school. Jen still went, hunting for goods for the shop, but Billie often had to forgo them because she worked nights. Despite getting home after three in the morning, she was determined not to miss out this time.

After a stop for more java at the drive-through, they travelled on to a farm on the west of town. There were already a dozen cars in the grassy field before the barn. Jen liked to come early before the new goods were picked over entirely. Inside the barn, the pair moved through aisles of cast off ephemera from previous generations. Jen cut a path straight to the clothing in the far corner and started searching through the racks.

Billie sifted through a mound of clothing heaped onto a table, ripe with the smell of mothballs. "Have you heard from Tammy?"

"Couple days ago. A quick call. Why?"

"I haven't seen her in days. Just wondering how she's doing." Billie tugged a coat from the heap and looked at it. A woman's coat, late 60s. "What about this?"

Jen sized up the garment. "Cute. Any damage to it?"

"Not that I can see," Billie said after a cursory examination.

"Put it in the 'possible' pile," Jen said and returned to the hunt. "Tammy's been busy with work. I know she's had a lot of night shoots."

"That's good. She'll keep out of trouble if she's busy."

Jen moved onto the next rack, shoving the hanging clothes back to gain some elbow room. "Why would you worry about her?"

"She gets bored if she's not busy," Billie said. "Then, she parties too much. Is she seeing anybody?"

"Tammy? She's probably rotating through a handful of guys. If there is someone, she hasn't mentioned it." Jen plucked a dress from the rack and tossed it over the coat Billie had found. "She gets bored easily with guys. She keeps threatening to go back to being bi-curious."

"I'm surprised she hasn't already."

"This is the definitely pile," Jen said, tossing another garment beside the others. Then, she looked at Billie with a wry smile. "Speaking of boys, how's your new boyfriend?"

"Stop."

"What? Aren't you two dating?"

"Barely," Billie grumped. She hated being put on the spot. "Not enough to refer to him that way."

"But you two are dating, right?" When Billie just shrugged, Jen pressed the issue. "Are you just hooking up?"

"It's not like that," Billie sighed. "But we haven't exactly gone on any dates. Not real ones, anyway."

Jen's face soured. "None? But he met us at the bar the other night."

"Well, there's one date. Sorta." Billie moved on to another table. "I'd kill for a plain old date, but it's just not in the cards, I guess."

"So, you're just getting to know him?"

"I wouldn't say that. We've spent a lot of time together, but the circumstances are always weird. Murder, dead bodies, haunted houses. Not exactly romantic." Digging deeper into a mound of clothing, she unearthed a pair of boots and held them up for Jen to see. "Definitely pile?"

"Oh yeah." Jen held up a skirt, pursed her lips in indecision, and tossed it onto the pile of possibles. "So, whatever happened with his fiancée?"

"They broke up."

"I figured out that part, but, I mean, was that before you two started up or after?"

Billie frowned. A touchy topic with Jen. "Nothing happened until after they split."

"That's good," Jen replied with no small sense of relief. "I'd like to get to know him better. We should have dinner together, the four of us."

"That would be nice." As soon as she'd said it, a warning bell sounded in Billie's head. "Not right away, but—"

Jen spun, her eyes sparkling with some idea. "You two should come over. Like a dinner party. Adam and I can make something nice."

"Oh," Billie said, trying to play up the enthusiasm in her voice. It sounded like a disaster in the making. "Maybe."

"Are you working Wednesday night?"

"No."

The gears were already turning. Jen's eyes sparkled. "We'll do it Wednesday. I can close the shop early and go home to prep. It'll be fun!"

"Don't get ahead of yourself," Billie said.

"Don't you want to?"

"Of course," Billie replied. Her friend's enthusiasm could often be a fault, sweeping things along before they were thought through. "Let me check with Mockler first."

"Would he be into it?" There was already a lilt of disappointment to Jen's tone.

"I'm sure he would, but he works odd hours."

They moved on, making their way through the clothing racks. Drawn to another table, Billie rummaged through an assortment of dishware and glasses to replace all the broken glassware in her kitchen.

"Try and convince him," Jen said. "I'd just like to get to know him."

"I will." Billie smiled at her friend's honesty.

"Look at this." Jen held up a raincoat, dark crimson and long. She tossed it to her. "Catch."

Billie held it up. "Swanky. Too flashy for me."

"You could use some colour. Try it on."

Billie slipped it on. A little long in the sleeves, but it felt right. She looked around, but there wasn't a mirror.

"It suits you," said Jen. "We can alter the cuffs if you want."

The material wasn't leather, but something synthetic and it was cold. Billie shivered once before realizing the chill wasn't natural. It still belonged to someone. She pivoted around to find the garment's owner sitting on a table of clothes. A woman around her own age, red hair and deep freckles. Billie stifled her shock, not wanting to alarm Jen.

The red-haired woman looked Billie up and down. "That was my favourite coat," she said. "My boyfriend bought it for me. Well, he stole it, but it was still a gift."

Billie's hand smoothed down the material, drawn to a spot on the left side. A hole in the slick material. The image of a knife flared quickly in her vision.

"Then, he had to go and ruin it for me," said the dead woman. "Just like he ruined everything."

Billie shrugged out of the raincoat.

The redhead slid down from the table. "I'm sure the hole can be fixed. Maybe your seamstress friend could mend it."

"No thanks," Billie hissed, tossing the coat away.

Jen watched her friend fling it off. "You don't like it?"

"Not my colour," Billie said.

The spectre drew closer. "You're the gypsy girl, aren't you? The one who can see us."

Billie turned away. "You got the wrong person."

Jen looked up, confused. "What?"

The redhead was undeterred. "I've always wondered what happened to him. He took off after ruining my coat. He probably just moved on, met a girl. Had a future that he stole from me."

Billie made for the door. "I'm gonna get some air. Holler when you're done."

Jen planted a fist on her hip at her friend's abrupt retreat. She retrieved the coat and found the damage in the material, already wondering if it could be discreetly stitched up. She heard Billie call back to her over the interior of the barn.

"Leave that," she hollered out. "Someone died in it."

~

Mockler swung the car to the curb before a narrow Victorian on Grosvenor Avenue. The driveway was blocked by a hockey net, the frayed ends of the netting flapping in the wind.

"Fer chrissakes," Odinbeck griped in the passenger seat. "I told those kids a hundred times not to leave the net out."

Mockler chuckled at his partner's grousing. Odinbeck had two daughters and a son, all of them hockey players. Mockler had even attended a few of their games. "Looks like they've taken over the whole yard."

"I'm gonna brain the lot of them," Odinbeck huffed as he clambered out of the car. "Thanks for the lift home. Get some sleep, huh."

Mockler mumbled goodnight, his mind elsewhere.

The older detective felt his radar ping. He bent down to peer inside the cab. "Hey. What is it?"

"Nothing," Mockler said. "Just a tough day."

Odinbeck scowled. "You got that stupid look on your face again. Like you're thinking too hard. Let it go, bud. It'll still be there tomorrow, whatever it is."

"Sure." Mockler put the car in gear. "G'night."

"I'm serious," Odinbeck said as he dragged the hockey net off the driveway and onto the lawn. "Let it go. Go home."

Detective Mockler assured his partner that he would do just that and swung the car back onto the street, roaring for the lights of King East up ahead. "Right after one more stop," he muttered to himself.

Neptune Avenue was quiet when Mockler rumbled up and pulled to the curb before the deconsecrated church with the blackened windows. A single car passed, its headlights flaring in the rearview mirror, then the street went dark again. Mockler killed the engine and sat in the dark car, watching the old church.

Just a second look, he told himself. That was all.

Dennis Burroughs had said something earlier about his son's interest in the occult that kept clanging inside the detective's skull. It collided with something that Gantry had told him about the old church on Neptune and the peculiar worship that went on there. He had dismissed it at the time as more of the Englishman's delusions, but it hammered up against the greasy feeling he had been left with after meeting the head of this dubious church with the blacked-out windows.

A quick reconnaissance pass, Mockler told himself. Nothing more. Five minutes and he'd take Odin's advice and go home.

The church doors opened and two men stepped out, lighting cigarettes under a bare bulb over the entrance. One of the men gesticulated with his hands as he spoke. His companion nodded and, then, they flicked their butts to the sidewalk and went back inside.

Mockler glanced at his watch. "Little late for a church meeting," he rumbled and then got out of the car.

The tall door swung open and Mockler stepped inside. At first he thought the lights were turned off, but, when his eyes adjusted he could see that the whole interior of the church had been painted black. The walls, pews, floor and windows were all brushed in flat black. Even the ceiling was painted. A few pinpricks of light glowed from candles in the darkness up ahead.

The only colour in the space came from an enormous cross suspended upside down over the altar, a deep shade of red. The effect was startling, making the hair on the back of his neck bristle.

He could see three men up near the transept of the church, but sensed there were more, hidden in the darkness. Two of them turned when the door clicked shut and immediately marched for the intruder. Big bruiser types, like linebackers dressed in black suits.

"You," barked one. "Get out. Now."

Mockler looked past them to the man near the altar. "Mister LaVey? Got a minute?"

The bruiser grunted at him again to leave, coming in fast and eager to brawl. He outweighed Mockler by a hundred pounds, but he stopped cold when he saw the badge in the detective's hand.

Szandor LaVey looked up from the oversized book he was consulting, a finger on the page to mark his place. Like the other two, he was clad in black and, against the black painted interior, he appeared as a disembodied head and pair of hands. "Detective, the church is closed which means you are trespassing. Unless, of course, you have a search warrant."

"I just had a few questions, Mister LaVey." Mockler walked up the aisle, casting his eyes over the nave. "Interesting colour scheme you chose."

LaVey slipped a ribbon into the page and closed the massive

book. "The church is closed to the public. I'll have to ask you to leave."

"I'm looking for some help, actually. I was hoping you could lend your expertise on an investigation."

"About the missing Englishman?"

"No," Mockler said. "About a homicide. One with a ritualistic aspect. To me, it looks like devil-worship, but I'm no expert. I was hoping you could help me identify it." He watched the man's brow rise up, intrigued by the notion. Appealing to someone's expertise always made them more amenable.

LaVey stepped down from the dais and approached the officer. "A homicide? Where did this happen? Who was it?"

"I can't go into any of the specifics of an active investigation, Mister LaVey, but there's a few details you could help me clarify." Mockler leaned against a pew. "The main thing I'm trying to discern is whether this crime was an actual satanic ritual or if it was just meant to look like one."

The church leader's hostility receded, replaced with curiosity. "I'll answer what questions I can."

"Great. Now, the victim was found naked in a wooded area. On his knees, with his arms lashed around a tree—"

"He?" LaVey interrupted. "The victim was male?"

"Yeah?" Mockler played up the role of ignorant rube, hoping to lure the man in more. "Is that significant?"

"It is. Most rituals require a female as the locus point. A male seems unusual."

"How so?"

"It depends on the purpose of the ritual, really. Certain fertility rites require a male. Some malignant rituals, too. Do you know what the purpose of the ritual was?"

"No idea. To me, it looked like human sacrifice."

LaVey folded his arms. "That is unusual. What else?"

"Here's the weird part," Mockler replied. "The victim was wearing antlers. They were actually attached to his skull. And there were symbols cut into his flesh."

"Antlers? That's barbaric. What kind of symbols?"

The detective produced his phone and flipped through the photo gallery. "This symbol was the common one."

LaVey squinted at the picture. "It's a simple pentacle. You see these everywhere."

"It's not a Satanic symbol?"

"Inverted like this, yes, but it's also a pop culture icon, co-opted by rock bands and Hollywood films. It's ubiquitous."

Mockler was discreet, observing the other man's reactions. Looking for the tell. Swiping his thumb over the screen, he brought up another image. A stylized X with arrow points. "What about this one?"

LaVey's brow furrowed as he scrutinized the picture. "This one is new to me. Are you sure this was deliberate? It looks like random cut marks to me."

"That's what I'm trying to figure out. So, it's not a symbol used in your practices?"

"I've never seen it before."

Mockler observed the man but no facial tics betrayed him. "What about the antlers on the head? Is that familiar?"

"I've never heard of that practice, let alone seen it done. I think, detective, that these details are meant to divert suspicion."

"This was only made to look like a Satanic ritual?"

"Yes," LaVey remarked. "Or it was done by someone with next to no knowledge of our beliefs. All religions attract their share of the deluded. Ours more than most."

"Do you know of any recent converts or visitors who seemed unstable? Or violent?"

"Not recently. A long time ago, we had an open door policy but that proved more trouble than it was worth. Now, we keep the door closed." LaVey adjusted the cuff of his jacket. "I can ask my staff if they've encountered anyone who seemed troubled."

Mockler produced a business card. "I'd appreciate that. Thanks for your time."

Szandor LaVey watched the detective cross back to the big oak doors. "Have you had any luck locating Gantry?"

"Not yet. He's still vanished."

"He's good at that. I'm sure he'll bob to the surface somewhere. Good night, detective."

Mockler nodded and went out the door.

CHAPTER 13

RETURNING HOME AFTER work, Billie couldn't stop worrying about Mockler. He had called earlier just to say goodnight after their opposing schedules had sunk any chance of seeing each other. Something in his voice had troubled her, a distractedness to it, but, when she had asked him about it, he said he was simply tired after another long day. After a few minutes of chitchat, she had asked if he was free for dinner the next night. Mockler had said he would make the time, but then seemed to deflate when she said that it was a dinner party at Jen's house.

After hitting on the idea at the flea market earlier in the day, Jen had already planned out a menu and even some fancy cocktails to mix, while pinning Billie down to a specific time. She told Jen that she would try but wouldn't promise anything until she had spoken to Mockler. Her date seemed indifferent to the idea.

"You don't want to go?" she had asked.

"I'm just surprised, to tell you the truth. I don't think I have a lot in common with your friends."

"That's because you don't know them yet. Jen just wants to get to know you."

"Ah. She wants to know if I'm good enough to date her friend?"

"Very funny," Billie had said. "She knows it's important to me. That's all. Will you come?"

"Of course. What time?"

"Eight. Will you have to work late?"

"I'll shift a few things around, but I'll make it."

That had made her happy. They said goodnight and she got back to work. Four hours later, she had begun to overthink the whole thing. Was he just being accommodating? Maybe he didn't like her friends after all? Was that the real reason for his reticence?

The apartment was quiet when she entered. More than that, it was empty. There was no presence in the flat at all.

Her eyes went first to the narrow window on the far wall, the one the Half-Boy used to gain entrance to the place. She had hoped it had been left open, the way he always left it, but it remained closed. On the off-chance that he had remembered his manners and closed the window after him, Billie had placed a scrap of paper against the pane. Any slight movement would have knocked it to the floor, but the tiny scrap remained exactly as she had left it. The small ghost hadn't returned home.

Normally that would have been good news, but it had been three days since the fiasco at the funeral home. Billie looked out the window at the city lights and wondered where the Half-Boy was and if he was all right. He was a ghost, she reminded herself. What could happen to him? He was like a tomcat, really. Free to roam the streets, he'd come home when he was ready to.

~

Six blocks east of the small apartment where the gypsy girl lived, a small figure emerged from a shadow and scaled the sheer wall of a brick building like some outsized arachnid. Its spindly fingers gripped the crevices of the brick as it pulled itself up and clambered onto a ledge three stories from the noisy street below with its unending chaos of cars and headlights and noise. The Half-Boy clung to his perch, looking for a way to escape the constant droning racket of the city streets. The noise was inescapable.

Haunting the interior of the tenement building on Barton, he had grown accustomed to the quiet of the space, the silence along its corridors and the space within the walls and the peace he enjoyed inside the home of the dark-haired gypsy girl. He had forgotten how loud and chaotic life on the streets was. It had been a long time since he had squatted among the filth of the streets, huddled under the gaslights for warmth.

That rare peace was gone now. The girl had jettisoned him from her life. She hadn't been the first to do so and he swallowed back the hot bitterness that burned in his gullet. His meager lot in life remained the same in death, to be shunned, turned away, cast out. Why had he thought that this latest refuge would be any different?

Perched on his ledge, he watched the street below with its horseless carriages and pedestrians going to and fro. Then, from the creep of his peripheral vision, he caught sight of two figures that were not unlike himself. A spectral pair that only he could see. Crossing the street below him, the figures drifted into a doorway. A moment later, he caught sight of one of them in a second-story window.

Reaching down, the boy without legs gripped the brick and mortar and scaled down headfirst to the street.

Hobbling up the staircase of the building, he could hear them talking in the rooms above. The building was derelict and empty, the voices of the pair the only sound within. Dragging his stumps along, he tracked the noise to a vast space that had once been a dance hall. A burned out chandelier hung cobwebbed from the ceiling. The south wall was all mirrors, cracked and cloudy with dust. The two spectres he had seen flitted about at the far end of the room. At first glance, they seemed an odd duo. The male was clad in the redcoat of a British soldier from a time when the land under them was a colonial outpost. An officer of some rank in his powdered wig and stockinged legs. His dance partner was of a more recent era. Her lithe frame donned in black leotard, her hair pulled tight under a ribbon, her feet bound in toe-shoes. She pirouetted in the Russian style, while the man stepped sprightly to a Scottish reel.

The mute ghost watched them dance, this odd pairing of the dead from different eras. The woman was a black swan of grace, her dark hair and features reminding him in no small part of the gypsy girl. Her partner clomped the boards in a rougher style, but the pair danced on, bowing and gesturing to one another in a singular dance of the dead sacred only to themselves. Blood from both of their open wounds dribbled to the floor as they twirled, but neither slipped or missed a beat.

The Half-Boy slunk out from his hiding spot in the hallway and hobbled into the dance hall. The dancers stopped immediately, sensing another presence in the room. The boy clapped his hands to show his appreciation, his gesture awkward and spastic, but he didn't want them to stop. He only wanted to cheer them on in their round-abouts.

He shriveled at the revulsion on their faces as they took his measure. Each of the dancers bled as profusely as he did from their open wounds, but they stepped back as if confronted with a leper. The woman turned her face into the shoulder of her dance partner to spare her eyes from the horrid sight. The soldier shooed him away with a linen kerchief in his hand as if dispelling a foul vapour. The pair retreated to the shadows and slipped into the cracked mirror as smoothly as dipping into a lake.

The legless boy stopped clapping, now alone in the decrepit ballroom. His hands dropped to his sides, his knuckles draping across the dusty hardwood of the old dance floor. Even his own kind rejected him. Turning away, he caught sight of his reflection in the wall of mirrors. A grotesque homunculus who dragged his pathetic frame along on his knuckles like some misshapen beast of the primate order. The hornet's sting in his breast kindled back at the reflection. He couldn't blame the spirit folk for their revulsion at his horrid appearance.

Nigh was the time to drift away, far from the judging eyes of both the living and the dead. Their scrutiny was too much to bear, much as it had been when he had scuttled along in the world of the living. Even, he remembered, in the time before the prison and the cruel moment when his legs had been shorn clean off by the drunkard with the sharp axe.

~

Finally, a real date. No spooky stuff, no angry spirits to disrupt their evening. Just dinner with friends, the kind of thing regular couples do all the time. Climbing into the passenger seat of Mockler's car, Billie had to pinch herself. Even this part was normal, being picked up by her date like it was prom night. He had even opened the car door for her. Not that she knew what prom was like, Billie recalled. She had skipped hers.

"You look great," Mockler said as he turned the ignition.

"Thanks. I tried." Billie felt her face flush, uncomfortable with compliments. She noted the smile on his face. Deep enough to crease a dimple in his cheek. "So do you."

Swinging the car back into traffic, Mockler twisted the rearview mirror and straightened his tie. "I wanted to go home and change out of my work clothes but I didn't have time."

"You always look good," Billie said. Her smile beamed. She liked complimenting him.

"Should I lose the tie?"

"Eyes on the road, officer." Taking a second look at him, Billie tugged the knot of his tie loose and slipped the whole thing from his collar. "I think that's better."

"Where are we headed?"

"Tisdale, just down from Cannon."

Mockler took a left at the next block. "Should we stop and get flowers or something?"

"I brought wine," Billie said, pulling the bottle from her bag to show him. "But flowers are good idea. Jen will appreciate that."

"Where's the closest florist?"

Billie cocked a thumb behind them. "Joanna's. Back that way."

"Hang on." Pulling to the curb, he swung the car around and shot back down to Barton. "Are you looking forward to this?"

"I am. I just hope Jen doesn't go overboard."

He looked at her. "What do you mean?"

"Jen loves dinner parties. Or anything with ceremony. She goes all out, so don't be surprised if there's a certain protocol to the evening."

"All right. Do you do this kind of thing a lot? The formal dinner parties and all?"

Billie shook her head. "Hardly ever, which is why Jen goes overboard when we do. You should see her Christmas parties. She's already got it planned out for this year." She pointed at something up ahead. "Just up here."

Pulling over, they climbed out and walked to the door. "I'm not big on flowers," he said. "Is there an etiquette to it?"

"Damned if I know. We'll just find something pretty."

"Hold up." He caught her arm and pulled her close. A kiss, then he smiled. "I missed you."

"Ditto," Billie said. She batted her eyelashes at him. "Hey, you wanna go park somewhere and make out before we hit the party?"

"Absolutely," he said. Billie noted the dimple in his smile had returned.

"They're beautiful," Jen exclaimed at the flowers offered to her. "Thank you." She ushered her guests inside to the narrow foyer of the house she shared with Adam.

"Thanks for having us," Mockler said. "You look great."

She really did, thought Billie. Jen's cocktail dress was an

early sixties affair with darts down from the fitted waist. Her hair was pinned up in a loose bouffant, her make-up subtle, but flawless. "Is that the dress you found on Saturday?"

"It is." Jen pivoted a small twirl. "After a quick darn to fix the hem."

"Where's Adam?"

"Out back, fussing with the coals again." Jen waved them through to the living room at the front of the house. Large with an immense bay window. "Come sit down. I'll get the cocktails."

"Nice place," Mockler said as Jen hurried for the kitchen. The room was a flawless mix of vintage pieces and modern touches, the lighting low and ambient. "It's like her shop."

"Jen's got great taste. I try to follow her style in the home decor department, but my place just ends up looking like a junk shop."

"You mean eclectic."

Billie rolled her eyes at him. She nodded at the food laid out on the coffee table. A charcuterie spread on a wooden cutting board. "Even this. Everything turns out perfect with Jen."

Jen swept back into the room with a tray of cocktails and her boyfriend in tow. "Ray, you remember Adam."

Mockler stood and shook hands. "Nice to see you again, Adam."

"You too, detective." Adam took the armchair beside Jen. "I'm glad you could make it."

"These," Jen said as she handed out the drinks, "are sidecars."

"Wow," Billie said, taking a sip of her drink. It was delicious and frosty. Even as a bartender Jen outshone her. "These are great."

"So," Jen said, turning to her guest. "Tell us about you, Ray. Where are you from? Where'd you go to school? What are your intentions toward my friend?"

Mockler laughed. "I think I'm getting grilled."

"She doesn't always give guests the third degree, I promise," Adam said. "Go easy on the guy, honey."

"Oh pshaw," Jen waved him away. "Why not get the details upfront. Besides, if you think this is bad, wait till you meet Aunt Maggie. Then, you'll be in for a grilling."

"I've met Maggie," Mockler replied. "She's very sweet."

Jen looked up in surprise. "You have? When?"

"We drove out to Long Point a couple weeks ago," Billie said. "When Ray opened up mom's cold case."

"Oh. Right." The oxygen flushed from the room. A tea candle guttered and Jen regained her composure. "I'd forgotten that."

Mockler turned to Jen's beau. "Jen said you got the barbecue going. What are you making?"

"Argentine ribs. It's a bit cold to be grilling outdoors. I had to feed it more wood to get the coals right."

"Sounds delicious. Are you a chef?"

"Graphic designer," Adam said. "I just mess around in the kitchen for fun."

Billie waved that notion away. "Don't listen to him. Adam's

an amazing cook."

Mockler raised his glass to his hosts. "Well, in that case, you can invite us for dinner anytime."

"You're a detective, right?" Adam leaned forward in his chair. "Homicide unit?"

"Yup." Mockler nodded and gave a half-shrug, leery of what was about to come next. Billie seemed to stiffen up next to him, as if she knew what was about to parlay. She was a psychic, he reminded himself.

"That must be a wicked job," Adam said. "Solving crimes and stuff. Murders, no less."

"It's a job. There's good parts and bad parts to it." He tucked into the tray of cured meat before him. "This is really good. Where'd you get it?"

"Cumbrae's," Jen answered, seizing upon the switch in topic. "They have great stuff there."

Reaching for the platter, Billie carried the conversation further along. "The place on Locke, with the pig in the windows?"

"No, the place out in Dundas."

Adam wasn't having any of it, his eyes locked on the man across the coffee table. "Still, that must be wild, figuring out clues and piecing together evidence. Building a case."

"It's different," Mockler said, smiling for propriety's sake.

Adam was just getting warmed up. "You ever take a crack at the Evelyn Dick case?"

"I have enough work on my desk. I don't need extra credit."

A slight chill tripped Billie's veins at the name. "Evelyn who?"

Adam guffawed. "Come on, the torso murder?"

Mockler dropped his hand over Billie's knee and gave it a squeeze. "It's nothing. An old case from the forties."

"Nothing?" Adam spat. "The woman killed her baby and cut her husband into pieces. It's like the most notorious case in the country."

"Eew." Jen elbowed her boyfriend. "Not exactly dinner conversation."

Mockler picked up his glass only to realize it was already drained. It had gone down quickly and he wanted another if he was going to have to play nice. "I wonder about the cops who worked that scene. What it must been like to inform that man's family that he was dead. That his head was missing."

"I guess," Adam replied. His eyes went down to his drink.

"Is there any more of this?" Mockler asked, shaking the ice in his empty glass.

"What about mob stuff?" Adam asked, blind to the hints. "You must have dealt with stuff like that?"

He looked at Adam. "Yesterday, I had to visit this very nice couple over in Glenview and tell them that their son was dead. That's the real test to the job. If you can stomach that task, you can keep going. If not, you sink like a stone."

Billie's eyes snapped quickly onto her date. "You had to do

that? You didn't tell me."

"Who wants to hear that stuff?" he answered. He took a breath and pushed down his ire, realizing too late how snippy he had just been to Billie. The young man's probing was irksome and he had lashed out at precisely the wrong person. "I'm sorry."

A lull in the conversation. Jen leapt at it, clutching Adam's wrist. "Should we check the barbecue? We don't want to char the ribs."

"It's fine," Adam said, a little too dismissively. He refocused on his guest. "I'm sorry, man. That must be awful. Was that the murder in the news? Up on the mountain?"

A grating ring filled the air. It was coming from Mockler's phone. Checking the screen, he got to his feet. "Excuse me. I need to take this."

Billie watched her date step out of the room to take the call. She could tell by his tone that it was work. Turning back, she levelled a hard gaze at Adam. "Dude, get a clue already."

Adam reared back, all innocent. "What?"

"He's not going to talk shop with you," Billie said. "He can't. So, just drop it."

"I'm just curious, that's all." Adam drained his glass and set it down. "Shall we talk about the charcuterie some more?"

"Adam," Jen said coldly. "Go check the barbecue."

"It's fine. I told you already—"

Mockler stepped back into the room, his phone still in his hand. "I'm sorry, I have to go."

"Now?" Billie shot to her feet. "It's your night off?"

"Something came up. I have to go." Mockler took a step in and pecked Jen's cheek. "I'm sorry about this. Maybe Billie and I can make it up to you?"

"It's okay," Jen said. "We'll do it another time."

Mockler reached out to shake hands with Adam. "Can I ask a favour? Will you send a piece of that barbecue home with Billie? I really want to try it."

Adam assured him that he would and Jen thanked him again for coming. Billie gripped Mockler's hand and walked him outside. "Can't someone else take the call?" she asked. "Whatever it is?"

"They said they wanted me on scene, so I gotta go." He pulled her close. "I'm sorry."

She pushed him away. "Go catch some bad guys."

A quick kiss and then he marched to his car and Billie watched him drive away. Nothing would ever be normal, she realized. Not even a simple dinner at a friend's house. A single thought kept buzzing in her brain like an insect trapped under glass. Would she and Mockler ever find time to just be a normal couple? Their track record did not foretell much hope.

CHAPTER 14

THE CALL WAS an unusual one. A break-and-enter at a church over on Sandford. Vandalism and destruction of property, but no body, no homicide. There hadn't even been an assault. Pulling up to the scene, Mockler saw a single police cruiser present, but its cherries weren't even flashing. Climbing out of the car, he couldn't figure out why the hell he'd been called to the scene.

Two figures stood on the wide steps before the church of the Holy Redeemer, their shadows cast long against the light over the front doors. One was a uniformed officer, the other a priest.

"Walton?" Mockler called as he approached the pair.

Officer Kate Walton descended the steps to greet him. Walton was five foot four with a slight build that belied her strength. Mockler had seen her drop men twice her size without breaking a sweat. A good cop with keen senses with whom Mockler had worked before. She had been the one who called earlier.

"Hi, Mockler," Officer Walton said. "Sorry to ruin your night off."

"That's okay. What do you got?"

Walton waved the cleric forward. "Detective, this is Father Ignacio Salvatore. Father, Detective Mockler."

Mockler clocked the man's age to be in the mid-50s, but his guess may have been skewed by the look of pale shock on the priest's face. "Father," Mockler said, shaking his hand. "I'm sorry to hear you had some trouble. Were you hurt?"

"No," said Father Salvatore. "I'm fine. Physically at least. My heart may have taken a knock at what they've done, but I'm not hurt."

Officer Walton nodded at the church before them. "Father Salvatore arrived about an hour ago to prepare for tomorrow. He found the doors broken in, the interior vandalized."

"Vandalized is understating it," the priest said. "What they did is obscene. I've never seen anything like it."

Detective Mockler noted again the shock rippling over the cleric's eyes but he still wasn't sure why he was here. "I see, but you didn't see anyone inside? No one was hurt?"

Walton turned to the shaken priest. "Father, I'm going to take the detective inside. Do you want to stay out here?"

"Yes. I can't look at that again."

Walton wagged her chin at the entrance and Mockler followed her up the steps to the doors. "I'm still unclear why I'm here, Walton," he said.

"I might be wrong about this, and, if I am, I apologize for wasting your time." Walton led the way through the doors into the church. "But take a look at it first. Then, you tell me."

The priest's words were apt. It was obscene. To the west of the nave stood a tall statue of the virgin on a raised platform where the penitent would light candles at her feet. These small votives had been swept away under the dripping carcass of some animal. It took Mockler a few moments to even identify the animal in question. It had been butchered into slabs of fur and blood, its entrails cut out and unspooled over the platform. The quartered legs of the animal ended in cloven hooves. Its head had been removed.

"Hell of a sight," Walton said quietly, observing the detective's reaction. "The eyes on that thing really gives me the creeps."

Breathing through the shock of it, Mockler studied the monstrous tableau. The head of the statue had been knocked clean off and it sat in a wet coil of intestines on the floor, the white plaster smeared with blood. The goat's head now sat atop the statue, plopped onto the neck of the virgin. The eyes with horizontal pupils looked down as if regarding the two police officers before it.

"Jesus Christ," grumbled Mockler.

"I'm surprised Father Salvatore didn't have a heart attack seeing this."

Mockler turned to the officer. "Did anyone see anything?"

"No one saw or heard anything unusual in the last few hours. Be careful where you step." Walton pointed at his feet. "The blood here on the floor? I didn't see it at first, but they wrote with it."

The detective took a step back to take in the mess on the floor. The spatter wasn't random, but it was difficult to make out. Climbing up onto a pew gave him enough of a perspective to hash out some of the blood pattern. One was a symbol, a triangle with what appeared to be hooks extended from it. The other splotchy pattern formed letters on the floor. SCRAAT.

"I have no idea what it means," Officer Walton said. "Doesn't sound like English."

"Who knows." Mockler took out his phone and snapped a couple photos of it before stepping down. "You still haven't told me why you brought me in, Walty."

The officer offered up a tiny shrug. "You're the expert on this stuff."

Why should he be surprised? The spooky rep was clinging to him like a bad smell, offensive and hard to shirk.

"It was that symbol, too," she said. "We've seen it before. At that old house on Laguna Road, where you had the dust-up with the freaky people in robes."

Mockler glanced at the uniformed officer and then dropped his gaze to the blood spatter again.

"I don't know if it means anything, but I thought you'd want to see it."

"Thanks. I appreciate that." Mockler leaned back against the pew and looked up at the goat's head perched atop the statue. "You're right about those eyes. Creepy-looking things."

"Do you think there's a connection between the two?"

I sure as hell hope not, he thought. The business at the Murder House was finished, the property bulldozed, but something of the same occult leanings linked the two as it also linked to the victim found in the woods lashed to a tree. The detective straightened up and turned to the officer. "You want some help processing the scene?"

"Chen and I can handle it. You can head home."

"I don't mind," he said. "It'll be more thorough with the three of us working it."

Officer Walton smiled weakly. "Thanks. Let me get Chen and we'll get started."

With the officer gone, Mockler stood alone in the desecrated church with the horrific mess on the west wall. Turning away from it, he puzzled out the possible meaning of the words painted in blood, but could make no sense of them. Taking out his phone again, he started typing the word into a search engine when he heard something move.

One of the hooves was quivering.

The hind leg had been quartered at the hip, completely severed from the flank end, but it moved, the leg coiling up, the cloven hoof bending back. Mockler's mouth went dry watching it undulate. The leg slipped from the platform and hit the floor with a wet thud, pulling down some of the tangled entrails with it.

The air went still, silence returning to the echo chamber of the church. Rationale demanded an answer and the detective skimmed through possibilities. A strange post-mortem seizing of the muscles? Early rigor mortis? A trick of the light?

When the severed goat's head cried out, Mockler simply turned and walked out the door, unwilling to witness anymore madness. The sound of the goat bleating followed him all the way out and, just before he ducked outside, he could have sworn the dead thing was calling out the strange word written on the floor.

~

The sting was acute and quick, like a needle into her lower spine. Billie gasped and the glass fell from her hand. Adam startled as it broke, assuming the woman was tipsy.

"Someone's had too many sidecars," he guffawed, going to fetch the broom.

Jen looked at the mess on her floor first and then the pain stitched across Billie's face. "Are you okay?"

"I'm sorry," Billie said. She knelt down to pick up the broken glass. "I'm such a klutz."

Jen fetched the garbage bin from under the sink. "What happened?"

"I don't know. Just a cramp or something." She dropped the glass shards into the bin. "I'm sorry, Jen. You went to so much trouble and the whole evening turned sour."

"C'est la vie." Jen reached out and touched her friend's brow. "You look a little piqued. Do you want to lie down?"

"I think I'll just go home before I wreck something else." Billie regarded her friend with some surprise. She had expected Jen to get upset over the broken glass or the ruined evening, but she wasn't. Her usually tightly wound friend seemed almost casual about the whole thing, dismissing it in French, no less. "You're sweet for putting up with me."

"Ditto," Jen said, her eyes meeting her friend's. There were fences that needed mending. "You sure you want to go?"

"I'm sure."

Adam came with the broom to sweep up the finer shards. Jen rose to her feet. "Do you want to lift home?"

"I'll cab it." Billie tugged on her friend's sleeve. "Walk me out?"

The night air was chilly as they stepped onto the porch. Billie slipped on her jacket and then turned to Jen. "I'm worried I'm going to screw this up."

"With Ray?"

"I thought everything was going to be okay now. It's all been so gonzo with him ever since we met, but when mom was found and laid to rest, I thought life would be normal again. Or at least not so complicated."

"You're being too hard on yourself, Bee. Things are always a bit odd when you start something new. It takes time to get to know one another."

Billie looked out at the street, the houses on the far side. "That's what I'm worried about. That he won't like what he finds."

"That's your self-doubt creeping in again." Jen reached out to fasten the top button on Billie's jacket. "We both know you have to keep that in check. Give him some credit. He's not the self-absorbed Peter Pan type you're used to dating."

Billie smiled, remembering what old friends were for. A quick hug and she shooed Jen back inside before she caught her death. She walked at a brisk pace up to Cannon Street but there wasn't a cab in sight. A residual ache throbbed in her spine from the earlier sting, an emphatic connection to another person. Shared pain. Digging out her phone, she called Mockler.

"Hey," she said when he picked up. "Are you all right?"

"I'm fine," he said on the other end. A little too quickly. "Why?"

"I dunno. I felt something. Thought you were in trouble."

"Nope. Everything's fine. How's the dinner going?"

Something seemed odd about his tone, but she couldn't be sure. "It was good. Quiet without you. I just left."

"So soon?"

"It was time." She squinted at the oncoming headlights, trying to spot a cab in the glare. "Are you sure you're okay?"

"Did you apologize to Jen for my exit? I'm sorry I had to abandon you there."

"She's fine. She understands." The street emptied of traffic and Billie marched on. "I hate this, Ray."

"What? That I had to skip out?"

"No," she interrupted him. "I've barely seen you in three days. And when I do, work takes you away from me."

"I'm sorry. It stinks, but I can't always skip out of it."

"I know," she said. The wind picked up and knifed clean through her thin clothes. She hadn't dressed for the weather. "I just miss you and I'm tired of stuff getting in the way. Why can't we be like a normal couple?"

"Maybe it's just not in the cards."

She hated that sentiment. And, in that moment, she decided to change the cards. Without thinking it through, she blurted out a crazy idea. "I'm staying at your place tonight. If I'm asleep when you get home, just curl up close to me. Deal?"

"Really?" His tone brightened immediately. "Are you sure?"

No.

"Yes," she said. "Where do you hide your spare key?"

"Under the flower pot. The big one with the dead flowers."

"Then, I'll meet you at home, mister detective."

"Deal."

She could sense his grin all the way down the ethereal phone connection. A cab appeared on the horizon, trawling east in her direction. She said goodbye and hung up, waving at the cab to stop. Climbing into the warm cab, the driver looked at her. "Where to?"

"Bristol Street."

CHAPTER 15

THE SPARE KEY wasn't under the flower pot. Billie put it back down and wondered if Mockler had forgotten it wasn't there. Had someone else used it? Looking over the porch, she looked under the mat and under the wicker chair, but no house key appeared. She fumed for a moment, feeling foolish and then went back to the big flower pot and tilted it over, but there was still nothing under it. Running her hand over the bottom of the pot, the key dislodged from the dirt it was stuck to and tumbled to the ground.

Crinkly leaves blew inside as she let herself in. The foyer was dark, the house beyond it as quiet as a tomb. She knew the house was empty, but couldn't quell her need to announce her arrival. Was that simple propriety or paranoia?

"Hello?"

The push of the wind against the window pane was the only sound. Turning on the lights, Billie crossed to the kitchen. The squeak of the old floorboards seemed shriekingly loud inside the vacant house. The kitchen was unchanged since she'd last seen it. Half-empty cupboards and two chairs stranded without a table. It still had the feel of a transient home.

Placing the key on the counter, she put the kettle on and opened cupboard after cupboard looking for the tea. There wasn't any. Mockler was more of a coffee drinker. Any tea in this kitchen belonged to the woman who used to live here and she had cleaned the place out when she left. Annoyed, Billie kept scrounging. She uncovered a jar of honey and noted two stray lemons on the counter. She'd fix that instead. The plan was simple. Make something hot to warm up and crash in front of the television until Mockler got home.

Did Mockler even have a TV?

Crossing into the living room, she took in the vintage suite he had salvaged for her, the mid-century modern stuff she liked. She still hadn't given him an answer about moving in together. The question was sure to come up tonight or in the morning. Tonight, she decided, would be a test. Maybe she could ease into the place and learn to live with its former history and old ghosts.

There was no television. In its place was a computer monitor atop a wooden box, the feed jerry-rigged into the cable. The screen turned blue when she hit the power button but there was no remote, no way to toggle a dial. She powered it off.

She wandered into the next room and hit the light switch. The dining room was empty save for a box on the floor and a broom leaning against the wall. A veil of warmth passed over her and she heard the faintest tickle of laughter in her ear. Residual energy from some moment of joy that had occurred in this room. Its intensity surprised her. She had kept her abilities closed off for days now, but something within the house was breaking through. Or was she unconsciously letting it come through. Biting down harder, the warmth and laughter evaporated. She didn't want to know what the occasion was that caused such joy. Had it been a birthday or some other celebration? Had he proposed to Christina in this room over a candlelit dinner? Maybe they had christened the dining room by having sex on the table?

Stop.

Billie stepped out of the room and killed the light. It amazed her how quickly her own thoughts could spin into poison that she was more than ready to guzzle down until she was sick. Go back to the sofa, find something to read and chill.

When she was little, her cuts and scrapes never healed properly because Billie couldn't resist picking at the scabs. As a woman facing her 30s, little had changed. She crossed the hall to the sunroom at the back. This room had been the art studio of the former woman of the house. The residual energy in this room was powerful and it ran hot.

She could almost see Christina in the room, working intensely at the easel, her eyes flushed with passion as if possessed. Despair ran alongside in an opposing stream of emotion. There the artist flung the canvas across the room and collapsed into a heap of self-loathing so deep it goosed the hair on Billie's forearms. Emotions of every colour ran electric in this studio like exposed wires, sparking and flaring as they crossed. There had been lovemaking in this room, but there had also been terrible fights, voices shrill with rage and booming with fury. The mixture of it all was as volatile as quicksilver and Billie thought she would choke on it.

Backing quickly from the room, she shut the French doors to the studio and hurried out the back door to breathe. The cold air flushed the toxic mix of emotions away. Off-balance, she lowered herself to the stoop and looked out over the backyard. There was energy out here too, but it felt different. His energy, she'd recognize it anywhere. He must have spent a lot of time out here alone. She wondered if the yard was where he came to put aside the day's misery and find some peace.

Did she honestly think she could ever live here? She didn't know if she would last a single night. What was she going to tell him?

When the wind got too cold, she slipped back inside, giving the studio doors a wide berth. Then, she heard the noise. Footsteps in another room. Someone in the house with her.

"Ray?" she called out. "Is that you?"

The footsteps in the other room stopped, but no voice called out in reply. Billie went still. Had someone broken in? Or had one of the dead followed her inside? She opened her heart by a fraction, just enough to sense if there was spirit present in the house, but she felt nothing.

A thud sounded from down the hall. The kitchen.

"Who's there?" She had to force herself toward the sound.

The doorframe splintered as a baseball bat smashed into it, the force of it an inch from Billie's face. She startled back to see a woman clutching the weapon in both hands.

Christina. Winding up for another swing.

~

"Get out!"

The baseball bat swung again, bashing the door jamb. Billie skidded backward, hands up to calm the woman down. "Easy. Put the bat down."

"What are you doing in my house?" Christina advanced with the bat clutched in both hands. A mask of anger twisting her features. "Get out!"

Billie backed further down the hallway, hoping she wouldn't get cornered by the woman. She seemed crazed. "Christina, put the bat down. Please. I'm not breaking in."

"Who the hell are you?" Christina spat, thrown off by the intruder addressing her by name.

"Just put the goddamn bat down and we'll talk."

The weapon lowered a half measure as Christina scrutinized the woman before her. "I know you from somewhere."

"My name's Billie. We met once." Billie watched the bat lower a little more, wondering exactly how to explain her presence to the woman who once lived here. "I'm a friend of Ray's."

The rage in the woman's eyes was swapped out for confusion as she squinted at the stranger. "Where is he?"

"At work."

Like a switch being flipped, the anger bled out quickly and the bat came down, dangling limply in the woman's hand. Christina glanced up at Billie and then looked away. "Right. Didn't take him long, did it?"

Billie felt her own fear burn off. "What are you doing here?"

"You don't get to ask me that!" The rage flared up briefly before dissipating again. The bat fell and rattled loudly against the floor and then Christina turned away. "Jesus Christ."

Her guts gave out, hating everything about this sordid scene. The last thing Billie needed right now was this drama. She could leave, just walk out the door and abandon the woman to her torment. Why was she even here?

Hearing the sound of the tap running, she crossed into the kitchen. Christina stood over the sink, splashing cold water over her face. When she straightened up, Billie took note of the red-rimmed eyes, the shaky hands.

Billie handed the woman a towel. "Are you all right?"

"Did he say when he'd be home?" Christina said, ignoring the towel.

"No." Billie watched the woman compose herself in a framed mirror. Even with the bloodshot eyes, Christina was dishearteningly beautiful and Billie felt small before it. Weakened almost, as if the woman's bearing was kryptonite. She had felt fragile enough experiencing the echo images of this woman in the house, standing before the genuine article was withering. Pushing it away, she steeled herself for the worst. "Why are you here?"

"Because it's still mine. Or half of it is." Christina looked over the nearly empty kitchen and then back to the woman in the doorway. "What's your name?"

"Sybil," she replied. She never went by her proper name. She wasn't sure why she did now.

"You're living here now?"

"No."

"But that's the plan, isn't it?" Christina's eyes ran up and down the interloper, coldly evaluating. "You two will be nested in soon. In my house."

"I won't live here."

"How noble of you," the woman sneered. "It didn't take him long to find someone new, did it?"

Billie clenched a fist, suddenly hating this woman with her perfect looks and snide derision. "Are you seeing someone?"

Christina didn't respond, but her lips pursed and her eyes broke away first. Billie had to push down the simple urge to march out, to walk away from this mess. She didn't need the hassle, but she didn't want to back down either, no matter how grey the issue of exactly who was the trespasser here.

Billie looked down at her shoes. The toes were scuffed, the boots not new. "I don't want to fight with you, Christina, but I don't want to get pulled into a mess that doesn't involve me."

Christina wasn't quite ready to call a truce. "Doesn't involve you?" she snapped. "You're right in the middle of it."

"This is between you and Ray, and I can't speak for him." Billie moved to the counter where her drink was. The mug was warm but not hot. "If you want to wait for him to come home, that's fine with me, but I'm not going to fight with you."

The house creaked it was so quiet. Christina let out a long sigh and sank into one of the chairs as if suddenly exhausted by it all.

"Do you want some tea?" Billie asked. She looked into her mug. "Actually, it's honey and lemon. I couldn't find any tea."

"He doesn't drink tea." Christina gaze held steady on the floor.

Billie blew on the mug, even though it was lukewarm. "Can I ask you something?"

The other woman shrugged without looking up from the floor.

"Have you two figured out what you're going to do with this house?"

"Neither of us wanted to deal with it at the time," Christina said. "I know he wants it. He loves this house, but I can't be tied to it anymore. I want out."

"What does that mean?"

The woman shrugged a second time. "It means we either sell it or he buys me out."

Billie slid down the cupboard and sat on the floor. "I guess the latter option is out."

"Who has that kind of money lying around? I suppose a payback arrangement could be made, but that would take a long time."

"And," Billie added, "it would bind the two of you together for a long time."

"There's that."

"Nothing's ever easy, is it?"

"No." Christina rose from the chair and brushed her hands together, as if she'd gotten them messy. Her fingernails were deep crimson. Crossing to the doorway, she noticed the splintered wood from where it had been hit. "I'm sorry for nearly taking your head off. Will you tell Ray that I need to talk to him?"

"Sure." Billie got to her feet. "Will you be all right?"

Christina ran her thumb over the battered wooden jamb. "I don't know what possessed me to come back here. Sometimes, I just charge into things before thinking them through."

"We all do that."

"Goodnight, Sybil."

Billie followed the woman out the front door to the porch just as a pair of headlights flashed their eyes. A car pulled into the driveway, the driver's side door swinging open. The look on Mockler's face was slackjawed confusion.

Christina marched past him to her car parked on the street. "We need to sell the house, Ray," was all she said.

Billie leaned against the post and folded her arms as Mockler's head snapped back and forth between the woman on the porch and the woman marching to the street.

Billie gave him a tiny wave. "Welcome home."

CHAPTER 16

SHE SHOULD HAVE checked the kitchen before offering to make breakfast. Billie managed to get the coffee brewing, but was stymied as to what to make. There were eggs, but no frying pan to cook them in. Checking the refrigerator a second time revealed no bacon, yogurt or fruit. There was no cereal or even bread to make toast with. Digging through a lower cupboard yielded a pot, but Billie was damned if she could remember how to poach or even soft-boil an egg. She always got the timing wrong.

Leaning against the counter, she rubbed her eyes vigorously to wake them up. Last night's sleep had been nil, interrupted constantly by awful dreams that terrified her in the moment, but, now, with the grey light of dawn, she could barely remember. An image or two lingered. One was of Christina sleepwalking through the house, her eyes without pupils, glowing eerily with a milky light. The other was of a man with flies in his mouth looming over the bed, while Mockler and Christina slept. Each time Billie had drifted back to sleep, another nightmare came, scaring her awake again.

It was the house itself that was haunting her, the residual energy of tension and bad blood that clung to every room. Her abilities, although closed off, picked up on the echoes of emotions and twisted around her REM sleep. Her initial reluctance to spend the night in Mockler's house was right on target, but she wanted to do it for him, to make an attempt at least. She didn't know what she was going to tell him, but she couldn't spend another night in this house, let alone live here.

Fortunately, the question of her moving in hadn't come up. Thrown off guard by Christina's sudden reappearance, he had apologized to Billie for having been ambushed like that. He must have imagined the worst because he seemed relieved to learn that they had had a quiet talk. She omitted the part about Christina almost taking her head off with the baseball bat.

They didn't have sex. The pop-in visit from the ex had put the kibosh on any romantic overtures. They had talked quietly for a while on the sofa, Mockler apologizing again for how she had been bushwhacked. The last thing he wanted, he'd said, was to have his past poison their relationship. It had been rocky enough. When he suggested that they get some sleep, Billie panicked anew, realizing again that she hadn't thought this through. There was no way in Hell that she was sleeping in the same bed he had shared with his ex. He'd think she was being silly, balking at that, but men didn't understand these things.

She needn't have worried. Mockler had sorted that out, leading her upstairs to the guest room. Smaller than the master bedroom, but he had been sleeping in this room since Christina had moved out. She asked why and he had told her that he never liked how the morning light filtered through the eastern facing windows. The guest room, he pointed out, faced west. She wasn't sure if she believed his answer, but didn't press the matter.

When he came downstairs, Billie was hovering over the pot of water on the stove. "That won't boil if you watch it," he said.

She leaned into him as he kissed her cheek. "How long do you leave eggs covered if you're soft-boiling them? Is it two minutes?"

"No idea. I never make them that way." He poured coffee into a mug and then took her cup. "Refill?"

"Please." Billie kept an eye on the clock. "Do you own a frying pan? All I could find was this pot."

"Most of the cookware was hers. I keep forgetting to get one."

"Then, how do you cook your eggs in the morning?"

"I don't," he said.

That tore her eyes from the clock. "What do you mean?"

Taking down a tall glass, Mockler took three eggs from the carton and cracked them into the glass. "Cheers," he said and then gulped it all down.

"Barf!" Billie just stared at him in disbelief. "That is totally vile."

"No, it's simple and easy. The four second breakfast. Done."

The thought of cold, raw eggs soured her appetite. "And you expect to kiss me with that mouth?"

He lunged at her, making kissing noises. She squealed, batting him away. "What other vile surprises are you keeping from me?"

"Did I mention my collection of severed heads in the meat freezer?"

"Oh shit." Taking the pot to the sink, she drained off the boiling water. "Damn."

"How many minutes was that?"

"I lost track," she said, flushing the eggs under cold water. "I don't suppose you have egg cups, do you?"

Rifling through a cupboard, he placed a small glass on the counter. "I have a shot glass."

"That'll do. Do you have time to sit with me while I eat eggs like a normal person?"

"I gotta run," he said, adjusting his tie. Coming up behind her, he slipped his arm around her waist. "You were tossing and turning a lot last night. Did you get any sleep?"

"A little," she fibbed. "It's always hard to sleep in a new place."

"Maybe you can catch some shut-eye later. Do you have plans today?"

"I'm going to stop by the Doll House. See the ladies. I'm working tonight."

"Damn," he groused. "Our schedules never line up, do they?"

"You could stop by the bar after work."

"If I finish up at a normal hour, I will." He set his bag on the counter and rifled through it, pulling out files and paperwork as he dug. "Have you seen my keys?"

"Did you check the bowl in the front hallway?"

"They're not there." He glanced over the kitchen one more time and then went out to the hallway. "Maybe I left them in my other jacket."

Billie set the egg in the shot glass and tapped at it with a butter knife. Shell fragments flew onto the paperwork Mockler had left on the counter. Gathering up the documents, she noticed a couple of large photographs tucked in the files. She snuck a peek and immediately regretted it. Two gruesome crime scene photos of a dead body lashed to a tree. The victim was naked, but she couldn't tell if it was a man or a woman. There was something coming out of the head. Horns?

"Whoa," Mockler said, sweeping back into the room. "Don't go looking at that stuff."

"Sorry, I snooped. What is that?"

He took the photos from her and stuffed everything back into the bag. "Just work."

Billie's mouth dipped into a slight grimace. "That looks really bad."

"It is." He kissed her forehead.

"Do you want to talk about it? I know you're not supposed to, officially, but I won't tell."

"You're sweet, but no," he said, heading for the door. "See ya later. Make yourself at home."

The floor shuddered as he shut the door. Billie turned to her breakfast, but pushed it away, her appetite gone. Dumping it into the trash, she put the cups in the sink and went to get her boots from the hallway. Making herself at home wasn't an option.

~

"It was a disaster," Billie stated.

"Don't listen to her," Jen shot back. "It wasn't a disaster."

Tammy wasn't sure who to believe, but knowing Jen's need for perfection in all things, she was inclined to side with Billie. "Doesn't sound all that bad," she said. "I mean, no one passed out or got food poisoning or anything."

"Lift it up a tiny bit," said Jen. "There."

Clutching the long shelf at each end, Billie and Tammy held the piece in place while Jen drove the screws in. A sliver of peace and Billie savoured it. Hanging out at the Doll House and kvetching over banal problems with her friends felt like old times. If only she could hang on to this.

"Are you finished?" Tammy groaned. "This is getting heavy."

"Almost there," Jen replied through the screws clamped in her teeth.

"So meeting the new boyfriend didn't go so well. Who cares? There'll be other opportunities." Tammy turned to look at Billie. "Unless you've dumped him already."

"Hilarious." Billie rolled her eyes. "I just wanted it to be nice, you know. Normal. But everything flopped as usual."

"You know," Tammy said, pointing at Billie, "for once, you set the expectation too high, not Jen."

"I don't do that," Jen peeved.

"Please," Tammy dismissed. "You set expectations for a trip to the corner store. But you?" Tammy turned back to Billie, "You normally don't expect much out of anything. This time you did. You set them too high. Jen's become a bad influence on you."

"Well, we can't all live in chaos, Tammy." Jen stepped back. "Okay, you can let go."

The shelf remained in place against the wall. Tammy brushed her hands off. "I don't live in chaos. I just don't cling to expectations; therefore, I don't get disappointed."

Even Billie wasn't buying that. "Come on. You don't set expectations?"

"Occasionally, but I don't fret if it doesn't work out. I just adapt." Tammy sat up, swinging her feet to the floor. "When I plan a photo shoot, I'll have a vision for how it will go, but things change and screw up or break all the time. I drop the vision, adapt to the screw-ups and roll with it. Nothing is ever perfect, but the good stuff never comes out of perfection or a plan going exactly as it was supposed to. Something better comes out of the unexpected, the chaotic."

"There's nothing wrong with setting your goals high or striving for perfection," Jen said.

"No. As long as you don't insist on perfection. Or the expectation." Tammy rose and pointed to the wall behind her. "Remember when you were renovating this place? You wanted this wall to be exposed brick, but when you and your dad tore off the drywall, there was no brick and you were so upset because it ruined your plan. But, you improvised and painted it hot pink. That looks way cooler."

"That's different," Jen dismissed.

"No, it isn't. You were in tears because it wasn't going to be 'perfect'. But, in the chaos, you adapted and came up with something better."

Jen folded her arms, unwilling to give an inch.

"The pink does suit the place," Billie conceded.

"So, what's your point?" Jen said. "We shouldn't have tried?"

"No, go ahead and try. Just give up the need for it to be perfect." Tammy pointed a finger at Billie. "You should throw the party next time."

"Me?" Billie leaned back. "No. My parties are always flops."

"That's exactly why you need to have one," Tammy insisted. "At your place. Zero expectations. Just us and Kaitlin, Adam and

Kyle. And your new beau."

"Zero expectations? You're expecting it to fail?"

Tammy marched over and pretended to knock on Billie's skull. "Hello, McFly? I'm not expecting anything, like I said. Just casual and no fuss. The way we used to have parties. Remember?"

"Those parties ended in trouble, remember?" Jen mimicked sarcastically. "God, do you remember getting trapped on the rooftop of Kaitlin's building? In our bathing suits?"

"See? That's the spirit!" Tammy turned back to Billie. "What nights do you have off this week?"

"Thursday."

"Thursday it is," Tammy declared, already dialing her phone. "I'll tell Kaitlin. Jen, you call Adam. And you, Billie, call your detective boyfriend. It's a date."

Jen blew her cheeks out in frustration, but reached for her phone. "I smell a disaster."

"Let's hope so," Tammy grinned.

~

Coming home, Billie made a silent wish before opening her door. She knew as soon as the latch clicked shut behind her that it hadn't come true. She sensed nothing around her. The Half-Boy hadn't returned.

Shouldn't she be happy about that? Doesn't that mean that he went back to the funeral home and sought out the warmth where he could cross over? He must have, she reasoned. His mission as her guardian angel was accomplished and there was no reason for him to stay. She went into the kitchen to put the kettle on, not wanting to contemplate the alternative.

Sitting with her feet up on the chipped coffee table, Billie looked over her small apartment. The party was a go, according to Tammy. Kaitlin and Adam had both confirmed. When she called Mockler she had expected him to be cool to the idea after the fiasco at Jen's, but he surprised her by looking forward to it. He said he'd make sure he was free that night and Billie reminded herself what Tammy had said about expectations.

Did she really do that to herself, setting expectations on things? No, she concluded, it was the opposite. She inverted expectations, assuming nothing would ever work out. When had she become so negative?

Pushing it aside, she realized that Tammy was right. Don't expect anything, just dive in and adapt as events change. Surveying the messy flat, she needed to get busy cleaning.

There was a sound at the door, a soft whooshing sound. She turned in time to see something slip under her door.

It was a small envelope of black paper. No name or label on it. She swung the door open but the hallway was empty. Whoever had delivered it was silent and fast. She closed the door, turned the lock and opened the black envelope.

A single slip of white velum, the note written in elegant

cursive with black ink.

Dear Sybil,

We need to talk. Call at number 6 Lorca Avenue this evening.

After sundown. Please. It's important.

Regards,

Cordelia

(a friend of the English fraud)

Billie checked the back of the card, but there was nothing there. She inspected the envelope and then read the note again. English fraud? She chewed her lip. Did she really want to meet another friend of Gantry's? Taking out her phone, she checked the weather to see what time the sun would set tonight. An hour from now. She had time to pay the visit and still get to work.

CHAPTER 17

SHE HAD TO locate Lorca Avenue on a map, having never heard of it. A street in the old money section of Durand, flanked by the rise of the mountain. She took the bike, despite the cold weather, after finding gloves and the black toque that Jen had given to her as a birthday present last year. At the time, she had thought the cap cute, with its grinning skull motif. Now, it simply seemed apt.

She set off at sundown, cycling through the core to the quieter tree-lined streets of the Durand neighbourhood with its big houses erected in a bygone era by steel barons and industrial tycoons. The pyramid-like monuments to the captains of industry who had built the Ambitious City. Lorca Avenue was a cul-de-sac at the bottom of Hess Street where ancient oak trees canopied the pavement below in a web of spindly branches. The address on the card was a massive Georgian manor set back from the street with a turret topping the gables like a spire. Of the many tall windows in the facade, only one was lit.

Leaning her bike against the stone veranda, she found a brass lion head on the front door with a hoop through its jaws. She rapped the knocker three times and waited. The door creaked open, revealing only darkness within, as if the interior lights were all dimmed.

"Come in," said a voice from within. A woman's voice.

Billie brandished the letter. "Hi. This card was slipped under my door?"

"Inside," said the voice. "Quickly, before you let in the chill air."

Stepping inside, Billie watched the door bang closed behind her. Engulfed in darkness, she bit her lip. "Uh, can you hit the lights? I can't see anything."

"Your eyes will acclimate in a moment," answered the voice. "Look to your left. Do you see the glow?"

The velvet pitch receded and Billie could make out a soft light framing the outline of a doorway. "Yes."

"Follow it."

Okay, Billie thought. The sudden plunge into darkness had startled her and her senses opened up involuntarily, throwing up a psychic web to warn of danger. She felt no threat from the woman in the darkness, so she moved toward the light from the other room. A library of sorts, from what she could make out. A fire blazed in a massive stone hearth, warming the space, but its light didn't carry far. Billie picked out two tall wingback chairs and a Persian rug before the fireplace, a wall of bookshelves on either side.

"This must seem strange to you, Sybil," said the woman, still invisible in the darkness. "Please, come near the fire where you can see better."

The flames rippled up the flue in a cascade of orange and yellow, the wooden logs crackling and popping in the hearth. Standing before it, Billie felt its heat thaw the chill in her hands.

"Thank you for coming," said the woman. "I apologize for the mysterious invite."

The woman stepped into the light and Billie felt herself gawking. She was taller than herself and, at best guess, a decade older, but mesmerizing as she moved into the light. Her eyes were heavy lidded, as if sleepy and her dark hair was streaked in strands of grey. Her pale hands clutched at a black shawl around her shoulders, pulling it tighter to keep warm. The woman made a slight bow, but did not offer her hand. "I'm Cordelia. Welcome to my home, Sybil."

Billie fumbled to reply, but felt herself numbed into gawking at the woman's features. She had to tear her eyes away to clear the fog in her thoughts. "Call me Billie. Everyone does."

"I know." The woman motioned to the tall chairs before the hearth. "Have a seat."

Billie sat before the fire and pulled off her hat and gloves. She studied her host as the woman took the opposite chair. Draped in black from head to toe, the woman named Cordelia looked as if she was headed out to some posh affair. Or a funeral. Billie surveyed the room around her, the walls stacked to the rafters with books. Potted ferns near the tall mullioned windows, a layer of dust over everything. "You have a beautiful home."

"Can I get you anything?" Cordelia asked. "Some tea to warm up with?"

"I'm fine." Billie unbuttoned her jacket, already too warm sitting this close to the fire. "I feel a bit disadvantaged here. You seem to know about me."

"I've been wanting to meet you for a while now. Your reputation is growing."

Billie stiffened up, her mind going immediately to an adolescent's understanding of the word. "My reputation?"

"As a medium," Cordelia said. "Your arrival has caused no small amount of stir within a certain community of people."

From the moment she had stepped across the threshold, Billie had felt a vague uneasiness nag at her. It now tilted into a clanging alarm of danger. She should have known better than to come here. The spookshow, it would seem, was not about to let her go without a fight. "I see."

"Are you still working at the tavern?"

The warning bells clanged on. "Yes," Billie replied. "Why?"

Cordelia folded her arms tightly as if chilled, despite their proximity to the open fire. "I'm surprised. I thought you would have set up shop by now."

"As a medium?" Billie shook her head. "No thanks."

The woman in the black shawl tilted her head, puzzled. "Why the reluctance? A seer as powerful as you would be in high demand. You need to hang out a shingle, my dear."

Was that what this was about? Another nutjob wanting her to contact a lost relative? Billie regarded the woman in the chair again. With her pale skin and dark hair, she seemed almost spectral. Cordelia was clearly no ghost, but something about her ragged at the periphery of Billie's senses, arousing it in spite of herself. "I've put all that behind me," she said.

Cordelia smiled. "I doubt that's possible. Besides, you're too young to retire."

"So you know Gantry?" Billie asked, changing the topic.

"I do," the other woman said. She shivered. "What happened to you? Why would you deny that part of yourself?"

"It's caused nothing but trouble. Did Gantry tell you about me?"

"He did. I was intrigued." Cordelia took the poker from the stand and prodded the embers in the fire. "Are you cold? I can put another log on the fire."

"I'm fine," Billie said. The room was almost stifling, but the woman in the shawl continued to shiver. "How do you know Gantry?"

"We're old friends. Occasionally enemies."

"Do you know what happened to him?"

Cordelia looked up. "That he'd been killed in the prison? I'd heard. That seems highly unlikely."

Billie agreed without saying so. "It sounds like one of his vanishing acts."

"Gantry was one of the reasons I wanted to talk to you. Did you see his body in the morgue?"

"I didn't get a chance," Billie said. "It disappeared."

"Leave it to Gantry to foul up his own demise. He should have pulled his vanishing act before getting stabbed in the back." The woman leaned forward, propping her elbow on her knee. "Sybil, what do you think happened to him?"

"I honestly don't know. With Gantry, anything's possible." Billie watched the fire crackle. "I hope it was all a trick and that he's sitting in a pub somewhere having a good laugh over it."

"As do I." The woman's gaze lingered over the flames, her eyes darkening as if she didn't believe her own words.

Billie studied her host. Her features were flawless, almost classical in their beauty. A face that launched a thousand ships. The phrase popped into Billie's head, but she couldn't remember where she had heard it before. "How did you know Gantry?"

"He came here one night," Cordelia said. "To the house. This was years ago. He came to kill me."

That snapped Billie's attention like a plucked piano wire. "Kill you? Why?"

"It's a long story. Gantry was a bit unstable back then." Cordelia rose from the wingback chair and swept forward, the fabric of her dress making a slithery sound.

Billie tensed, as if the woman was going to attack her. Or swoop down over her in an amorous drape. Either way, Billie felt her pulse quicken in a heady confusion of fear and anticipation. She noted, almost idly, the woman's bare feet peeking out from the cascading hem of the long dress. An oddly rustic touch to the refined sleekness of her attire.

"Sybil." Cordelia settled onto the ottoman at Billie's feet, tugging the black shawl tight again. "Give me your hand."

The dizziness amplified with the woman's proximity and Billie shuddered, unable to tear her eyes from Cordelia's. Their colour seem to change under the flickering light of the hearth, one moment blue, the next green, then orange. Cordelia held out her hand, palm up like a penitent waiting to receive the Eucharist.

Voltage crackled at the touch of her skin, followed by a numbness so cold it stung. Not quite the same chill that Billie experienced from the dead, but close. Akin to but something other.

The woman turned Billie's hand over and traced her finger down the lines of her palm. "Your lifeline is interesting. It splits off at several points and then fades away."

"What does that mean?"

Cordelia tilted her hand to the light from the fireplace. "Do you have children?"

"No. Does that mean I will?"

"Possibly, but there are so many of them. I believe it has

more to do with the souls you encounter in your life, each one taking a piece of you with them."

Billie shivered, the chill from the woman's touch was leeching up her arm. "Your hands are cold."

"I am always cold." Rather than releasing her guest's hand, Cordelia tightened her grip. "Did Gantry ever talk to you about an impending darkness?"

"Darkness?"

"Something he feared," Cordelia said. "Few things truly frightened that man, but that was one, this looming threat that he insisted was coming."

"He mentioned it, but never said what it was." Billie tugged her hand back. "You're hurting me."

The woman's grip locked more, her nails digging into the flesh. "He must have said more than that. He said he's preparing for it, that he needed to be ready."

"Let go."

Cordelia's eyes hardened, the irises changing colour again. "I believe you were part of his preparation for what was coming. Tell me what you know."

"Stop!" Ripping her hand free, Billie shot up and backed away from the woman. She tried to rub her numb hand back to life, but that only made the pain worse. Cordelia rose from the ottoman, her dress slinking up a slithery sound. Billie took a step back, eyeballing the doorway in case she needed to run. There was something wrong with this woman with the cold hands and it was wrong all the way through her. "What are you?"

"I'm no pale apparition, if that's what you're asking." Cordelia crossed to the fire and spread her hands before the flames to warm them. The study was tropical from the fire, but still the woman pulled the shawl tight like she couldn't get warm.

Billie gathered up her jacket and gloves from the chair. She no longer cared what this woman's secret was, she just wanted to get out. "I'm leaving. Don't call on me again."

Cordelia looked up as her guest strode for the door. "Something is loose in this city, Sybil. Something dangerous."

Billie stopped. "What is it?"

"I don't know. But I believe it to be part of this threat that Gantry was so maddeningly vague about." Cordelia folded her arms and turned to face the young woman. "I'm sorry I hurt you."

The pain in Billie's hand subsided to the throbbing of pins and needles. "How do you know this thing is loose?"

"Can't you feel it?" Cordelia spat, shocked. "Out there in the dark, slithering through the streets?"

"I don't feel anything," Billie replied, neglecting to inform the woman that she had kept her talents strangled and muted. "Goodbye, Cordelia."

Cordelia remained still, listening to the young woman's boots rap against the marble. "Be alert, Sybil," she called out. "And keep your back to the wall."

CHAPTER 18

WHEN THURSDAY NIGHT came, Billie felt like a hypocrite. After admonishing Jen for needing to have everything perfect, Billie had spent the day sweating every detail. After cleaning the apartment, she rushed out to a handful of shops for food and booze. Back home, she fretted over the playlist, the lighting and what to wear, wishing she had planned this better. When Jen and Adam arrived, punctual as ever, Billie wasn't even dressed. Jen shooed her from the kitchen, telling her to get ready.

Kaitlin, Kyle and Tammy arrived together. Jen had rearranged the food on the coffee table and soon everyone was tucking in, drinks in hand.

Billie lit a few more candles and dimmed the overhead light. She turned to Tammy. "I thought you were bringing a date?"

"So did I," Tammy said. "Turns out my date is an idiot who can't read a calendar."

"Is this someone new?" Jen asked, her wine glass held

daintily at the stem. "Or someone we know?"

"His name's Clive. He's in a band."

"Of course he's in a band," Kaitlin chided. "Let me guess, he's playing later tonight and wants you to go."

"Worse," Tammy groaned. "He has band practice. He wanted me to come by the rehearsal space."

"Eew!" Jen cringed. "I thought we'd outgrown that phase, being the groupie girlfriend."

"We did," Tammy confirmed.

Adam looked at his date with disbelief. "You used to be a groupie girlfriend?"

"What girl hasn't?" Jen shrugged. "It's the worst, hanging out on a stinky couch watching your boyfriend's crappy band mangle a song. Double-eew."

Billie hovered over her guests from her perch on the arm of the sofa, sipping a beer and feeling completely disconnected from her own party. So far, everything seemed fine, but she kept fretting that she'd forgotten something and, checking the time, wondering when the rest of the food should be brought out. She still needed to prepare the croquettes and sling them into the oven. She figured that would go over well in an hour or so, once her guests were well into their cups. And, then, there was the matter of her own date. Glancing at the clock again, she crossed to the window and looked down at the street.

"Billie?"

She turned around to find them all looking at her. "What?"

"You okay?" Tammy asked.

"Yeah. Why?"

"We were just wondering where your date was," Jen chimed in. "He's the guest of honour, isn't he?"

"He's on his way," Billie said, stepping away from the window. A white lie. Mockler had assured her that he would be there when she had spoken to him earlier in the afternoon. He was now an hour late and hadn't returned any of her texts. "Who needs a refill?"

"We're fine." Kaitlin patted the seat beside her. "Come sit. You look too tense."

Squeezing into the cramped living room suite, Billie settled in next to Kaitlin. "I'm sorry. I don't know where he is."

"He's out catching bad guys," Adam said, saluting Billie with his glass.

"Or he's at the donut shop," grumbled Kyle.

"Don't be an ass," Kaitlin scolded.

"What?" Kyle protested. "It's true."

"Ignore him," Kaitlin said, about to nudge her friend, but Billie rose and crossed to the window again. "Billie, don't take him seriously."

"I'm not." Billie peered down at the street again. An odd tug at her guts pulled her back to the window and she expected to see his car pull up on Barton Street below. Over the last five months, she had experienced more than just the usual tug of heartstrings when it came to the detective. More than once, she had felt an eerie bond with him, emphatically sharing his pain or fear when he was in danger. With the strange pull to something outside the window, she could only guess that their emphatic bond was growing tighter and his proximity had triggered her inner alarm bell. What else could it be?

His car was nowhere to be seen among the ones parked below. Billie scanned the buildings across the way, the dark windows and empty doorways. No unearthly faces peered up at her, no lonely phantom stalking her home.

The door swung open and her date appeared. Mockler swept in with a bottle of wine in his hand and a sheepish grin on his face. "Sorry I'm late."

"The man of the hour is here," belted out Tammy.

Billie met him halfway. "You had me worried for a second. You got held up at work?"

"Like always." He tossed his coat over a chair and slipped an arm round her waist. "Things went haywire just as I was about to leave. A suspect went apeshit in the box."

She put a finger to his lip, where the skin was swollen in an angry red lump. "Did you get hurt?"

"It's nothing." He nodded at the guests seated round the coffee table. "How's the party? Did I miss anything?"

"Do you want some ice for that? It's looks raw."

"Nah. I'd kill for a drink though."

Billie tilted up and kissed the corner of his mouth, careful to avoid the swollen patch on the opposite end. "Done."

Mockler squeezed in among the guests and joined the chatter. Billie looked on, happy to see him get along with her friends. He enquired about Jen's shop and Tammy asked rude questions about being a cop. Adam chatted with him about the Ti-Cats and, when the conversation tipped over to the NHL, even Kyle warmed up and joined in. Mockler was funny and engaging, often spinning the banter back to Billie like a tennis ball served over the net.

Mission accomplished, she thought. Her new man was thick as thieves among her friends. So why, Billie fretted, couldn't she just relax and join in the fun? She had felt the same odd distance as before, as if observing the proceedings from faraway rather than being in the midst of it. A persistent nagging prickle kept tugging her attention back to the window. What the hell was out there?

Tammy was in the middle of another lewd tale so Billie slipped away to the window again. The street looked unchanged. Light traffic, stray newspapers rippling down the pavement like tumbleweeds. Was her radar off? Maybe keeping herself closed off this long was adversely affecting her senses. Then, she remembered what Cordelia had said earlier, about something dangerous loose in the city. Was this it? This vague threat she had warned of?

Down on Barton Street, something slunk out of the shadow of a doorway. Small and misshapen, it glanced up at her before dragging itself into the darkness of an alleyway. Something wasn't right about the way it moved, skulking off like a wounded animal.

"Oh my God..."

Mockler straightened up. "Billie?"

No reply came. Mockler watched his date sprint out the front door.

Billie hammered down the stairs hard, leaping the last three steps. Landing hard in heels hurt, but she swallowed the pain and burst out to the street. No traffic, nothing but the wind moving. She bolted across the street for the alley beside the dry cleaners. She stopped the moment she was engulfed in the darkness between the two buildings. Squinting, she could just make out a dumpster and a tumble of trash piled up against the side of one building. Beyond that was perfect night, a Stygian gloom that swallowed everything.

For one tiny moment, she considered the idea that her eyes had played a trick on her before realizing that this small phantom was what had been drawing her to the window all night. Who else would it be?

"Where are you?" she called out, the heels of her good shoes crunching over the debris on the pavement. "I can't see you."

Nothing moved. The wind vanished, dropping a heavy silence over the filthy alley.

"Please," Billie begged. "Don't run. Let me find you."

Stillness. There was only one way to find him now. Taking a

deep breath, Billie exhaled slowly and turned the lock on that secret part of her heart, opening herself up all the way.

A tinkle of glass echoed further down. A bottle rolled out from behind a stack of rotten wooden pallets. Billie ran to it.

She almost didn't recognize him. He seemed withered in appearance, little more than an opaque husk stretched over a fretboard of bone. His spindly frame swam in his tattered garments as if drowning in oversize clothes. His small eyes gaped blankly as if his wits had been stolen during his exile like some half-pint Lear lost on the heath.

She rushed to scoop him up, but the boy flailed and tried to crawl away.

'Stop," she pleaded. "It's me. I'm not going to hurt you."

Backed into a grimy corner, the Half-Boy covered his head with his hands as if anticipating a fist.

Billie knelt before him cautiously, not wanting to frighten him anymore than she had. What had happened to him? He seemed more animal than boy, like a stray dog left to hunt for scraps in the streets of a hostile city. Had she done this to him?

She reached out to take his wrist. He flinched as if stung, but the spectral flesh became solid in her hand and she pulled him close. A moment's hesitation before he crawled into her arms and clung fast. She cooed into his mangled ear that everything was going to be okay now.

Lifting him up, Billie turned to leave, but found the exit blocked. The dead surrounded her on all sides. They clogged the alley north and south, more drifting in from the street or scaling down the walls of the buildings around her. All drawn to her beacon like sharks smelling blood in the water. Some gnashed their teeth and others pleaded for help and some simply wept, their hands reaching out like beggars to her.

"Get out of the way," she said. "All of you."

Butcher, baker and candlestick maker, the assembled dead pressed in further. Billie plowed through them with the boy in her arms. The nearest ones tumbled back, falling into the ones behind as the ghosts parted before her as she made for the street.

No music sounded from her apartment as she approached her front door and she wondered if everyone had left. The boy clung to her, his face buried in the crook of her neck. Her guests turned in unison as Billie crashed her own party.

"Billie, where did you—" Jen hurried to her, but stopped cold, her eyes going wide. "Oh my God, what is that?"

At first, Billie assumed that she would simply look odd with her arms out before her, clutching thin air, but the horrified looks on her guests' faces said otherwise.

"Jesus Christ," Adam blurted. "What happened to that kid?"

"Was he hit by a car?"

"His legs are gone! He's bleeding all over you."

They could see him. All of them could see the little boy with the amputated legs in her arms. Without realizing it, she had rendered the ghost corporeal. It sapped her strength, her knees buckling as the boy became heavier in her arms.

"Should we call an ambulance?" Kyle said.

"He's gonna bleed to death for Christ's sakes!"

The only member of the party not panicking was Kaitlin. She simply looked on in awe. Billie turned to her. "Where's Ray?"

"He's out looking for you," Kaitlin answered. Her eyes dropped to the boy. "Who is he?"

"I wish I knew." Billie ignored the torrent of questions from the others and crossed to the sofa. The dark blood flapping from his wounds spattered over the floor as Billie eased the boy down. His small fists, clamped tightly round her neck, had to be pried away.

Adam was already dialling 911, while the others flapped about in a panic over what to do. Billie felt a chill crawl over her skin and, when a candle guttered, her stomach dropped. She snatched Kaitlin's wrist. "Kaitlin, you have to get everyone out of here."

"What?" Kaitlin sputtered, confused. "Why?"

"It's going to get very crowded in here. It won't be safe."

The lamps flickered on and off, strobing the room in pulsating light. Another candle went out.

"What now?" Kyle growled.

The dead were already inside with them. The temperature plummeted suddenly, the guests watching their breath mist the air before them. The music garbled into static and a bottle tipped over and rolled across the floor. Adam jumped out of its way like it was dangerous. "What the hell is going on?" he snapped.

The salt barrier over the threshold must have been swept away with so many people going to and fro. The dead souls had followed her home, crowding in the corridor and bottlenecking through the door in ones and twos. They lurched and drifted toward the gypsy girl in the room but Billie watched in horror as a few went after Kaitlin, reaching out with their skeletal hands for her hair, touching her cheek. Kaitlin recoiled, feeling their cold invisible touch.

"Get away from her." Billie charged at the ghosts swarming her friend. Something in her growl made them shrink away. "Get everyone out, Kaitlin. Please."

Kaitlin corralled her friends to the door. "Everybody out! Party's over!"

Jen wouldn't budge and Adam demanded to know what was going on, while Tammy griped that the party was just getting started. When the first lightbulb exploded, they all jumped out of their skins. When the coffee table rushed across the floor under its own power, its legs screeching loudly on the wood, they all bolted for the door. Kaitlin glanced back once at Billie before following the others into the corridor and down the stairs.

A plate spun through the air, splattering onion dip against the wall and Billie shrieked at the rancorous souls to get out, get out, get out. The dead fled through the door and slipped through the cracks in the walls to escape until only a single figure remained, framed in the doorway.

"Billie?" Mockler said.

CHAPTER 19

MOCKLER TOOK IN the disaster. The dip smeared against the wall, the broken glasses on the floor and the table thrown across the room. "What the hell happened?"

Billie knelt on the floor before the sofa. She didn't respond.

"Billie, are you hurt?" Mockler moved quickly, stepping around the broken dish. "Where did you disappear to?"

"To help a friend," she said.

"Who?" When she didn't respond, he brushed the bangs from her eyes. "Look at me. What friend?"

"The boy." Billie wagged her chin at something before her. "The one I told you about."

He spun about, but saw nothing. The sofa, a throw pillow tumbled to the floor. "The one who won't leave?"

"But he did leave. I sent him away," she said. "It almost killed him."

"Killed him?" Mockler studied her. He had seen Billie laid

low by grief and hot with anger. He had seen her frightened for her very life, but this, this faraway look of despair seemed new. "He's a ghost, isn't he?"

"Doesn't mean it's not true." Her eyes were blurry and she wiped them clear. The boy came into focus again, coiled up and shivering on the sofa before him. A string of spittle hung from his wet lips. The solidity he had gained from her touch had faded, rendering him invisible to the man in the room. Billie lowered her chin. "I've been so stupid."

"Don't go there."

"I was greedy. Thinking I could have it all."

He fetched the tissue box from the shelf and placed it at her feet. "Tell me, but don't speak in riddles. Just be plain with me. Please."

"I tried to push it all away." She plucked a tissue out. "The ghosts, my abilities, the whole damn thing. I thought I could shut it out forever."

"And the boy?" Mockler glanced behind him again, but no child materialized.

"I tried to show him how to cross over. He must have thought I was rejecting him." Balling up the damp tissue in her hand, she reached for another. "God knows where he's been all this time. Lost, I guess."

"This is the boy who won't speak, right?"

"He *can't* speak," Billie corrected him. "His tongue was cut out. God, he's just a little kid. I wish you could see him."

"How old do you think he is?"

She watched Mockler cast his eyes over the room again before realizing she was wrong. The others had seen the boy in her arms. They had even seen the blood that forever dripped from his wounds. Billie tucked her legs under her and scooted closer to the sofa. "There is a way."

"What are you doing?" he asked.

"I want you to see him. Take my hand."

He took her outstretched hand, uncertain if he actually wanted to see this child she spoke of. Billie reached out to the sofa and the lights dimmed immediately, as if the wattage was being throttled. A small dark form billowed up from the sofa cushions like smoke taking shape. Startled, he almost let go of Billie's hand.

"Hold tight," she whispered to the detective. Then, she turned to the smoky darkness bubbling on the sofa and cooed softly to it. "Wake up."

He was small, his thin hands peeking out from the threadbare sleeves of a coat that looked two sizes too big for him. His head was tilted down, concealing his face under the brim of a putrid newsboy cap. Mockler's eyes were drawn to the ghastly wreckage of his legs. The wounds were wet and fresh looking as they bled onto the cushion below him. When the child's small hands clutched hers, he almost pulled Billie away.

Billie offered a thin smile. "It's okay. He won't hurt me."

"You're shivering," he whispered. Her hand felt cold in his.

"I know." She gave Mockler's hand a squeeze of reassurance and then turned back to the boy. "Hey. I want you to meet my friend. Don't be shy."

The boy rotated his head and met the man's stare. Mockler steeled himself to keep from pulling Billie away again. The child's flesh was pale and his black eyes glistened with an unearthly sparkle. His cheek was purpled in bruises and the corner of his mouth had been cut open. The white flesh flapped loosely with each movement. His eyes narrowed into slits of suspicion at the man holding the woman's other hand.

"Easy," Billie cooed. "He's not going to hurt you."

"Billie," Mockler hissed. "Are you sure this is safe?"

The boy backed further into the sofa, as if ready to bolt. Billie looked back at Mockler. "Shhh. Don't talk."

She whispered something to the boy that Mockler couldn't make out, but it seemed to put the child at ease. She turned to Mockler again. "Take a look at him. When do you think he lived?"

Mockler scrutinized the ghost. The shabby coat and rancid cap. The boy's hands were small, but they were calloused and raw, grime encrusted under the nails. "Hard to say," he whispered. "A century ago? Maybe more."

"I need to know who he is," Billie said. "Will you help me?"

Mockler nodded, studying the boy anew. His garments, the loose coat. "Will he empty his pockets for you?"

Billie released Mockler's hand and whispered something to

the boy. He dug into his pockets and placed a few items in her palm.

Mockler inched closer. "What does he have?"

"A blue marble." Turning the items over in her palm, she held up a large coin. "An old penny."

"Is there a year stamped on it?"

She tilted it to the candlelight. "1902."

"What else?"

"There's a length of red ribbon. Satin maybe. And a small knife."

He looked up at her. "A knife?"

She lifted something, dangling it between her fingers. "It's odd looking. Can you see it?"

"Barely. What's odd about it?"

"It looks homemade," Billie said. "It's just a piece of sharp metal with twine wrapped around one end for a handle."

"Is that it?"

"That's everything." Billie handed these small treasures back to their owner. The lad hid them away among his person. "Thank you," she said softly.

Last among the articles was the ribbon. The Half-Boy folded it carefully and pressed it to his lips before tucking it away.

"What does that mean?"

"I don't know," Billie said. She touched the boy's wrist. "Is that special, that ribbon? Did it belong to someone?"

The boy just stared back at the woman, his face blank as

stone.

Mockler scratched his chin. "Look inside his cap. Maybe there's a name stitched there. Or a label."

Billie whispered to the boy again and he slid the cap from his head and gave it to her. His thin hair was crudely cropped, as if barbered by someone who had no knack for the task. Bald patches of coarse scalp shone through here and there on his large head. "There's a label," she said, "but it's worn out. I can't make out the maker's mark."

"Take a guess."

"Wait. There's a name here." She moved closer to the light. "Stitched under the bill."

"Can you make it out?"

"Arch?" she said, squinting at the cap. "No, Archibald." Billie looked up at the boy, her eyes brightening as they opened wide. "Archibald Crump. Is that your name?"

The boy flinched. His mouth hooked into a sour grimace as he snatched the cap away and squared it back onto his head. Dropping to the floor, he galloped away.

The detective tensed up. He could no longer see the legless child, but he heard the slapping of his hands against the floor as he ran off. "Where did he go?"

"He's gone." Billie pulled closer to him, her eyes still bright. "Do you think that's his name? Archibald?"

"Hard to say. His reaction was odd."

"Archie," she uttered, as if testing the sounds of the word.

"My God. Archie."

He asked her to spell it for him, writing it down precisely in his notepad. "It's a good start. The date on the penny too."

The flash of delight stayed in her eyes. She took Mockler's hand. "I need to know more. How he lived and how he died."

"We can try," he said as he closed the notepad. "But it won't be easy with a death this old. Just temper your expectations, okay?"

"I will," she grinned and leaned into him, resting her temple against his shoulder. She whispered the word again in reverent invocation.

Archie.

~

"I told you," Kyle snipped the moment they arrived home to the condo on Stinson Street. "I told you Billie was trouble."

"Don't start, Kyle." Kaitlin tossed her coat onto a chair and crossed to the kitchen sink. Her head was splitting.

"I can't believe we all fell for it, too," Kyle went on. "Running out of there like scared little kids."

Kaitlin ignored his baiting, rooting through the cupboard where they kept a bottle of pain relief handy. "Where's the Advil? Did you use it all?"

"Where we always keep it." Kyle brushed past her as he plucked a beer from the refrigerator. "How did she do it? How did she pull it off? The lights and stuff falling over?"

The pill bottle was hidden behind a honey jar. She took it down and shook it. No rattling sound within. "Kyle, what's the rule about the Advil? Whoever empties it, replaces it."

He wasn't listening. "Did she rig the place beforehand? Was someone helping her orchestrate it all?"

"She didn't fake it, Kyle!" Kaitlin hurled the empty container into the trash. "It happened. Wrap your head around it already."

"Jesus Christ, you fell for that shit?" Looking at her, he mimed a fake flush of surprise. "What am I saying? Of course you fell for it."

Kaitlin kneaded her temples. "How can you question it? After everything that's happened? It's real, Kyle. Wake up!"

He scoffed. Kaitlin watched him sneer and chug back the beer, almost in contempt. She had been through a literal Hell of the paranormal and even Kyle, with his stubborn refusal of anything that defied logic, had experienced it. Yet, now, he blew it off, like it was all a bad joke. "You don't get it," she said. "After all of this, you still don't get it. Do you?"

"No, I get it." He swiped the back of his hand across his mouth. "It's plain as day. She hoodwinked you. Not that that was hard, was it? You've always been into this shit. Tarot cards and Ouija boards. My mistake was keeping quiet about it. I figured, no, Kaitlin's got her head screwed on right. This is just a phase. She'll move past it and then everything will be fine. But no. Your insane friend says she can see ghosts and you fall for it hook, line and sinker!"

This was going to end badly and Kaitlin knew it. She walked away. "I'm not having this discussion again."

"Because you know I'm right," he snarled. "Your friend Billie is a nutjob looking for attention. She'll stop at nothing to get it, end of story. The chick is trouble and she's a complete fraud. And you? You fucking fell for it."

"Shut up!"

"It's always the quiet ones," he said, dropping onto the couch and digging for the remote. "The weirdo mousy chicks who turn crazy on you. Do yourself a solid, babe, and broom her."

The TV clicked on, the sound of the hockey game booming loud over the room. Maybe it was the mindless chatter of the commentators that pushed Kaitlin over the edge, maybe something else. She snatched the remote from her hand and killed the screen. Then, she threw the remote to the floor and stomped it under her bootheels until it shattered.

Kyle blinked at her with a stupid look on his face. "What the fuck is wrong with you?"

"Get out," Kaitlin seethed. "Get out and don't ever come back here. We are OVER!"

He laughed. She couldn't believe it, but he laughed at her. He turned back to the television like there was something still on the screen. "Gimme a fucking break."

"Fine. You stay." Kaitlin snatched up her bag and her coat and yanked open the door. "I'm leaving. I'll send someone for my stuff. I don't ever want to see you again."

He failed to heed the tone in her voice and shrugged it off. Kyle was of the belief that whoever got the last word in an argument was the winner and kept that faith now. A dismissive wave of his hand and a condescending tone. "You'll be back," he derided.

She wanted nothing more than to slam the door shut with a thunderous bang, but it levered slowly on a hydraulic swing arm that gently eased the door home to avoid any such slamming. Disgusted, she simply turned and marched for the stairs.

CHAPTER 20

"WHERE DO WE start?" asked Billie.

Getting an early jump on the day, they ran out the door to get coffee before Mockler left for work. The pair of them yawned and rubbed their eyes against the brightly lit cafe. Neither had gotten much sleep after the party had been crashed by ghosts.

"We start with what we know," Mockler said, producing the notepad from his pocket. He flipped through to the last scribbles taken down. "Male child, Caucasian. How old would you say he is? Or was. You know what I mean."

Billie wrinkled her nose as she guessed. "Ten? I'm no good at guessing kids' ages."

"Let's say eight to 12 years of age," he stated. "Severe trauma to both legs, tongue severed. Possibly accidental, but more likely a violent assault. The penny you found in his pocket means his death occurred after 1902. Do I have that right?"

"What do you mean?" she asked, looking at him through the steam of her coffee cup.

He lowered his voice. "I'm assuming the stuff in his pockets was there when he died. Or do ghosts collect things after they die?"

"It was there. So, we narrow it down to anytime after 1902. Wouldn't his death be in the police records?"

"I hope so, but we're talking about an incident from a hundred years ago. I've never had to go back that far with a case."

She was a little annoyed at his caution, but refused to let it spoil her mood. "Regardless, we have his name. I still can't believe that's his name after all this time. Archie. Like the kid in the comics."

"Don't settle on that as fact, Billie. It's just a name stitched into a hat. That doesn't mean it was his."

"Who else would it be?"

"Maybe it's not his cap," Mockler shrugged. "Maybe it was second hand or he found it in the streets? Stitching a name into a cap would have taken time, if his mother did it. Or it would have cost money to hire a seamstress to do it. The boy doesn't look all that prosperous."

"Don't be such a Negative Nancy," Billie said. "It's his name. It has to be."

"It probably is. I hope it is. But don't make assumptions, and don't fall in love with your assumption." He checked his watch.

"I gotta run. What are you up to?"

"I'm going to the library. The local archives might have something."

"That's a good idea. Look through the newspapers from that year and beyond. It's a slog going through it all, but the microfilm might turn up something."

Gathering their things, they stepped out into a cold wind and an overcast sky.

"I'll check in with you later." He walked toward his car, digging out his keys. "Good luck, honey."

A kiss and then she waved goodbye. She felt silly that her heart had thudded hard hearing the tiny endearment from him, but it left a smile on her lips that lasted the whole way home.

~

The first search attempt was a washout, but that was to be expected with an incident this old. An obligatory general scouring of police records from his desk terminal turned up no information on the name Archibald Crump and the searchable database of homicides only went back as far as the late 60s. Digging deeper meant a trip to the archive depository off site. Mockler looked over the schedule for today to see if there was anywhere to slot in a trip to the depository.

He rolled his chair back to look into the next cubicle. "Odin, can we push back the follow-up with the McMartin woman?"

"Again?" Odinbeck looked over his glasses at the younger detective. "Gibson ain't gonna like that. She wants that mess tied up with a bow before sending it down to the crown prosecutor."

Mockler scratched his chin. "I'm gonna call McMartin, see if we can move the follow-up to the end of the day."

"Don't leave an interview to the end of the day, butthead. End of the day means the kids come home from school and she's busy getting dinner on the table. It's chaos." Detective Odinbeck slid the glasses from his nose. "Did something come up?"

"Not officially. Just something I want to look up in the archive depot, but they close up shop at four."

"Archives? The hell you want there?" Odinbeck turned back to his screen, dismissing the question with a wave of his hand. "On second thought, I don't even want to know."

Mockler shot up and grabbed his jacket. "Tell you what, I'll take care of the interview with McMartin. You can double-check my report in the morning before we toss it upstairs. Deal?"

"Knock yourself out, kid," Odinbeck laughed.

~

"Here ya go," said the clerk as he slid three enormous books onto the counter.

Mockler looked down at the oversize volumes before him. "That's it?"

"The records only go back so far," said the clerk. "A lot of stuff gets lost or destroyed over the years. It thins out the further back you go. Whatever has survived gets bound into volumes like this."

The volumes in question were two feet tall by a foot and a half wide, bound in hardcover that was dusty and smelled of mildew. Each oversize volume was four inches thick with the years in question embossed into the cover. Mockler pulled the nearest one closer, its cover declaring 1902 - 1904. Opening it, he leafed through its yellowed pages. The typeset was achingly minuscule.

"It's killer on the eyes," the clerk said. "What is it you're looking for?"

"The death of a child, possibly a homicide." He turned another fragile page and his heart sank at the blur of type. "Sometime after 1902."

"A child's death?" The clerk's smile faded. "That's a tough one. It might not even be documented in here."

"Why not?"

"A lot of times, the death of a child went unreported. A lot of adult deaths went unreported too, but a child's death was considered a family matter and, therefore, private, no matter the circumstances."

"Even a homicide?"

"Yes, sadly. Child mortality was shockingly common back then," the clerk said. "And reporting it to the authorities would only bring unwanted attention to the family. Especially if that family was poor or newly immigrated. They did things the old way, keeping it in house."

Mockler flipped the pages again, trying to discern a pattern or classification to the dense information on the flimsy paper. "Is there a trick to indexing this stuff? These crime reports seemed jumbled together with no division by subject." He ran his finger down a column of type. "You got a death here, followed by a fire at a blacksmith, then a drunken brawl at a pub on King."

"The classification is simply chronological. The incidents recorded by date alone."

Mockler closed the book and surveyed all three thick volumes. "I may have bitten off a bit more than I can chew here. Any chance I could take these home with me?"

"Officially no," reported the clerk. Then, he leaned in to whisper. "But if you promise to treat them gently and return them in two days, no one will be the wiser."

"Thanks," Mockler said. Stacking all three books under his arm, he checked the hallway to make sure it was empty. "I promise to take good care of them." He turned to wink at the clerk, but the man behind the counter had already vanished into the back storage room.

~

Two hours into her search of the microfilm archives, Billie's eyes began to blur from the scroll of old newspaper pages. She leaned back from the screen and rubbed her eyes, losing hope that she would find anything useful here.

She had arrived at the Central Library shortly after saying goodbye to Mockler, finding her way up to the Local History and Archives Department on the third floor. A polite librarian named Debbie walked her through the process of accessing the archives on the microfilm files and feeding the spool of film onto the machine. Once she had mastered the controls to get the negative squared up in the screen, Debbie showed her how print any pages she needed. Tingling with anticipation, Billie began scanning through the newspapers of 1902, scrutinizing the fine typeset and archaic language for anything relating to the death or dismemberment of a little boy.

Nothing appeared. Pages and pages floated by in the screen, but she found no articles pertaining to a child's death, let alone any hint of the legless ghost child who had become part of her life. The crime reports she saw related only to adult deaths and not one obituary mentioned any children at all. Speculating that the death of a child simply didn't merit an obituary at the turn of the century, she made a note to ask the librarian about it later.

Pushing through another roll of film, she got up to stretch her legs before feeding a fourth spool into the machine. All of the eager anticipation pent up over finally finding an answer to her mysterious companion had completely dissipated, leaving behind an oily film of hopelessness. Finish the roll, she bolstered herself, then go hunt down some lunch. If she had the strength, she'd come back for another try later. Scrolling through the last of the film, her eye caught something and she wound the pages backward and scoured the print again. What had hooked her attention had been a single word.

Séance.

There, in a lower column of small print, the tiny headline read *'An Invitation to a Séance'*. Billie skimmed through the article, a simple notice of a séance being held by a supposedly renowned clairvoyant in the Tea Room of the Lavender Hotel on Bay Street, May 4, 1903. She had seen three séance invitations already but something about this notice had ripped a tingle up the back of her neck like nothing else. It was the name of the 'famous clairvoyant and spiritualist medium'.

Archibald Crump.

~

The West Town Bar and Grill had a quiet atmosphere if one hit it at the right time and time was something they didn't have a lot of. He was winding down his workday as she was heading off to start hers. They settled on the upscale diner as a halfway point to spend what little time they had. Mockler was waiting for her at a table near the window when she came through the door and searched the faces inside. His smile lit the moment he saw her.

"Hey handsome," she said as she kissed him. She was still surprised at how easy the flirtation bubbled out. It never had before, often fumbling out in an awkward jumble, but it came easily with him. "You look tired."

"Long day." He leaned back to take a look at her. "You look gorgeous."

"It helps with the tips," she said, shrugging off the compliment. Sitting down, she saw two pint glasses on the table.

"I ordered for you," he said by way of explanation. "I know you don't have a lot of time."

"Thanks." She clinked her glass against his. "Tell me about your day. What made it so long?"

"Lots of detail stuff, tedious as hell." Mockler shrugged. "That's all."

Billie searched his eyes. "You don't talk about work much anymore."

"I don't?"

"No. How come?"

He shrugged again. "I don't want to bore you with it."

"You can bore me with anything you want," she said, meaning every word. He smiled at that and she liked the way his eyes crinkled as he did so. "Did you get a chance to check the records on our friend? I was hoping we could compare notes."

"Sure." He took out his phone. "But be warned, I don't have a lot of notes to compare to. The police archives from that era are pretty slim. I poured through a third of it today without finding anything that even remotely comes close. In fact, I found very few reports of children's deaths at all."

Billie straightened up. "I found the same thing looking through the newspapers of the time. Didn't kids die back then?"

"Child mortality was high, but it was rarely reported. Most deaths were considered family matters."

"That's just weird," Billie stated. "It's almost callous."

"Life was different. Kids died all the time. That's why people had big families back then, knowing that some of the kids wouldn't make it." Mockler sipped his beer. "Did you get a chance to hit the library today?"

"I did," Billie said proudly. "I got schooled in using the archives, and I think I found something." Digging into her bag, she produced a sheet of paper and unfolded it against the table. She pointed at a narrow column of type. "Here."

She watched his reaction as he skimmed the piece. His eyes shot up to lock on hers. "Archibald Crump?" he said.

"How weird is that? At a séance no less?"

"I don't know what to make of it," he said. "Did you find anything else with this name?"

"That's it."

He read the notice again. "According to this, Archibald Crump is a clairvoyant holding a seance in a high end tea room. There's no way a child is putting on a séance."

"That's what I thought. I suppose it would be too much of a coincidence if there were two people with that same name."

He scratched the stubble on his chin. "Unless they're related. The boy in your apartment might be Archibald Junior."

"Maybe." Billie took the page and read the notice again. "I'm going back to the library tomorrow. There's got to be more to this."

Mockler scrolled through the contacts on his phone. "Do you know the bookshop over on Ottawa Street? The rare book dealer above the beauty supply place?"

"The one with the weird sign? I've never gone up there."

"The owner is a guy named Armand Barrow. He's a historian, big into local history. Talk to him. He might know about this Crump character." Scrounging up a pen, he scribbled the number into the margin of the page. "Call him first. He keeps odd hours."

The food came and they tucked into their plates. Between bites of a clubhouse sandwich, Mockler asked "Have you talked to your friends about what happened?"

"I called them to apologize," Billie said. "Jen's a little pissed. She thought it was a prank."

"Do you want to try this? It's really good." He cut a piece and put it on her plate. "Jen still doesn't believe in your ability?"

"We just don't talk about it. It's awkward."

"Do you think she'll ever come around?"

His phone chirped before she could answer. Checking the message, Mockler looked up at the entrance and waved at someone.

"What's going on?" she asked, turning to see a woman making her way to their table.

"I had an idea, if you're up for it." He rose to greet the woman. "Liz, thanks for coming."

"I don't normally make house-calls, but you said it was important." The woman was small with long grey hair scrunched into a high ponytail. She had a large sketch pad tucked under her arm and she turned to Billie. "Hi. I'm Liz."

Billie shook the woman's hand. "Billie. Have a seat. Are you hungry?"

"I ate already." Liz settled into a chair beside Mockler and looked around for the waiter. "I might have a glass of wine though."

Billie glanced at her date, waiting to find out what this was about. Mockler smiled. "Liz is a sketch artist. She works with the force a lot."

"That must be interesting," Billie said, glancing at the woman's sketch pad again.

"It is, but it can be difficult too, asking someone to describe the person who hurt them." The woman placed a number of pencils on the table and turned the pad to a fresh page. She looked at the detective. "So? Who are we sketching?"

"I thought it might help if we had a visual," Mockler said to Billie. He reached out and put his hand over hers. "Do you think you could describe your friend to Liz?"

Billie leaned back in surprise. "Is that necessary?"

"No," he said. "But sometimes it helps to have a sketch to use as a guide."

Billie set her fork down. "I'm just not sure I can describe him all that well."

"There's no right or wrong," Liz said, selecting one of the pencils from the table. "Just do your best and we can adjust as we go along. Start with the basics. Sex, age, height."

Billie folded her napkin in her lap, wondering how best to describe the boy to the artist across the table. She started with his approximate age and his small size. She described his threadbare clothes and natty cap, the features of his face. She told Liz of the amputated legs, but omitted detailing that the wounds were always fresh and how the severed stumps never stopped bleeding. She spent a moment describing the way the boy held himself, his constant slouch. She glanced at Mockler and he gave her a wink as they watched the woman work the sketch with different grades of pencils.

"I gotta say, this is one of the more bizarre renderings I've done." She laid her tools aside and handed the sketchpad across to them. "Is this the boy you saw?"

Billie took the pad and Mockler leaned into her to see. The rendering was finely detailed and seemed to capture the essential sadness of the tragic little boy. It wasn't so much the features of his face, but the boy's posture, the way his shoulders hunched and his head dipped as if in eternal shame.

"Wow," Billie said, looking up at Liz. "That's really good."

"Thanks." The woman packed away her pencils. She took the sketchpad back, tore the drawing out and handed it to Billie. "I hope it helps."

"It will," Mockler assured her. "Thanks for meeting us, Liz."

The artist finished her wine and said goodbye. Billie couldn't stop staring at the drawing.

Mockler propped both elbows on the table. "What do you think?"

"It's so odd seeing a picture of him. Your friend is really talented."

"She's good at teasing out the details from people." Mockler held the sketch at arm's length to gain perspective. "Sad little guy, isn't he? Like something out of a Dickens story."

"I gotta run," Billie said, checking the time on her phone. "Will you make me a copy of that?"

He handed it to her. "You keep the original. Just photocopy it for me."

"Okay. Thanks." She leaned in to kiss his cheek. He needed a shave. "How do you feel about giving me a lift to work?"

"I'd love to."

CHAPTER 21

"ARCHIBALD CRUMP," STATED the man behind the desk. "Clairvoyant and showman. Exposed as a fraud."

"Fraud?" Billie asked, looking up with surprise at the man. "How do you know?"

"There are two threads to every history," said Armand Barrow. "The official history of the public record and then the obscure, often darker truth stitched underneath it. One just needs to know where to look."

Barrow's Rare Books was a cramped space above a beauty supply shop on Ottawa where the musty smell of old books was mitigated by the aroma of hair product from the shop below. Proprietor Armand Barrow, a short man in his late 50s, was a curious study of contradictions. The glasses hung around his neck from a chain and his grey beard gave him a grandfatherly charm, but the tattooed forearms and Cannibal Corpse tee-shirt made him seem like a biker misplaced inside a book shop.

Heeding Mockler's advice, Billie had called ahead to book an appointment with the book dealer. When Barrow had asked what it was about, she had said she was trying to find info on an obscure clairvoyant, adding that Detective Mockler had referred her. Barrow asked her to spell the name of the individual and then told her to come by after noon. Clearly, the rare book dealer had done his homework.

Still parsing the man's riddle about twin histories, Billie chewed her lip before venturing another question. "Was Archibald Crump a child clairvoyant?"

Barrow arched on eyebrow. "Child? No, he was in his 30s when he set out his shingle here in Hamilton. Why?"

"No reason," Billie said. "You said he was a fraud?"

"He was exposed as one. The exact details are obscure but he was quite successful for a time holding séances and private divinations. Then in 1906, something happened and he was chased from stage one night and almost murdered by a mob."

"What did he do?"

"That part is still a mystery," said Barrow.

Billie propped an elbow on the counter. "So, he was a fortune teller?"

"Yes. Spiritualists and séances were all the rage in the early part of the century. Crump was a Scottish emigre who claimed to come from a long line of diviners back home. He even claimed his ancestors were seers to the court of George the Third. Here, have a look at this." Barrow reached under the glass and unfurled a small poster. *'An Evening of Spiritualist Wonder and Cabinet Seance with the astounding Archibald Crump'*, read the headline in archaic font. The lurid illustration showed a man in black tails and trim moustache gesturing over a skull.

Billie lingered over the illustration. The man pictured was clearly not the Half-Boy. So, what was his connection to the child? "Where did you find this?"

"The curse of a collector, I'm afraid. A wee bit of everything in here."

She ran her finger over the lurid poster. "So Crump ran séances for a while, but was proven to be a fake?"

"Either that or he gave a bad fortune to the wrong person," Barrow grinned, scratching his belly. "I think he was run out of town in 1906, during the riot."

"Riot?"

"Rail strike. The local workers were in a labour dispute with their bosses and shut down the trains. The mayor called in the army to break the strike. All hell broke loose, city in shambles. Crump disappeared during the chaos, never to be seen again."

Billie pursed her lips in thought. "How do you know all this stuff about Crump?"

"The spiritualist movement of that period has always been a hobby of mine. There was a fair bit of it here in town. In fact, there were even chapbooks produced during that era." Barrow turned to the shelf behind him and produced three small hand-printed pamphlets and laid them across the counter. "Sort of an early newsletter produced by the adherents of the spiritualist movement."

Billie fanned the brittle chapbooks across the glass. The covers were yellow with garish typography in red and black. *The Eye of Horus Society.*

Barrow tapped the third booklet on the end, with its crude rendering of a dove over a pyramid. "There's a few references to Crump in this one."

"How much?" Billie asked, picking it up gingerly. The cover was loose, straying from its interior pages.

The book dealer looked at the young woman and then looked at the chapbook in her hand. "Fifty?"

"Dollars?" Billie protested. "There's barely 50 pages in here. And it's falling apart."

Barrow shrugged. "It's a rare document from a curious period of local history," he said, as if that countered any dispute to its value.

Billie scowled, but dug into her pocket all the same. Working bar usually meant having wads of cash, but all she came up with were two wrinkled $20 bills. "Forty is all I got."

Armand Barrow shook his head in dismay, but took her cash anyway. "You're practically robbing me blind, young lady. Maybe I should call that detective friend of yours and inform him of a robbery in progress." Winking at her, he slipped the purchase into a brown paper bag and handed it to her. "Happy reading."

~

"So that's it?" Tammy asked. "It's over?"

Kaitlin nodded slowly. "Yeah. I think so."

They were seated on the couch in Tammy's apartment, where Kaitlin had crashed the night before. This incident hadn't been the first time Kaitlin had sought refuge after a fight with her boyfriend. When she had shown up late last night, Tammy didn't press her for particulars of the quarrel, she just got the extra bedding out and the two of them killed a bottle of pinot noir.

When Kaitlin asked to stay a second night, Tammy knew it was serious. A night away from Kyle was usually enough for Kaitlin to cool off and go back with a clear head to sort things out. Camping out on her couch for a second night was new territory and it troubled Tammy.

"And this is all because of what happened at Billie's?" Tammy asked.

"That was the tipping point." Kaitlin picked up her glass and looked at the dark vino within. "We've been having problems for a while now."

That was news to Tammy. "You two always seem solid to me."

"We're good at keeping it private. Putting on a good show for everybody."

"Clearly." Tammy reached for her glass, wondering if she

should order in some food. Neither of them had eaten since getting home from work and it looked like they were about to repeat last night's decimation of red wine on the couch. "But what was it about Billie's that tipped it over?"

"Kyle can be so condescending when he wants to be," Kaitlin said. "Especially about anything I have an interest in. He used to, at least, be respectful of it, but, now, whenever anything comes up about the paranormal, he just gets nasty with me."

"He kinda has reason to," Tammy pointed out. She backtracked when she saw anger flash in her friend's eyes. "That came out wrong. I'm not saying he's right, but maybe it scares him. You almost died because of it, remember?"

"Don't take his side," Kaitlin snarled. Then, she smiled. "Bitch."

"I'll never be on his side, dumbass. I'm just saying maybe he's scared and it comes out all wrong. Dudes are shit at saying what's really eating them. Instead, they pick ridiculous things to bitch about."

"That I can recognize, but then it turned mean. I know he never believed in any of that stuff but he would at least tolerate it. But, now, he taunts me with it, going out of his way to belittle me for being gullible. I'm just sick of it."

"I'm sorry, honey. I had no idea it was that bad." Tammy patted her friend's hand. "Well, you can stay here as long as you want."

"Thanks. I'll find a place soon, I promise."

"Don't sweat it. I miss having a roomie." Tammy rose from the couch with a grunt to retrieve her phone from the table. "I'm gonna order some takeout from across the street. You okay with burritos?"

"Sure," Kaitlin said as Tammy went into the kitchen. She looked at her glass, thinking she should probably slow down, but took another sip anyway. When a chill passed through her, she looked for a blanket to wrap over her shoulders, but there wasn't one. Tammy was simple in her furnishings. Functional with few comforts. She rose to get her sweater from the chair, but an abrupt pain shot through her abdomen like a hot blade. It stole her breath, but she managed to set her glass down without dropping it. Her first thought was the wound in her belly, but it was healed over. Had something internal ripped loose, a stitch below the surface? It had been weeks now.

The second pain ripped across her back like a bone-studded whip flaying the flesh. She gasped to call Tammy, but the third flash stole her voice. A stroke, she thought. I'm having a stroke. Then, she thought, I'm too young to be having a stroke.

Kaitlin shut her eyes against the pain and, when she opened them again, she was somewhere else. Not Tammy's warm apartment, somewhere cold and damp and very dark. The ground under her was frigid stone and grimy with muck. A small light filtered in through a crack in the wall and something passed before the dim light, blocking it. When her eyes adjusted, she saw a dark figure before her. The face was covered by a hood, two dark eye-holes cut through the material, but she could see no eyes within. The cloaked figure held a flail in his bloodied fist, with leather thongs that rattled from the sharp studs embedded in each string.

Her tormentor was fast, lashing out again with the flail. Kaitlin felt it tear across her cheek, flinging her across the floor, almost colliding into a tin bucket against wall. The water within the bucket spilt and she saw her face reflected in its rolling surface, but it wasn't her face that looked back, it was a man's face. His cheek was split and blood dripped into the water where it dispersed. Kaitlin blinked twice before recognizing the face in the water's surface. If only she could remember his name.

"What was that noise?" Tammy said, coming back into the living room. Kaitlin was on the floor, thrashing in some kind of seizure. Tammy dropped to her knees and tried to hold her still.

"Kaitlin, what's wrong?"

Kaitlin's jaw worked up and down, the teeth snarling as she uttered one word over and over. Tammy strained to listen but, it didn't make any sense.

A name.

Owen.

~

The desk in the corner, untouched for months, was a graveyard of old interests and abandoned hobbies. There was an old Hasselblad camera that Billie had found at a yard sale two years ago. Alongside it were three rolls of shot film waiting to be developed and two contact sheets of older test photos. Tammy, who had inspired the interest in photography, had helped her learn the basics of the trade and mechanics of picture developing. The old Swedish camera, a precise and beautiful piece in and of itself, had sat untouched for almost a year.

Next to the camera was a vintage sewing box of pink wicker with a coiled handle. The clasp was broken and the lid didn't close properly anymore. This inspiration had come from Jen, whose talent and skill with material Billie had always envied. Further crowding the desk were re-purposed baby food jars filled with beading, spools of wire and small tools. Kaitlin, when Billie had first met her, made her own jewelry.

These artifacts of lost interests had gathered dust when Billie realized that what had inspired each of them was not the craft in itself, but the passion of those schooled in them. Tammy, with her photography; Jen's love of creative design and Kaitlin's patient skill with wire and bead. The passion was what Billie had been after in her search for her own vocation and now the sight of these relics and unfinished creations was simply depressing.

Gathering up the detritus of her old pursuits, she packed it away into a box and slid the box under the desk. Cleaning the desk with a rag, she set up her cranky laptop, a notebook and three books from the library on the history of Hamilton. Squared up atop the pile of books was the small chapbook from the book dealer that had cost her 40 clams. The wall above the desk was cluttered with postcards and pictures torn from magazines. These came down and the push-pins reused to fix a small map she had photocopied from a library book showing the layout of the city in 1904. Next to this map she tacked the pencil rendering of the Half-Boy from the sketch artist.

She took a moment to approve the set up. She was now ready to tackle a new pursuit but there was one critical aspect that separated this pursuit from the others she had boxed away; passion. She was determined to unlock the true identity of the lost boy who had become a part of her life. Eager to dig in, she started with the pricey little booklet titled *The Eye of Horus*.

Thirty minutes later, Billie was ready to chuck the useless thing out the window. *The Eye of Horus* was little more than a gossip rag for some arcane inner circle of enthusiasts of the spiritualist movement at the turn of the century. There were a few essays on the use of the Tarot, water-witching and the existence of faeries, all written in dense, flowery language that only seemed to obscure their subjects rather than elucidate them. There were pieces on phrenology, palmistry and séances by practitioners of these subjects that were basically early advertorials. There was a review of a recent Houdini performance in Montreal and a review of a carnival sideshow called the Lesser Orphans of Cairo. The archaic language was giving her a headache and she wondered if she'd have better luck with the library books. Flipping through the rest of the chapbook, she found more of the same but the last two pages were letters to the editor. These were not as stuffy as the articles and a few missives were even gossipy, with one spiritualist accusing another of being a fraud. Juicy. The last letter in the column made her sit up when she spied a familiar name: Archibald Crump.

The letter was glowing praise from an admirer who had recently consulted with Crump in an effort to contact a deceased relative. Describing Crump as the real McCoy, the admirer stated that her mind had been put at ease after the spiritualist had contacted the spirit of her late mother to ensure that she approved of her recent engagement. The correspondent did, however, find Crump's methods unusual, not the least of which was the inclusion of the little boy at the table. Explaining the child's presence, Crump had reassured her that children, with their unbiased minds and pure hearts, were the ideal conduits for the spirit realm and not to be alarmed if the ghost of her dead mother spoke directly through the little boy.

Billie felt her heart double-thump with excitement. She read the letter a second time to hone in on the details. Crump used a child in his séance routine, a little boy. Could it be a coincidence or was it possible that the child described in the letter was in fact the Half-Boy? The tattered cap he wore in death was a hand-me-down from Archibald Crump.

She spun around in the chair and looked over the apartment.

It was empty. She widened her senses, like a sonar ping, and swept the place. The boy was close, but remained hidden somewhere.

"Come out," she said aloud. "I want to talk to you."

Nothing stirred. If anything, the lad's presence dissipated from her senses as if he'd slunk away.

She got to her feet, her muscles jittery with excitement at the possible connection she had unearthed. Had she finally tracked him down? Adding to the gleeful discovery was the odd inclusion of the paranormal, the boy's use as a sort of intermediary between Crump and the spirit of this woman's late mother. Was that more coincidence or did it hint at some hidden reason why the boy had been drawn to Billie in the first place?

Her phone went off before she could puzzle out any more. "Hello?" she said without checking the caller display.

"Bee? It's Tammy. Can you come over here? It's an emergency."

"Emergency? What's wrong?"

"It's Kaitlin," Tammy said, her voice tinted in panic. "She's had some kind of fit."

"Then take her to the hospital. Is it her injury?"

"That's what I thought too, but she's says it's not. It's weird, Bee. Like, spooky weird. She didn't even want me to call you."

Billie covered her free ear, as if that would clarify what the other woman was saying. "What do you mean spooky weird?"

"Billie, please. Just get over here. Now!"

"Okay. I'm on my way." Billie hung up, reached for her coat and ran for the door, but something in her peripheral vision made her stop.

It fluttered to the ground like a feather, but she couldn't tell what it was at first. The apartment seemed the same until she noticed that the drawing of the Half-Boy rendered by the sketch artist was gone from the wall. It had been torn to pieces and lay scattered over her newly cleaned desk and the floor around it.

The boy was nowhere to be seen, but she could feel an echo of his presence in the room, faint and fading like he had just fled.

~

Detective Mockler sat with his feet propped up, fighting to keep his focus trained on the cramped typeset. Nestled against his lap was one of the oversized books, the second of the trio he had borrowed from the archive depository. All three volumes were due back tomorrow and he still had a long way to go, but his brain was fried from scouring the archaic records filed by the constabulary of a century ago.

A missile dropped from overhead like a bombing run, landing squarely on the book. Mockler flinched, catching the object before it tumbled from his lap. A crinkly paper bag, one corner damp with grease.

"Bombs away," declared Odinbeck as he dropped into his chair. "Time for your three o' clock jolt."

Mockler lifted the bag as if it was dangerous. "What is it?"

"Quick pick-me-up," Odinbeck said. He nodded at the massive book in his partner's lap. "You still searching that?"

"Yup." Mockler peered inside the bag to find a huge donut with a thick glaze of pink frosting. "Where did you find this?"

"New coffee place on John Street. I scoffed at the idea of gourmet donuts. Then, I tried one. Shazam." Odinbeck reached over and took the giant book from Mockler. "Lemme see this thing."

Removing the pastry from the bag, Mockler admired the decorative icing swirled into a flower and then he bit into it. Heaven.

"Here," Odinbeck said, tossing two stapled pages at him. "Have a look at this."

Mockler scanned the bold print. "The tox screen?" he asked, crumbs falling onto the paper. "On who?"

"Antler man." Odinbeck wet a finger to turn the onionskin pages. "Our mysterious vic in the woods. They pumped that poor son of a bitch up with everything."

"Opiate derivative, sodium pentothal," Mockler said, reading out the bullet points. "Morphine? Jesus."

Odinbeck ran his finger down the columns of type as he skimmed the page. "A real cocktail of stuff. Muscle relaxants, too. They had him doped to the gills. I hope the poor bastard didn't feel any pain."

"Anything rare in the mix?" Mockler asked, turning to the

second page in the toxicology report. "Something we could focus on."

"Not really. Everything coulda been lifted from cancer meds or bought on the street." The older detective sat up, holding his finger in a certain place on the page. "What is it you're looking for? A child's death?"

"Yeah. A boy. Why?"

"Is this him?" Odinbeck wheeled his chair closer, keeping his finger cued to a certain passage. "Body of a child, washed up in the harbour. Possible boating accident. Legs missing from cadaver."

Mockler blinked stupidly for a moment before snatching the massive tome back, his gaze laser-beaming on the text. He had squandered a day and a half scouring these pages to no effect only to have his partner track it down with a breezy effortlessness. He read the pertinent details a second time. A child, male, both legs severed at the upper thigh.

He almost ignored his phone when it lit up. He was curt answering it, annoyed at being disturbed now. "Mockler."

"Ray?" Billie's voice, something not right in her tone. "I need to see you."

Sliding the giant book onto his desk, he pressed a finger on the passage so as to not lose his place. "Can it wait? I'm in the middle of something here."

"No," she said. There was no mistaking her tone. Stone cold gravitas. "I'm at Tammy's. You need to get down here now. One oh-four Sherman South. Please."

Slapping a sticky note onto the passage, he slammed the book close and tucked it under his arm. "I'm on my way."

CHAPTER 22

"WHY DIDN'T YOU want to tell me?" Billie asked.

Kaitlin was on the sofa with her knees tucked up and a blanket around her shoulders. "You said you quit. You didn't want anything to do with it anymore." She shrugged. "I wanted to respect that."

"Quit?" Tammy shifted her gaze to Billie. "Quit what? Being psychic?"

The glare in Tammy's eyes was cold and Billie winced under it. She looked up at Kaitlin, shivering on the sofa. Her skin had taken on a waxy sheen and there was a red mark on her brow from where she had hit her head during the seizure. Hadn't she been through enough already? "Kaitlin," she said, reaching out for her hand. "I screwed up. Again. I shouldn't have brushed you off when you wanted to talk. I should have listened to you."

"I get it now," Kaitlin said. "Believe me, I get it."

Billie lowered her eyes, feeling unworthy of her friend's

grace. She seemed destined to forever make the wrong choices. The attempt to shut out the spookshow forever had been foolish, not to mention selfish. It had isolated Kaitlin and spurned the Half-Boy when both needed her. How could she have been so thoughtless?

She pushed away the suffocating remorse. There would be time to crucify herself over it later. Right now, something had happened and it was troubling. "Are you sure it was Owen?"

"Positive. It was like I was inside his head. I could feel everything he was feeling." Kaitlin touched the spot on her cheek where she had felt the whip flay her skin. "It still hurts."

"How is that possible?" Tammy interjected, looking at Billie. "I thought you were the one who's psychic?"

"I don't know. It's not like there's an instruction manual to this stuff." Billie turned back to the woman shivering on the sofa. "Could you see where he was? Did anything look familiar?"

Kaitlin shook her head. "It was dark and cold. Like it was underground. That's all I could see."

The entry buzzer sounded and Tammy left the room to see who it was. Kaitlin went on. "He was in so much pain, Bee. I think they're going to kill him."

"He tried to kill you, Kaitlin."

"That wasn't him," Kaitlin countered. "That awful woman was using him. Owen's not a bad person. He's just messed up."

Tammy stepped back into the room. "Bee? Your boyfriend's

here."

~

"Do you believe her?" Mockler asked.

Billie nodded her head. "Kaitlin has some ability. I'm not sure what exactly it is, but it's real."

They had stepped into the kitchen to talk quietly, while Tammy took care of their friend. The detective scratched his head, mulling over what he'd just been told. "So, Kaitlin has this seizure where she suddenly feels what this Owen kid is feeling?"

"Basically," Billie said. "It's a flash of empathy with the other person. Don't ask me exactly how it works because I don't know. But Kaitlin has a connection to certain people and when the other person experiences extreme pain or stress, it's like it's happening to her, too."

"Even with a guy who tried to kill her?"

"They'd both been possessed by Evelyn Bourdain," Billie suggested. "Maybe that was enough to bond them."

"And she didn't see the person attacking her? Or Owen, I mean?"

"She said it was too dark."

Mockler leaned back against the counter, his face darkening. "Shit," he muttered quietly.

"What is it?"

His eyes stayed on the floor. "Do you remember Owen's

friend, Justin?"

"How could I forget? They were both there at the Murder House."

"He's dead. He was found in the woods, tied to a tree stump and cut open in some kind of ritual."

"What?" She took a step back, as if distance would render his statement sensible. "Are you sure it was him? When did it happen?"

"Eight days ago. We positively identified him."

She shook her head, still trying to make sense of it. "Why didn't you tell me?"

"I don't know if it has anything to do with you or what happened at that house. It looks like something else." Mockler rubbed his eyes. "You'd been through enough already. I wasn't going to tell you about it unless I knew for certain it had something to do with you."

"He was killed in some ritual," she fumed. "How could it not?"

"You told me that the Bourdain woman was gone after the house went up in flames and the whole place was bulldozed. You said she was gone."

"She is gone," Billie said. "I'm sure of it."

"Then, there's something else going on. Who knows what else those two were into."

"But you still should have told me. After all this? Jesus."

"You're right." He sighed, shoulders stooping. "I didn't want to burden you with it if I didn't have to. You said you wanted to put all of this behind you."

Billie held her tongue. She understood what he was saying, but it didn't extinguish the ire souring her guts. She took a breath and said, "For the record, I don't want you to protect me or shield me from things, but I do need you to be open with me. About everything. Okay?"

"Fair enough," he said.

"Good." Billie reached for her coat. "Now, show me where this happened."

"What?"

"The crime scene. I want to see the place where Justin died." She cut off his protest before he uttered a word. "No arguments. Let's go."

~

The lights of the city were left behind as they drove the dark country roads to a place called Crooks Hollow. The quaint houses gave way to the occasional farm in the distance and then they too faded until there was only the yellow stripe of the road lit up in the headlights.

"Take the wheel," he said.

"Why?" she asked in surprise.

"Just hold it steady for a second."

Billie gripped the steering wheel as Mockler reached behind

to find his suitcase in the backseat. Sliding back into position, he rifled through its contents without taking the wheel.

Keeping the car on course from the passenger side was awkward, especially at the speed they were travelling. "Uh, do you want to pull over so we can change places?"

"I got it," he said, taking the steering wheel again. He held out a manila folder. "Here. You may as well see all of it."

Opening the folder, Billie slid out the crime scene photos. Unprepared, she turned away for a moment before steeling her gut and looking back. It was impossible not to wince at the sight of the body lashed to the tree or the bloody wounds up and down his skin. It looked as if he'd been attacked with a wire brush. "What did they do to his head?"

"Those are deer antlers. They were drilled into his skull." He watched her grimace at the horror of it. "They also carved symbols into his flesh. There's photographs of them in there."

Billie's stomach churned at the images, but she kept flipping through the pictures until she found the snapshots he referred to. "That poor man."

"He was doped up on a lot of stuff, including morphine. He may not have felt much pain when they did that to him. Do you recognize any of those?"

"No," she said. "None of these look familiar."

"I compared these markings to the glyphs found at the Murder House. None of them matched. I don't think there's a correlation."

Billie squared up the loose photographs and closed the folder. "So, whoever did this to Justin has nothing to do with the Murder House? It's just a coincidence?"

"I'm not so sure. These two guys were obsessed with the paranormal. They may have encountered the perpetrators through that, exactly the same way they got mixed up with the Bourdain woman." He slowed the car, keeping an eye out for a landmark in the darkness of the trees. "Gantry once told me that there's an occult underground operating in the city. Not amateur stuff like these two kids but wealthy, well-connected people who operated some kind of network."

"He told me that, too, but Gantry said a lot of weird things." She slid the folder back into the bag. "Do you think this underground network is involved here?"

"It's just a guess at this point. One of many." He drove on, crawling the car along. "Keep your eyes peeled for a sign that says Crooks Hollow Mill."

A bank of trees hemmed both sides of the dark road like a fortress wall. The only light came from the vehicle's headlights, the only sound that of the tires grinding slowly over the cracked asphalt.

"I think I found the boy," he said. "Your friend."

Billie turned quickly. "Oh my God, so did I." She had almost forgotten about it in the chaos. "What did you find?"

"A small note in the police archives, dated 1906. The body of a child washed up in the harbour. Both legs were missing from the thigh down."

"That has to be him," she said, thrilled at the find. "What else did it say? Was there a name?"

"No, that was it. Just the discovery of the body."

Billie's brow furrowed. "That's it? The police find a dead child and that's it?"

"It may have gotten lost in the chaos," he said. "The body was found on November22, the day after a huge riot in the city. A lot of people got hurt that night, some of them died."

"I remember seeing something about a strike."

"It was bloody. With the rail workers on strike, the city called in police forces from all over the area to break up the crowds. A sheriff actually read the Riot Act and then everything blew up. It was brutal. I think the boy found in the harbour was just added to the casualty list and not investigated properly."

"Did he drown?"

"The report didn't say. It's possible he could have had some accident and then fallen into the water. I doubt we'll ever know for sure."

"It must be him," said Billie. "The severed legs, the date occurring just a few years after the date on the penny in his pocket."

Mockler kept scanning the wall of trees. "What did you find?"

"A reference in an old booklet. It mentions Archibald Crump's séances, and how he used a small boy as part of his act."

"A boy?" Mockler asked. "Was it his son?"

"The letter didn't say."

"Why would he use a kid in a séance? Is that normal?"

"Not that I know of," Billie replied with a shrug. "According to the letter, Crump claimed that the boy was some kind of conduit that allowed the spirits to come through."

"The kid was a psychic?" The detective slowed the car even more. "Jesus, this just gets weirder by the minute."

"It has to be him," she stated. "The severed legs, the date corresponding to the penny we found in his pocket. Crump using a boy in his act, which is where the boy got the cap from. It all adds up."

"Except we still don't know his name."

She looked out at the dark forest and then turned back to the detective. "Do you think this Crump guy killed him?"

"It's possible. The severed legs could have been an accident. Maybe he fell into the path of an oncoming train. But you said his tongue was cut out. It seems more likely he was murdered." Mockler stopped the vehicle altogether. "There's something else. The spot on the waterfront where the body washed up."

"What about it?"

"I looked it up. That spot is now where Pier Four Park is. The same place where you almost drowned." Killing the engine, he nodded at something on the starboard side of the car. "We're here."

Two flashlights followed a pathway that wound through the inky woods. Beyond that was the complete darkness of night in the countryside. When they came into the clearing, Billie saw strands of yellow police tape strewn among the muddy leaves. Mockler swept the beam of his flashlight over the scarred trunk of an old oak. There hadn't been any rain in days and the blood stains were still visible.

"This is where he was found," Mockler said.

Billie stood still, her boots already covered with mud. She looked over the old tree, mentally overlaying the scene from the photographs.

"Are you, uh," Mockler fumbled for the words, "sensing anything?"

"I need a second."

He went quiet and watched her. Billie took a breath and closed her eyes. Then, she began to fidget, small ticks in her shoulders, her neck. Her hands became restless, rubbing together as if cold. She opened her eyes and circled the trunk slowly.

"He was scared," Billie said. "His head was all messed up. All these crazy thoughts, and then panic and fear."

"Was that the drugs he was pumped with?"

"I think so. It's all crazy." She turned away now and then as if something out in the darkness had caught her attention. "Whoever did this to him, there was more than one person."

"How many?"

"Five or six? Maybe more."

"Can you describe them?" he asked.

"Not really. They're wearing dark clothes. Their faces are hidden from me." She stopped cold and then backed away quickly. "Oh no. That's not good."

"What is it?" Mockler took a step closer. The fear in her eyes was real, her hands moving faster in their manic wringing.

"Something bad was here. Something really, really bad." She looked up as he walked toward her and waved him back. "Don't go near it."

He trained his light up and down the knotty bark. "What is it?"

"I don't know, but it's not good. These people tried to bring it close, to summon it." Billie backed away even further. "I don't want to be here anymore."

"Is it dangerous?"

"I don't know. Can we go?"

He took her hand and they marched from the clearing without another word. Billie was tense, her hands wringing endlessly when they climbed back into the car. He fired the engine, spun it around and stomped the pedal. Two miles down the road, he reached out and took ahold of her hands.

"Are you all right?"

"Yeah. Just keep driving."

"You said they tried to summon something."

"That's what the ritual was about. Justin was the bait or the offering. I don't know, it's all messed up."

He nixed any further questions, wanting her to calm down. Her restless hands slowed with every mile they put behind them. Billie finally exhaled loudly and leaned back into the seat. He drove a little further before trying again.

"This thing they were after. Do you know what it was?"

"No. I felt it out there, like it was circling overhead, but I don't know what it is."

They passed a farm on one side, then a house, then two. Civilization. He looked at her. "What about Justin? Was he there?"

"No," she said. "All I saw was the echo of what happened."

The car merged with the traffic coming down Highway Eight and the lights of Dundas sprinkled before them. "I'll take you home," he said.

"Can we keep driving? Down near the rail yard?"

"What for?"

"I'm not sure," Billie said. She was chewing her lip and the restless hand-wringing had started anew. "I'll tell you when we get there."

CHAPTER 23

"STOP HERE."

Mockler swung the car to the curb, but his faith had ebbed to a dim ember that this stop would pan out. Following Billie's lead, he had driven around most of the Gibson end without any luck. This location was their sixth visit so far. Each time, Billie had looked over the buildings only to declare that it wasn't the place. When he asked what exactly she was looking for, Billie had been unable to describe it. She simply asked to keep driving. He slid the gear into park, expecting more of the same. "Is this it?"

No answer. She had already bolted from the vehicle, leaving the passenger door to bounce on its hinge.

"Billie?"

She was 30 paces out, looking up at the building looming before them. A brick edifice built in the panache of the late industrial boom, but long abandoned, the windows ugly with plywood. Mockler came alongside Billie to find her transfixed by the building behind the dipping branches of the trees. "What is it?"

The wind whistled off the wasteland of the empty field to their left. "The men who took Justin to the woods," she said. "They were here. In this building."

Mockler looked at the boarded up doors and then back to Billie. Her eyes had taken on that eerie gaze they had whenever she peered beyond the veil. They were going inside. Exactly how, he wasn't sure. He told her to wait and ran back to the car. When he returned, he held two Maglites and an iron prybar. "Let's go around back."

The fence was low and easily traversed. The rear of the building was a raw scar where an adjoining structure had been torn down long ago. No locked doors, just more boarded up windows. Mockler approached one and drove the prybar into the seam, angling the board loose. When it fell to the ground, he climbed over and reached back to help her.

Disturbed by the broken seal, dust clouded the funnels of light from the flashlights. The beams played over the bubbled plaster and the peeling paint of the walls. The rubble on the floor was rusty and sharp and they'd both need tetanus shots if they weren't careful.

"Doesn't look like anyone's been here in a long time," he said.

Billie stood by the opened window. "They didn't come in this way."

"Okay," he replied, watching her. Her eyes had lost none of their earlier intensity. "Do we know what we're looking for?"

She shook her head. "Sorry."

Through a doorway and into a corridor. He trained the light east and then west. "Which way?"

"Down," she said.

Not what he'd expected. Finding the stairwell took some time, treading over the rubble in the dark. The air grew damper as they went down one flight and then, at Billie's insistence, another. A dank sub-basement of old stone walls and oily puddles on the floor. It stank of mold and raw earth.

"This way," Billie said, continuing forward.

"Hold on. We're pretty far down. If we get turned around down here, we're gonna have a hell of a time finding our way back out."

"We have to keep going."

Mockler reached out for her. "What's down here?"

"I honestly don't know," she said. There was no way to describe the strange pull that kept calling out to her. At least nothing that would make any sense to him. The magnetic tug at her guts was unsettling, but oddly familiar. She had experienced it once before, during her first fateful visit to the Murder House, an irresistible lure to something hidden inside. It had led her to break open the concrete floor then, opening a sinister can of worms that had engulfed them all. "But I have to find out."

"Hang on." Mockler swept the light over the floor, scouring the ground.

"What are you looking for?"

"Something sharp." Reaching into the debris, he came up with a metal file, dark with rust. "This might work." Scraping it against the wall, the pointed end of the file left a thin line across the stone. "It'll have to do. Lead on."

They continued on, Billie leading the way deeper into the subterranean corridor, her shoes splashing on the wet floor. Mockler stayed close behind, scraping the tool into the wall to leave a trail they could follow if they got lost.

The corridor bisected another. Peering down the left-hand passage, Billie saw a faint glow.

"There's a light up ahead," she whispered.

Mockler hesitated. This blind search was too reckless, stumbling around this deep in the dark. He didn't want her to go any further. "Can you sense what's down there?"

"I can't tell." She tugged her arm away, impatient to go on.

"Let me go first," he whispered. "Stay behind me, stay quiet."

The grit on the floor crunched underfoot too loudly as they crept forward. Mockler eased his firearm from its holster and kept it down as they approached the doorway. A soft pool of light illuminated a square of floor. Flattening against the wall, Mockler eased cautiously into the doorframe.

A vast room lit with two portable lanterns. Two individuals, both clad in dark clothing, both bent over a table working at something. Another glance revealed a third person in the room, prone on the table. This individual didn't move, possibly unconscious as the two others bent over it.

Owen, he thought. The missing partner of the man found in the woods. These freaks were preparing him for the same ritual.

The two figures straightened up and turned to the doorway, almost as if they knew the detective was there all along. One reached for something behind him.

"Police!" Mockler stormed into the room, gun drawn. "Get down on the floor!"

Neither figure obeyed. One clutched a machete, raising it high overhead and swinging it down at the unconscious man on the table.

Mockler aimed and fired. Then, the lights winked out, plunging the room into utter darkness. Noise crashed around in the dark, furniture tumbling and glass shattering.

He swept the flashlight over the room, but both men had vanished. Mockler cursed; he had the one with the machete dead in his sights. He must have hit him, but the room was empty save for the unconscious man on the table. He barked at the darkness for the men to show themselves, but nothing stirred. How could they have fled so quickly?

"Ray!"

Keyed up, he flinched when Billie jostled into the doorway behind him. "Billie, get back."

Training her lightbeam at the long table, she gasped when she saw the man atop it. "Who is that?"

"Owen," he said. Moving into the room, he swept the light and the aim of the gun over the space and back again, expecting the dark figures to pop out at them. If they did, he'd simply put them down.

Billie rushed past him to the unconscious man on the table. Mockler heard her gasp again. "Oh God," she choked. "It's him."

Pushing in, he looked down at the face lit up in the beam of light. It wasn't the missing ghost-hunter.

"Gantry…" she uttered.

~

The two canisters left by the west exit door had been placed there for a reason, a contingency plan should the unthinkable occur. The two men racing up the stairs of the abandoned factory needed that contingency now.

The first man to the exit was already spinning the cap from the spout. He kicked the can over and 16 litres of gasoline glugged out onto the dirty floor. Splashing through the gurgling fuel, the other man cursed his companion for not waiting until he was clear. Now his shoes were wet with econo-grade gasoline.

"Shut up and move," snapped the taller man. He poured the second canister onto the cracked tile. "Get the door!"

Tipping the jug, the two figures splashed a trail of fuel out the door, down the concrete steps and out into the gravel of the adjacent lot. The man with the wet shoes fumbled out a box of wooden matches, but snapped the heads of the first two in his haste to light them. The third one lit and its flame arced through the air as he threw it. The slime trail of gas went up instantly, snaking back across the lot, up the stairs and through the open door.

There was a great whooshing sound and the grimy windows of the factory flared up in a hot orange glow. The two men watched the flames for a minute longer before squeezing through a gap in the chain link fence. Only one of them looked back as they marched briskly through a brown field of dry grass.

~

Billie couldn't believe her own eyes. The wily trickster who had guided her into this upside down world of the paranormal lay stretched out before them, pale as a fish belly.

"Is he alive?" Mockler asked.

She pressed her fingers to his neck. "There's a pulse."

"What the hell have they done to him?"

John Gantry lay on some jerry-rigged version of an operating table, his arm hooked into an intravenous drip. Sensor pads were taped onto his chest and his temples; the wires snaked over him and were patched into two dusty hospital monitors. Strands of wet gauze were bandaged over small wounds across his sternum and up his neck. Next to the table was a stand cluttered with surgical instruments. Mockler poked through the mess of scalpels, forceps and clamps, all still bloodied.

Billie ripped the wires away. "We have to get him out of here. Pull that tube out."

"We need an ambulance," he protested.

"No ambulance. You and I are getting him out." She turned back to the man on the table and thumbed open his left eye. "Gantry, can you hear me? It's Billie. Wake up."

The pupils rolled around lazily without drawing focus on her. A slow gurgle issued from Gantry's throat, but whether it was an attempt to speak or a death rattle, Billie couldn't tell. "Hurry," she urged the detective.

"Billie, we can't just drag him out of here. The man's almost dead." Mockler shook his head at what he was saying. "He is dead, for Christ's sakes! We need a medical team here."

"And what, take him to a hospital? What then? He goes back to prison?"

Mockler gritted his teeth together. He ripped the needle from Gantry's arm and tossed the tubing away. "Find something to cover him with."

Billie found a thin sheet among a clutter of medical tools and they threw it over him. Hoisting the man up, each draped an arm over their shoulders and carried Gantry along. The corridor was narrow and difficult to negotiate with the limp figure between them.

"Stop," Mockler said. Handing Billie his Maglite, he said, "I'll carry him, you lead the way."

Mockler threw the man over his shoulder in a fireman's lift and Billie went on ahead, lighting the way and clearing obstacles from their path. Over the sound of their footfalls splashing through the wet floor, another sound ragged at Billie's ear, but she couldn't place it. The stone corridor was like an echo chamber, amplifying and distorting sound.

Following the scrape mark on the wall, she led the way to the bottom of the stairs. An old desk was set against the wall and Billie pushed the debris from it, clearing the surface. "Hold up," she said.

"What is it?"

"Something's wrong," she said, going up the stairs. "Wait here."

Taking the steps two at a time, Billie raced up to the landing and leaned over the railing to look up. The exit above was where the noise was coming from, an angry popping and snapping sound. Light filled the stairwell above her and she felt the heat push down from the inferno raging overhead.

CHAPTER 24

"WE NEED TO find another way out," Billie said, bounding back down the stairwell.

"What's that noise?"

"Fire." She watched his face pale. "The stairs are blocked."

Mockler looked back down the stone hallway. A labyrinth of corridors to get lost in, all of it cloaked in darkness.

"Come on," Billie said, already tugging at Gantry's limp frame. "There's got to be another way out of here."

He hoisted the man over his shoulders again. "Lead the way."

Scrambling back the way they came, Billie swept the light beam around, searching for an exit sign. Around a corner and up another corridor, she spotted one halfway down, its red glass catching the light. Pushing through the door revealed a stairwell, but smoke was boiling down the steps toward them.

"Keep looking," he growled.

They pushed on, racing on down another turn in the

passageway. Billie kept looking back at Mockler. With the dead weight slung over his shoulders, he was losing momentum, the strain of it shining in his bared teeth. Another exit sign appeared. Billie slammed the door open to find another smoke-choked stairwell. The flames were visible through the fog. Pulling the door closed, she found Gantry on the floor with Mockler kneeling over him, wheezing.

"The whole building is on fire," she said.

"Let me catch my breath."

"I'll carry him," she said, tugging at Gantry's arm. "You lead the way."

"Billie, he's too heavy. You won't get far."

Didn't people in desperate situations get a burst of adrenalin that gave them superhuman strength? Hadn't she read that somewhere? Mothers lifting a car to free their trapped children? She had a crazy notion that it would kick in for her, too, that she'd toss the Englishman over her shoulder and race for the next exit like it was nothing.

She couldn't even get him off the ground. Maybe she just wasn't desperate enough.

The walls shook as an explosion from above rocked the foundations of the building. Debris and dust rained down from overhead. Panting, she looked at Mockler. "What if we hid somewhere, in a room with a fire-door? Maybe the fire won't reach us down here?"

"The smoke would still kill us. There's no way to keep it

out." Mockler wrapped the unconscious man's arm over his shoulder, ready to lift him again. "We just have to keep trying."

"Wait."

"We don't have time, Billie."

She gripped his arm to stop him. "Just give me a second."

Rising to her feet, she took a breath to calm the jack-hammering of her heart. It was a long shot, but they were out of options. She opened up to the other side and uttered a simple phrase into the realm of shades.

Help us.

"What are you doing," grunted Mockler.

"Shh."

Nothing happened. No spectral figure materialized before her. She expected the Half-Boy to appear, rushing in to the rescue as he had so many times in the past. Was she too far away for him to hear her? Maybe the fire was masking her cries for help.

Further down the corridor, something moved in the darkness. Billie opened up her heart all the way and a figure loomed from the inky pitch like it was glowing.

She took a step closer, trying to get a better look. "I know you," she said.

"You shouldn't be down here," the figure said, although it had no mouth, only a ragged piece of jaw that flapped wetly from one hinge. A young man without a face, just the cratered catastrophe left by a shotgun blast.

"We have to get out of here," she said. "Do you know a way

out?"

"There's a tunnel," the ghost said. "I'll show you."

She turned to Mockler and helped lift Gantry onto his shoulders. "Time to go."

They moved on, a strange expedition through the dark as the fire raged above. Billie kept one eye on the pale figure before her and another on the man behind as he grunted under his burden. They came to a metal door.

The dead youth nodded at the rusty swing handle. "I'd open it for you if I could."

She began to panic when the handle refused to budge. She tipped her weight into it, but the handle remained seized.

"Hit it with something." The youth looked over the floor. "The brick yonder."

She found the brick that he indicated and hammered the stubborn handle. The smoke was souring the air and she hit it again. It clanged down, the door popping open.

The hinges squealed when she yanked it open and Mockler ferried his burden through. They resumed their march, Billie keeping one flashlight trained behind her to light Mockler's path. They came to a silo with a winding metal staircase. The steps clanged under their feet as they went up and Billie heard Mockler straining harder to force himself up. One more door and they tumbled out into a cold wind. Gantry flopped over onto the ground where Mockler all but dropped him.

Billie scanned the area around them, trying to get her

bearings. Across the street, the night was lit by the torrent of flames eating its way through the old factory building. Forty yards away, but she could feel the heat of it on her face.

"Thank you," she wheezed to the young man without a face, but the ghost was gone.

~

"I still think we should take him to a hospital," Mockler rasped, out of breath.

"We're here now," Billie replied. "There's no sense arguing about it anymore."

John Gantry lay unconscious in Billie's bed. His face had a waxy slick to it and his breathing was ragged. The debate over what to do with the injured man had rekindled once they found the car. The detective pressed for the hospital, but Billie was adamant that they return to her apartment. Ferrying the dead weight up the two flights of stairs to her apartment had almost wrecked them both after the escape from the bowels of the burning building.

"What if he dies here?" Mockler coughed, his throat seared from smoke inhalation. "Do you really want him, of all people, haunting you?"

The thought of Gantry as a ghost knocking around her apartment was unsettling. He was creepy enough in the real world. "He's not going to die."

Mockler gave the prone man the once over. "We don't even know how badly he's hurt. Leaving aside the fact that he's officially dead."

Billie left the room, returning with a bowl of water and a washcloth. Dabbing the dried blood and soot away, she assessed the various incisions to his chest and arms. "None of these wounds look that serious."

"What about the stab to the back?" Mockler asked, referencing the assault Gantry had suffered while incarcerated.

Billie tossed the cloth into the bowl and took hold of the man's shoulder. "Help me roll him on his side."

Mockler grunted with disapproval, but helped her roll the body over all the same. Six angry wounds puckered the flesh of his back, ragged and red like they were infected. He heard Billie gasp at their severity.

"He needs a doctor, Billie. Simple as that."

She turned to him, her eyes bright. "He knows a doctor. I met him once. What was his name? Jim?"

Something clicked. Mockler dug out his wallet and began tossing the contents out onto the floor. "Jameson. A surgeon."

"How do you know that?"

"Where is it?" Mockler grumbled, sifting the crush of business cards on the floor. He snatched one up and showed it to her. "I met him too."

The ex-surgeon stood in Billie's small bedroom 20 minutes later looking down at the pale man in the bed. "I knew it was too good to be true," Jameson griped, speaking directly to Gantry. "Why couldn't you stay dead?"

Billie fired a look at Mockler, but the detective just shrugged, unsure of what to make of the exchange. Jameson had initially refused to come. After barking at Mockler for calling so late, he had withered at the request to come and help the slippery Englishman. Mockler could almost hear the air leak out of the ex-surgeon like a balloon deflating, but Jameson knew the score. Taking Gantry to a hospital was out of the question.

Billie softened her tone as she addressed the man. "Can you help him?"

Jameson discharged an odd laugh, almost cruel. "You realize that we'd all be better off if we just dumped him into the harbour now, don't you?"

"It crossed my mind," Mockler said. He needed to nudge the doctor along. "But it's late and none of us are really up for premeditated homicide."

The ex-surgeon had brought his medical bag with him, a vintage collapsible case of black leather with his initials embossed in gold leaf. Laying it on the floor, he undid the clasps and then pulled the sheet down to expose the injured man's torso. Plucking out a pair of delicate scissors, he began cutting away the filthy bandages.

Billie hovered over the man. "Is there anything you need?"

"Scotch, over ice."

"I meant for Gantry," she said.

"Warm water and cloths to clean him up with. Gauze if you have any." The man slipped a pair of glasses from his breast pocket, slid them onto his nose and looked at Billie. "The number for a competent exorcist, if you know any."

She forced a smile. "We're going to be awhile, aren't we?"

"I'm afraid so. Better make that scotch a double."

The couple took turns doing nurse duty as the doctor attended to the wounds, stitching the patient up cold without anaesthetic. Gantry stirred once, a slight spasm followed by a brief spat of muttering. Jameson declared it a good sign. Billie got the man a drink after that.

Another hour passed and the ex-surgeon packed away his instruments, announcing that he had done all he could. The rest was up to Gantry. He rose and stretched his neck before addressing the couple. "One of you will have to monitor him for the next day or so. Talk to him. Try and wake him. A good smack across the face might do the trick."

"So, he's going to make it?" Billie asked.

"Hard to tell with that one. How many times can you cheat death without it catching up to you?" Reaching into his doctor's bag, Jameson pressed a handful of pills into Billie's hand, each one individually wrapped. "Administer the blue ones twice a day. If he's in pain, give him the green ones. They're morphine."

"Morphine?" Billie startled. "Is it that bad?"

"Bad? For someone who was carted away in a body bag, I'd say he was doing remarkably well."

"How did he do that?" Mockler asked. "He was declared dead and taken to the morgue. How is he still alive?"

Jameson took up his kit. "With Gantry, who knows? My guess is that the manipulative bastard is simply too pigheaded to die." The ex-surgeon marched for the door, wiping his hands over his trouser legs as if he was no more than the neighbourhood repair man. "Keep me posted."

~

"Who do you think those men were?" Billie fell back onto the sofa, her nerves frayed from the adrenalin come-down. "And what do they want with Gantry?"

"I wish I knew," Mockler said as he settled beside her. "They must have taken him from the morgue."

Settling back, she propped her feet onto his lap. "And brought him back to life?"

Mockler shook his head, unwilling to venture an answer.

Billie watched him rub his eyes as the adrenalin crash hit him, too. "Hey," she said, gently prodding him with her toes. "You did good back there. Saving Gantry."

"You're the one who got us out of that hellhole. I just carried the luggage." He stopped rubbing his eyes and his hand dropped to her ankle. "Did you know we would find him there?"

"No. It was just this pull I felt. Why?"

"Those two incidents have to be related," he said. "The man killed in the woods and you finding Gantry in that basement. I just don't know what it could be."

"Maybe Gantry can tell us when he wakes up."

If, they both thought but neither said aloud. *If he wakes up.*

Mockler turned to her. "Did you sense any connection? Or see anything about those two goons in the dark clothes?"

"Nothing. Those two were blank to me." She watched his eyes droop. "Here. Why don't you lie down? I'll go sit with Gantry for a while."

"Don't get up," he said, his hand locking around her ankle. "I'm fine right here." Then, apropos of nothing, he said, "You need to eat more."

"Huh?"

"I can get my whole hand around your ankle."

"Oh. You like girls with thick ankles, is that what you're telling me?"

"Winter's coming. Time to fatten up before the snow falls."

She smiled. "We'll go visit Maggie. She'll feed us till we can't fit out the door."

"Have you talked to her?"

"I should call. It's been a while." Billie sunk further into the cushions and looked up at the man on the other end of the sofa. "I like having you here," she said.

Smirking, he leaned back and closed his eyes. "Wait till I start snoring. You might change your mind."

She had meant to close her eyes for only a minute, but the cushions under her were too soft, molding to her frame. Waking later with a hard jerk, she leaned up on an elbow to see the clock on the wall. A minute had turned into two hours. Mockler remained in the same position, leaning back against the sofa. His snoring was low and rumbly, but not loud enough to wake her.

He's going to have a stiff back if he spends the night like that, she thought. Swinging her feet to the floor, she puzzled over how to get him into a more comfortable position without waking him.

The floor creaked behind her. She turned, startling.

Gantry stood before the window, looking out at the city. The sheet from the bed wrapped around his shoulders.

"Gantry?" she said, rushing to him. "Are you all right? How do you feel? What happened to you?"

He didn't turn to her or speak; his eyes vacant like that of a sleepwalker. Billie bit her lip, wondering what to do. She took his arm and tried to gently tug him back to the bedroom. "Everything's okay," she cooed. "Let's get you back to bed."

He wouldn't budge, his eyes never breaking from the window. She'd have to wake Mockler to get the injured man back into bed.

"You..." he groaned.

"What?" Billie jerked. "Gantry, what did you say?"

"You should have left me there," he said.

CHAPTER 25

GOING BLIND WAS a fear that Owen Rinalto had carried with him since the eighth grade, watching his grandfather lose his sight to cataracts. He remembered how helpless the old man became, how fragile and dependent on his grandmother for everything. The powerlessness of it was what had frightened Owen the most, planting in him a lifelong sensitivity to his eyes.

Now, he was blind too, just like his grandpa.

The primordial darkness of his cell had atrophied his sight to nothing. Even when his captors pushed open the door and dragged him out, he was blind. A faint glow in the darkness, but that was all. No forms or colours, just black with a pinprick of light. Helpless, just like grandpa.

They carried him up a flight of stairs and through a door before taking him into what felt like a much larger space. They dropped him to the floor and Owen felt himself spinning around as if cast off into space. They had injected so much shit into his veins that he feared he'd never get straight again. He was no stranger to drug use, having tried everything offered to him but he'd stopped cold when he met Justin and the two of them began exploring the paranormal. Encountering the supernatural was enough of a head trip, you didn't want to do it high.

Voices echoed around him, the men addressing one another in the dark. All Owen could do was listen.

"He looks weak," said one voice. A low gravel tone of authority and disdain. The superior. "How bad is he?"

"Fit enough," said one of the others, the servile ones.

"Cut the psychotropics," said the superior. "And feed him some protein. His time has come."

"Now?" questioned the other subordinate. "But the next moon won't appear for another ten days."

"Recent developments require that we move up the timeline."

"Developments?" asked one of the lower ranks. "What happened?"

"Gantry was discovered. Two individuals broke into the site and took him. We need to move things along."

"Broke in? When?"

"Earlier this evening," boomed the chieftain. "One of them was a cop. Possibly the detective who's been hunting Gantry."

"Did Elan and Morris escape?"

"They did. They torched the place. I had hoped that the fire consumed Gantry and his rescuers, but it was not to be." The superior paused for a moment and then, continued. "Therefore, the Englishman remains a threat. We need to perform the ceremony now, before he interferes."

"Not if we find him first. He couldn't have gone far in his state."

"Possibly," the chieftain rumbled. "What about this ally of his? The gypsy girl? Do we know where she lives?"

"Yes."

"Then, put a team together. If the Englishman is there, kill him."

"What about the psychic woman?"

"Eliminate her, too."

Owen strained to hear more, but the men had ceased talking. Blinking his dry eyes, a faint sluice of hope came over Owen. Maybe he wasn't going blind after all. With his eyes adjusting to the faint ambient light, he could see that everything around him was painted black. The floor, the walls, the pews beside him. Was it a church?

"Clean him up. We need him to be the sacrifice, the least he can do is look like one."

Footfalls echoed again. Owen couldn't be sure, but it seemed that the boss had left the room. Before he could hear anymore, he felt himself jerked to his feet and pushed along.

"Pretty pet," said one. "You get to play an important role in all this. You get to be dolled up and made to look pretty for the entity circling overhead. You ought to be proud."

They were going to kill him. Of that, there was no doubt. And they were going to do it sooner rather than later. He was thrown to the floor and then he heard the squeal of a faucet being turned. The water was icy when it hit him.

~

John Gantry looked like a ghost seated on Billie's sofa. With his blasted stare and quivering lip, the expatriate Brit could have been mistaken for one of the many lost dead that Billie had come across since discovering her gift. Or a wasted rock star, Billie thought, coming down after a particularly nasty binge.

He hadn't spoken since the enigmatic gurgle at the window and Billie wondered if this really was a case of sleepwalking. Gantry sat hunched with the sheet around him, gazing out a thousand yards. The tea she'd made for him sat untouched and a thread of drool dangled from his lips.

Mockler folded his arms, observing the pale man. "The look in his eyes worries me. Maybe his mind is gone."

"It's just shock," Billie said. "He'll come around."

"The man was dead. That's gotta do a number on one's mind." Mockler winced as he stretched the kink out of his back, his muscles creaking after falling asleep in a sitting position. "What was it he said?"

"Something about leaving him behind," she said with a shrug.

"Sounds like gibberish," Mockler said.

The man on the sofa twitched. "Clueless as ever," Gantry

wheezed. "That's a shocker."

The couple in the room startled. Billie rushed closer. "Gantry? You awake?"

His eyes rolled slowly to hers. "I'm not sure. Is this Hell?" He tried to smile, but it came out all wrong, looking more like a perverted grin. "Alright, Billie?"

"I'm fine. Worried about you." She pressed her fingers to his brow. No fever. "I don't know how to help you. How do you feel?"

"Bright as a daisy," Gantry muttered. "After it's been stomped under a hundred jackboots."

Billie shared a glance with Mockler. "Are you thirsty? Hungry, cold, anything?"

"Cup of tea would be nice."

"It's right in front of you," Mockler said.

"Tah." Gantry reached for it but his hand was too weak to grasp it. He gave up. "I'd murder someone for a smoke, but I seem to have misplaced my fags. Along with my clothes, it seems."

"Gantry," Mockler broke in, "what happened to you?"

"Issat you, Mockler?" Gantry rumbled. "Run down the shop for a pack of ciggies, would you? Navy cut. There's a good lad."

Mockler shook his head, eyes up to Billie. "You'd think dying would leave someone a little humble. Not in this case."

Billie studied Gantry. His movements were slow, as if simply turning his head took concentration. She patted his bony knee.

"You should rest. The questions can wait till later."

"No." A flicker of life sparked in Gantry's eyes. Hot, almost angry. "I don't ever want to sleep again."

"Maybe some black coffee would help," Mockler suggested.

"The ciggies would do better." Gantry's smile still wasn't working, a lopsided sneer more like.

"I'll be damned if I'm running to the corner store for cancer sticks."

Rising to her feet, Billie squeezed the detective's elbow. "Get the coffee. Make it strong." She looked back at the vacant-eyed man shrouded in the bed sheet. "I'll sort the rest."

The cigarettes were old and stale, a half deck that Gantry had left behind in her flat a month ago. She had been laid up at the time, sick as a dog after witnessing an evil man bricked up into a wall by a cohort of angry ghosts. Gantry had spent a few days looking after her. She wouldn't say he 'nursed her back to health.' It was more like he hung about to make sure she didn't die on him.

The smell of it was awful, but Gantry seemed to come back to life as he hoovered the nicotine down. The glassy blankness in his eyes slowly hinted at their usual glint of cruel glee. "Cor," he groaned. "Jesus didn't feel this bad crawling out of his tomb."

Spewing blasphemy, Billie thought. He must be feeling better. She ventured a question. "What happened to you?"

"Some bastard stabbed me in the back. Those other tossers,

they just ran right over me."

"You were pronounced dead," Mockler added. "They tossed you in a body bag and dropped you at the morgue. Then, you vanished."

"Did I?" Gantry crushed the cigarette into a makeshift ashtray. "Neat trick."

Mockler gritted his teeth, steeling himself for a long string of riddles from the slippery eel. "Did you plan that somehow? Did you get up off the slab and wander off?"

"Something like that," Gantry said.

"How?" Billie asked. It was best to be skeptical around the man.

"Trade secret, luv."

"Quit the bullshit already," Mockler bit. "How did you do it?"

"Just a bit of hocus-pocus. Nothing fancy, mind you, just journeyman stuff." Gantry brought the coffee to his lips slowly, his movements still shaky. "I knew those bastards were coming for me. So, I worked up a quick plan to get out of prison. It worked up to a point. Rising up from the slab is not like pulling a rabbit from a hat."

Billie stayed quiet. She didn't put anything past Gantry these days. She could see that Mockler was another story. He didn't know the Englishman as well as she did. The homicide detective still operated in a world of logic and facts.

"For the record, I don't swallow a word of that horseshit,"

Mockler warned. "But, for the moment, let's roll with it. You wake up and just stroll out of the morgue. Then, what?"

"It was more of a crawl, really. Hands and knees, like a sick dog. I was halfway down the hall when they found me."

"Who?" Billie asked. "The staff at the morgue?"

"That's what I thought at first," Gantry said. "But then they started stomping me with their boots. When they threw a hood over my head, I guessed they weren't the morgue attendants."

"Who?" Mockler spat.

"Aside from their boots, I never got a look at them. They tossed me into a van and off we went. Everything's hazy after that." Gantry reached for another cigarette. "I was laid out on a table in a dark room. There were two of them, both with surgical masks hiding their faces. They juiced something nasty into my veins, kept me higher than a flipping kite."

Mockler waved the smoke away. "What did they do to you?"

"They had questions. I wasn't in the mood to chat so, they got clever with the knives and the clamps. Amateurs, really. No knowledge of pressure points."

"What did they want to know?"

"Everything," Gantry said. "Trade secrets, like I said. Operations. They asked about the Bourdain woman and the Murder House. My associates, my past. All kinds of things."

"Associates?" Mockler leaned in, nodding at their host. "You mean Billie? They know about her?"

"They'd heard rumours about a powerful psychic, but not

much more than." Gantry noted the concern in both of their eyes. "Don't worry, I told them bugger all."

Billie furrowed her brow. "You said nothing? Didn't that just make it worse?"

"Oh no, I prattled my arse off. Reams of utter gobshite and occult nonsense. They lapped it up, the stupid sods. Even taking notes at one point. I wanted to see what they fixated on, which ridiculous tale tickled their fancy."

"Why?"

"To twig who they were. They were after power. Knowledge and secrets." A shudder passed over him, spilling coffee from the cup in his hand. Gantry set it down and looked at his rescuers. "How did you find me?"

"Billie tracked you down," Mockler replied. "We drove around half the city till she zeroed in on that building."

"I see." The man in the bed sheet seemed peeved. "It didn't occur to you to look until now?"

"Don't be an asshole," Mockler said. "We looked high and low for you. Billie more than me."

"You were hidden," Billie said. "Whoever took you knew how to mask your presence from me."

"What changed?"

Billie sipped her tea. "Ray was showing me a crime scene. An occult one. An image of a building flashed in my head. That's where we found you."

"The two incidents must be related," Mockler added. "The

people responsible for the crime must be the same ones who abducted you."

Gantry's eyes narrowed. "What sort of crime are we talking about?"

"Homicide," replied Mockler. "Victim killed in what appears to be a kind of ritual. Symbols were cut into his flesh and horns attached to his head."

"Horns?" Gantry spat. "What sort? Goat horns or antlers?"

"Antlers."

"Shite."

A shudder passed through the Englishman, his face darkening. Billie exchanged a glance with Mockler and then asked, "What is it?"

"You need to show me this crime scene," Gantry said. He looked down at the sheet he was wearing. "After I find some clothes first."

"You're in no shape to go anywhere," Billie stated. "You need to recuperate."

"I need to see this bloody thing, before it's too late." Gantry shot to his feet, but vertigo overwhelmed him, causing him to teeter like a tree ready to timber. He dropped back onto the sofa. "Once the room stops spinning, of course."

"What's so important about it, Gantry?" Billie asked.

"Trouble is coming. And I'm nowhere near ready for it."

Mockler crossed the room to the front door to retrieve something. Billie touched the sick man's brow to test his temperature again. "Is it this threat you keep hinting at? The approaching evil something-or-other?"

"Rising darkness," he corrected her.

"Whatever."

"Not whatever. There's a difference."

"Does it matter?" she huffed.

"Depends who you ask—" Something dropped into Gantry's lap, cutting him off. A plain manila folder. "What's this?"

Mockler took his seat. "The crime scene. In glossy colour. Have a look."

Gantry opened the folder and went through the photographs, examining each one carefully. Silent, the hard set of his eyes falling away and tipping into something close to fear. "Give me the details," he said. "Who's the lad?"

Mockler gave him the bullet points. About the victim being Justin Burroughs, lately of the Paranormal Trackers and the chaos at the Murder House. The details of his death, the symbols and about his missing ghost-hunting pal, Owen Rinalto. He summed it up with how the investigation had stalled out.

Gantry held up one of the photos. "The time stamp on these pictures. Is this the date the body was found?" The detective said it was. Gantry stared at the picture again. "What's the date today?"

"The 17th," Billie said.

"When's the next full moon?"

Mockler raised an eyebrow at the question but Billie did not.

She checked her phone. "The 25th. Christmas day."

"That gives us eight days," Gantry fumed.

"Until what?"

"Until they try again," stated Gantry. "Presumably with the other kid, Ollie."

"Owen," Mockler corrected him. "They're gonna pull another ritual?"

"Quick as ever, detective." Gantry got to his feet again, slowly this time. "We need to crack on."

"Stop," Mockler ordered. "You need to explain this. Properly. No enigmatic bullshit, no sly riddles. Just the truth."

"Not in a bloody bedsheet I'm not. I need some clothes first. Shower, too." He shuffled for the door.

"Where do you think you're going?" Billie demanded, going after him.

"Back to H.Q. to clean up. I'll be back in a tic."

Mockler followed him to the door. "You can barely stand, Gantry. Sit down."

"Bollocks. Just need some fresh air is all." Gantry turned to address the detective, but a queer look fell over his face as he fell against the wall and slid to the floor. "Whoops."

"Back to bed, tough guy." Billie scooped the downed man's arm and looked up at Mockler. "Help me get him up."

"Let him crawl back," Mockler said with no small hint of disdain. "I've carried his sorry ass enough for one night."

Billie's glare was withering and Mockler relented, lifting the limey back to the lumpy sofa. Gantry crumpled forward, his head cradled in his hands. "Better fetch a bucket," Gantry groaned.

Billie lunged for the wastebasket under her desk and thrust it under the Englishman just in time. She and Mockler backed away as the injured man wretched into it. Gantry wiped his mouth and looked up at the other two, his face paled and slick with sweat. "I still need some clothes."

Mockler scowled. "I'll go get them. When I get back, you're gonna spill everything. Where is this place of yours?"

Gantry cursed as he scrounged up a pen from the coffee table and wrote something on a scrap of paper. "The green door at the end of the hall. The closet in the back room." He handed it across to the detective. "Get the gear, but don't touch anything."

Mockler looked at the address scribbled on the paper. "Right. You got a lot of expensive furnishings in this rat hole of yours?"

"No. Just a lot of nasty stuff. Some of it bites."

The detective glanced at Billie and then back to the man clutching the bucket. "Behave yourself while I'm gone and do everything Billie tells you." He marched for the door. "I'll be back in a flash."

The apartment shook as the door slammed shut. Gantry grinned like he was having a grand time and then he stuck his head back into the wastebasket and dry-heaved.

Frowning, Billie dashed into the bathroom for a proper bucket and a dampened washcloth. When she returned to the sofa she found her guest leaning back against the cushions, catching his breath. "Why do you make everything so hard?" she asked.

Gantry raised his head to answer, but panic lit into his eyes and he thrust his face back into the bucket.

Billie perched onto the arm of the sofa and waited for the dry-heaving to pass. "Sneering at everything is the easy way out," she said quietly, almost to herself. "Being kind is hard. It takes strength to be gentle and kind. Didn't anyone ever tell you that?"

Gantry lifted his face from the bucket, panting hard. His eyes narrowed, as if contemplating her words. Then, he spoke. "If you quote Morrissey one more time, I'm going to vomit up a vital organ."

CHAPTER 26

THE ADDRESS SCRIBBLED on the scrap paper was a narrow wedge of brick on Catherine Street that had once housed a drugstore. The entrance was around back, up a rickety fire escape that rattled precariously under Mockler's steps. The hallway was rank and speckled with trash, but at the far end loomed the green-painted door that Gantry had promised. Reaching up, Mockler ran his fingers over the dusty lip of the doorframe until he found the key and unlatched the door.

Hitting the light switch, the overhead bulb flickered intermittently as if poorly wired. The space was narrow and cluttered from floor to ceiling with what, to Mockler, looked like trash. A hoarder's burrow, somewhere between a used book shop and junk dealer. Shelves lined almost every wall where old books and magazines were crowded for space with odd statuary and bizarre-looking instruments. A stuffed raven stared out from one shelf, its black plumage and glass eyes frosted with dust.

Mockler picked his way through the stacks of oddities on the floor into the main room where a large desk straddled the north end, lousy with documents and an overflowing ashtray. Opposite the cluttered desk was a kitchenette with very little counter space and a single sink heaped with dirty cups. The icebox was an antiquated Kelvinator with a chrome hinge handle. It reminded Mockler of the one his parents had in the basement, a relic used for extra space. He gripped the handle, but stopped before opening it. Would it surprise him to find a severed human head in John Gantry's fridge? Or even a whole corpse stuffed inside, the remains of some poor bastard who had gotten on the wrong side of the slippery Englishman? He yanked the handle and the whole refrigerator shook as if balanced on wobbly footing.

The detective was almost disappointed to find no human head staring back at him from the shelves of the icebox. There were cartons of old take-out and half empty jars of condiments, but most of the space was occupied by cans of beer, English ales and Czech pilsners. The Kelvinator, like the rest of the place, resembled a demented bachelor's pad by way of an obsessed hoarder. It seemed almost too cliché. He was about to close the fridge when he heard something move within. Bending down, he caught sight of something slithering inside the icebox back behind the cans of beer. Dark and scaly like the skin of a snake, it undulated past the crusty bottle of ketchup. Mockler slammed the door shut, rattling the fridge on its wobbly stand.

"Okay," Mockler muttered to himself. "Get the clothes and

then get out." He scanned the apartment again, wary of any other nasty surprises creeping out from behind the stacks of junk.

The back room was a marked contrast to the rest of the place, clean and orderly, no junk strewn here. The bed was big and tastefully done, the spread complimenting the colour of the walls. There were even a few throw pillows on it, an oddly feminine contrast to the stanky man-cave feel of the outer room. The closet was tidy and organized, Gantry's dark suits hung properly. It seemed almost bi-polar, the pristine orderliness of the bedroom versus the junkshop chaos of the other room.

Shrugging it off, Mockler gathered up an armful of clothes and crossed back into the outer room. The cluttered mess of the place was stifling, the overstuffed shelves rendering the air claustrophobic and stale. Halfway to the door, something caught his eye and he stopped to take a closer look. Teetering on the edge of the bookshelf stood an enormous glass carboy with a wide flue and something dark bobbing in its chemical depths. Here was the severed head that he had expected to find in the icebox, a ghastly orb pickled in its formaldehyde bath. Male, 40s to 50s, with a straggly beard and a lot of hard living etched into the lines of the face. Both ears were docked from the man's head. A brittle yellow label was fixed to the glass, scribbled penmanship in blue ink. *Edward John Dimond.*

Mockler studied the gruesome exhibit, trying to discern the plastic seam or rubber joint that would give the piece away as a prop, when the eyes popped open and the severed head stared back at the man through the heavy glass. The mouth chomped open and shut soundlessly through the chemical liquid as if screaming for help.

The clothes fell to the floor. Mockler cursed, scooped them back up and ran. He glanced back once before slamming the door. The head was spinning in its formaldehyde, the mouth still screaming.

~

Gantry sat slouched with the bucket between his knees, as still as a stone Buddha. He hadn't spoken a word since Mockler left and Billie thought he had fallen asleep in the sitting position. She chewed her lip, wondering if she could ease him down onto the sofa without waking him.

"I'm awake," he said.

Billie sat on the coffee table across from him. "Feeling any better?"

"No."

His reply was oddly frank, with no veneer of mockery to it. It matched the wasted slant of his eyes and the trembling in his right hand.

"Are you cold?" she asked.

"Freezing."

Fetching the blanket from the armchair, she draped it over his shoulders and settled back onto the coffee table. "This place is drafty. I can turn up the heat if you'd like."

Gantry didn't respond, like he hadn't heard anything.

"Hey." She touched his knee. "What is it?"

He folded his arms to still his trembling hand. "Just not in a chatty mood. Being dead will do that to you."

"That must have been terrifying," she said, unsure of how to respond. How do you console someone who's been dead?

"I don't think all of me came back."

"What do you mean?"

He shook his head slowly. "Something isn't right. Down deep not right. I feel bloody hollow." Gantry's eyes darted about the room like a bird flitting from perch to perch, unable to land. "If I had a poetic inclination, I'd say I came back without a soul."

"I don't know if that's possible." She studied him anew, this uncharacteristic introspection. "Are you getting sicker? You seemed almost chipper earlier."

"That was a poker face, for your boyfriend's benefit," he mumbled. "Pride's always been my downfall."

"I see. No poker face for me?"

"You're different," he said.

She smiled. He reached for his cigarettes, but she stopped his hand. "Why don't you lay off that for now? Go get some sleep."

"The Florence Nightingale thing is getting a bit much," Gantry groused, but he dropped the pack all the same. He turned around, looking over the apartment like he had misplaced something. "Where's that little bastard of a pet you keep?"

"He's not a pet."

"He's a fucking junkyard dog is what he is. Did you finally give the tosser the heave-ho?"

Billie crossed to the small window that the boy often left open. "I tried to help him move on, but that blew up in my face. So, I'm trying something new."

"An exorcism?"

"Your rotten humour's coming back." Pushing back the curtain, she scanned the street below. A couple walking arm-in-arm were the only pedestrians within view. No sign of the little ghost creeping along the side of a building. "Mockler and I are trying to find out who he was."

"Oh?" he sneered. "With you and Scooby-Doo on the case, I'm sure you'll crack that mystery in no time."

"Be nice," Billie scolded. "He carried your sorry butt all the way out of that deathtrap."

"Then, we're even." Gantry snatched up the crumpled pack and lit up. "So? Have you dug up anything on the legless wonder?"

"A few things. He died in 1906. His body was found in the harbour. And he used to be part of an act put on by a clairvoyant."

Gantry sat up. "Clairvoyant? You're joking."

"This guy used to put on séances and he used the boy as a medium. The conduit, he called him." Billie took one of the printed pages from her desk and handed it across. "This guy."

"Archibald Crump," Gantry said, reading the old advertisement. "Sounds like a complete git. Was he the boy's dad?"

"Dunno. That's as far as we've gotten."

"That's more than coincidence, the boy being a medium," Gantry stated, reading the column a second time. There was no reply. Gantry turned to her. "Billie?"

"Someone's here," she said, her eyes on the front door.

"I don't hear anything," he said.

The door blew in with a thunderous crack, as if kicked open by an explosion. Three dark-clad figures stormed inside, rushing the startled psychic and the shivering man wrapped in a bed sheet.

~

Running errands never sat well with Detective Mockler. Running errands for that no-good limey prick was even worse. Locking the door to Gantry's flat behind him, Mockler had a wicked notion to call Odinbeck and have the cramped apartment seized for evidence. Just to piss off Gantry. The only thing that held him back was Billie. She might need the slippery bastard's help.

Despite what had occurred over the last few weeks when Gantry had helped them to locate the remains of Mary Agnes Culpepper, Mockler still resented the fact that Gantry was a part of Billie's life. Disaster followed the man around like a puppy dog and he didn't want Billie caught in the fallout of any of that fool's madness.

The truth of the matter was that John Gantry was still a wanted criminal. He was duty-bound to arrest him. Billie would be furious with him, but, at least, she'd be out of danger with the man locked up. The real crux was whether he himself could betray the man like that now, after everything that had transpired.

Parking across the street from Billie's building, Mockler climbed out and opened the backdoor to fetch the bundle of clothes from the backseat. The sound of shattering glass made him turn around. Shards of it rained down across the pavement. Mockler looked up to see the source, a third floor window in the top apartment. Billie's flat.

~

There was no time to react. Billie's jaw dropped, frozen in shock at the intruders storming the apartment. She felt Gantry shove her away.

"Billie," he snarled. "Run!"

She counted three of them before she was slammed into a wall by gloved hands and thrown to the floor. Gantry, naked save for the sheet and weak as a newborn foal, went down even faster. It was over that quickly.

The knee pressed into her back kept Billie pinned flat to the floor. She screamed at the invaders to get out, to get off of her. The gloved fist smacked hard across her mouth as the brute barked at her to shut up. Squinting through the sting, she saw Gantry struggle against the intruder until he crumpled under a rain of blows.

There was little to distinguish the men who had burst in. They were clad in black fatigues like a SWAT team, their faces masked under inky balaclavas. For a moment, she thought this violent raid was a mistake, that these men were a police assault unit busting down the wrong door, but the way they viciously beat the Englishman told her otherwise.

"The target's subdued," said one of the men.

"Check," said another. "Is that the gypsy?"

"Has to be her," hissed the one with his knee hammered into Billie's back. "What do we do with her?"

"Take her with us. Bind them."

Billie panicked, kicking her feet, trying to buck the man off, but it was hopeless. Her wrists were yanked behind her back and she felt a plastic tie wrap over them. All she could do was curse at them, spitting a blue streak of obscenities at the invaders.

She stopped cursing when she felt something shift in the room, a subtle change in the atmosphere. She almost smiled when she felt the temperature plummet as a cold wave passed over her. The cavalry had just arrived. He always did.

"Hostile!" barked one of the men.

All three shot to their feet, heads up, alert to any danger.

Billie caught a glimpse of something scuttling across the ceiling like an enormous spider. There was a flash of snarling teeth as the Half-Boy dropped onto the heads of the assault team. A wicked thought flared through Billie's mind as she watched him.

Hurt them.

The moment was brief, hope snapping off and blowing away in the wind. One of the black-clad invaders had a weapon of some kind, a dark metal contraption that didn't look anything like a gun. The sound it emitted was so sharp it hurt her ears. The Half-Boy bounced off of the piercing noise, scrabbling away as if he was on fire. Charging across the floor, his teeth popped in an outraged snarl as he sprang at the invaders. The weapon came up, levelled a full frontal blast and the boy was blown clean out the window, shattering the glass as he was ejected into the night.

The pain in her ears scrambled her thoughts. What had they done to him? How could they hurt something that was already dead? Clamping her hands over her ears, she saw the dark men confer, but she couldn't hear a word they were saying. She couldn't hear anything at all beyond a high-pitched tone that whined hot in her eardrums.

To her left, Gantry struggled to get up. A thin line of blood trickled from his ear. Billie watched helplessly as he was kicked down under a heavy boot. The plastic ties came out as the marauders set about binding the Englishman's wrists. The one with the strange weapon slung the device behind his back and turned on her but, then, he suddenly froze, looking past Billie to something at the door.

Mockler. Gun locked in both hands, the barrel aimed at the intruders. He was barking something as he advanced, but Billie was deaf to it. The dark men took a step back. One of them hurled something at the floor and white light exploded across the room. Billie fell backward as her retinas were scorched, now blind as well as deaf.

CHAPTER 27

THE FIRST SENSE to awaken was touch. A low rumbling through her bones that puzzled her until she recognized what it was. She was in a car, driving somewhere. The stinging in her ears had subsided but the sound was muffled. She wondered if she would have permanent hearing damage. Her vision was a different story, clouded by a white flare that didn't recede no matter how many times she blinked.

She felt a hand on her wrist and knew immediately that it was Mockler. He was on her left, which meant that she was in the passenger seat. She could hear his voice, but his words were squelched by the ringing in her ears.

"Where's Gantry?" she asked. "Who were those men?" She kept asking questions, but was unable to hear her own voice, let alone his. She felt his hand squeeze hers. A signal. Stay calm. Everything's going to be okay. At least, that's what she hoped his gesture meant.

The hot flare in her retinas had dimmed by the time the car shut down, allowing her to just make out the exterior of his house as she climbed out of the car. Gantry brushed past her, a hazy outline as he stumbled out of the backseat. The detective took hold of their arms and led the pair up the porch steps. Once inside, she was settled onto the old sofa where she sat with her head down until the nausea passed.

Music filtered through the ringing in her eardrums, a jazzy musical riff like something from an old movie. Lifting her head, Billie turned to the sound to find an unlikely sight. John Gantry was leaning over the old Hi-Fi cabinet in Mockler's living room, sifting through old record sleeves.

"Hey," she said, grateful to hear her own voice.

"Do you hear that?" Gantry said. He adjusted a knob on the old sound system. "So warm. They don't make 'em like that anymore."

Gantry seemed a new man. Gone was the bedsheet and the blasted void in his eyes. His hair was still wet from a shower and he was dressed in a familiar dark suit, but somehow Gantry still managed to look haphazardly thrown together. She wondered how much of it was pure affectation. He turned and hollered into the next room. "She's up!"

"Ouch." Her back muscles squealed in protest as she straightened up. "How long was I out?"

"Long enough for your friend to make himself look pretty," Mockler said as he came into the room. "How do you feel?"

"Dizzy," she said. "But at least I can hear you. What happened back there?"

"We were hit with this." Mockler placed something into her open palm. A metal cylinder with holes bored into the barrel. "Flashbang grenade."

Billie turned the piece over in her hand. "A grenade?"

"It doesn't explode shrapnel; it disorients a target with light and sound." Mockler took the cylinder back. "This is military grade. Whoever these people are, they're dangerous."

"Let's not give them too much credit," Gantry said. "They're a pack of tossers in Rambo gear."

"They had you flat on your face, didn't they?" Mocker challenged. "These are the same people who held you captive until we sprang you. Let's not underestimate them."

"How did they know where I lived?" Billie got to her feet, steadying herself. She looked to Gantry. "And how did they know you were there?"

Mockler's gaze was unfriendly. "Did you tell them about Billie?"

"I told them bugger all," Gantry snapped. "You know that."

"Then, how did they track you down?"

"Clearly, they have a few tricks up their sleeves. Minor hocus pocus."

Mockler shook the grenade in his hand. It rattled. "I wouldn't call this minor. These people are hardcore. We need to know who we're up against. Time to spill the beans, Gantry."

"I'll sort these fuckers; don't worry about that. Just stay out of the way and I'll bring you their heads on a platter."

Mockler crossed the floor, chest puffed. "Not with Billie in danger. You need to cut the man of mystery bullshit and level with us. If not, I'll just take it into the office and make this an official police matter."

The two men were nose to nose. Billie shook her head at the posturing. "For God's sakes, don't start."

"Aye, bring in the filth," Gantry scoffed, too caught up in the brinkmanship to hear the woman. "I'm sure the constabulary will handle this mess forthwith. Exactly how are you going to explain your involvement in this, detective?"

"They can fire me for all I care, asshole. At the very least, they'd ensure that Billie was safe rather than leave her in the lurch like you."

The threat of violence rippled in the air. Fed up with the blustering, Billie had no stomach for playing referee anymore. The overhead light flickered rapidly, stuttering the room in strobes of light. "Enough. I'm in no mood to referee another punch-up. Just sit down and shut up."

Mockler stepped away. He had sense enough to be shamed. Gantry sulked, unwilling to give up the juvenile posturing. "He started it."

Billie massaged her temples, dreading the whopper of a

headache coming on. "Gantry, you said that we have eight days until they try another ritual with Owen. What are they after? And what does it have to do with you?"

Gantry stepped toward the window that looked out onto the backyard. "I made a mistake a long time ago. And I've been paying for it ever since. Others have paid the price too."

His voice trailed off. Billie watched the Englishman, his face turned away. Whatever he was digging at was buried deep, so she waited for him to continue but he went silent.

"Who paid?"

"Ellie," he said. "She paid the most."

"Who?" Mockler snapped, impatience lacing his tone. Billie gripped his wrist, returning the non-verbal communication of earlier. Let him speak.

Gantry leaned back against the mahogany stereo cabinet. "In 2006, a construction crew was excavating a carpark in Norfolk when they broke open a hidden tomb. Archaeologists from the uni were called in to identify it. Their best guess was a minor lord from the late medieval period, but they were wrong. I was a hundred miles away at the time, pissed out of me skull in Covent Garden, but my radar went off like an alarm when that crew broke the seal on that tomb. I got my arse up there in a flash to have a boo. I knew straight away this wasn't some two bit chief, but something much more interesting. It was the burial site of Margaret Read of King's Lynn, burned at the stake in fifteen-ninety for being a witch. Now, most people executed for witchcraft were completely innocent but old Margaret was a different story. A true matriarch of power, and Margie knew lots of secrets.

"Being the arrogant prick I was, I wanted to know her secrets. So, I conjured her. A little hocus pocus, like a trawl line down into the underworld, and I dragged the old girl to the surface. Margie was none too pleased to be disturbed, but everything blew up in my face when I realized she wasn't alone. Something else had scratched its way to the surface with her."

Here, Gantry paused to light a cigarette, the look in his eyes far away. Billie felt Mockler grow impatient beside her. The more outlandish the tale became, the more he fidgeted. She clamped his wrist harder to keep him still.

"Old Margaret, she was the real deal. A true witch, but not the wicked kind from the fairy tales, yeah. When they burned her, Margie's heart leapt from the fire and left a mark on a wall that's visible to this day. Her village was being decimated by something evil and Margie was trying to get rid of it. That's when she was accused by the church of witchcraft and lashed to the stake, but old Margaret, she was a fighter. Just before they set fire to the kindling, Margie invited the demon into her and they both went up in flames. The old girl sacrificed herself to save the very people who had condemned her."

"Hold on," Mockler interrupted, no longer able to stay quiet. "Did you say demon?"

"I did. That's why her heart burst from the flames, still

beating. Margaret had gone down fighting and, stupid me, when I conjured her back, that thing came, too." Gantry blew smoke from his nostrils, like some nether thing himself. "Then, it got loose."

With a flourish of defeat, the detective rubbed the bridge of his nose. "I don't want to hear anymore."

Billie looked up at Gantry. "Is that what happened to Ellie?"

"He's a spiteful bastard, this one," Gantry nodded. "With a flair for cruelty. Instead of coming after me directly, it skulked about, waiting to see who I cared about. It took hold of Ellie on a June night. We had gone round to see some friends, but Ellie said she wasn't feeling well. So we went home and she went to bed. I found her the next morning on the stoop, stark naked in the rain. Her eyes as lifeless as glass. That's when it started. Ellie was never the same again."

Piecing together the hints that Gantry had dropped since she'd met him, Billie guessed what happened next. "You performed an exorcism."

"Bingo. And I failed. Ellie died. The filth suspected me of murder. I went underground for good."

"What happened to the demon?" Billie asked, faltering over the last word.

"It got loose. I've been chasing it ever since. Manchester, Glasgow, Oslo, Madrid. Then, finally here." Gantry locked eyes with the detective. "That's when you and I crossed paths."

Mockler's hands dropped into his lap. He looked pale. "The

Jane Doe in the tenement."

"It's last victim," Gantry confirmed.

Billie took a breath, trying to take all of it in. "Why did it come here? To Hamilton?"

"It followed me this time. I came here to locate the source of the biggest psychic blip ever to flash across me radar."

Mockler's eyes went from the woman beside him to the man leaning against the Hi-Fi cabinet. "You mean Billie."

"The demon trailed me here and, decided to have a little fun taking possession of a transient girl squatting in an abandoned tower block. By the time I found her, it was too late. The bastard had his teeth in her. Still, I tried to exorcise the scum, but I failed. Again. You know the rest of the story."

Gantry looked away and the room grew quiet. Billie felt Mockler grow restless beside her, impatient and frustrated at what he had just heard. The detective hated this spooky stuff, this bizarre, nonsensical otherworld of the supernatural that had infested his life since the two of them had met. She didn't blame him and wondered if there was a limit to his patience. Or his sanity.

She waited a moment before breaking the silence. "This thing. Does it have a name?"

"It has lots of names, most of which are unpronounceable. Or misleading." Gantry retrieved the manila folder and flipped through the crime scene photos. He handed one across to her. "Its common name is Skratte."

Billie held the photo up for Mockler to see. A close shot of a glyph carved into the victim's flesh. "Skratte?"

"Old Scratch," Gantry said, nodding at the photo. "That's its mark there."

"That's the connection?" Mockler asked. "The people who abducted you and the victim in the woods. This demon thing?"

"They're trying to summon it," Billie concluded.

"Close," Gantry said. "It's already here. They're trying to give it form."

"Meaning what?"

"Its powers are constrained in this world, but, with a physical form, it can do so much more damage. That's why it keeps possessing people, but the possession is too traumatic. It kills the person it inhabits."

"But it keeps trying?"

"What else can it do? It's either that or go back to where it came from. No, Old Scratch has had a taste of freedom. It wants more."

Mockler turned the photographs over. "So, these people offered the victim for it to possess? Knowing it won't last?"

"They must have found a way to solve that problem. Or they think they have. To keep the demon from killing its host." Gantry shrugged. "That's my guess."

"Why Justin?" Billie asked. "Is there a link to the Murder House? Or Evelyn Bourdain?"

"Not directly. Justin's involvement with Bourdain just made

him vulnerable to the paranormal. These arseholes must have smelled it on him. Or they were keeping an eye on what happened at the Murder House."

Mockler rose and crossed to the window that looked out on to the backyard. "What happens if it works? If these people give this thing a body that it won't kill, what happens then?"

"Well," Gantry grinned, "pardon the cliche, but, all hell breaks loose."

Billie slid the gruesome photographs back into the folder, unable to look at them anymore. "That's why they took you, wasn't it? They knew about your history with this Scratch thing."

"They had lots of questions about it. I didn't put the two together at the time. I thought they were just fishing for anything they could find."

"What did you tell them?" Mockler asked curtly.

Gantry growled. "Do we have to go through this again? I told them a bunch of malarkey."

"Are you sure? Maybe there's no coincidence here. They interrogate you, then they try and pull this demon trick?"

"Piss off, Mockler." Gantry's warned. "If I'd let something slip, I'd own up to it."

Billie got to her feet, feeling the urge to move, to do something. She didn't want to ask the obvious question but someone had to. "So, what do we do now?"

"The rest is straight-forward," Gantry said, pulling the

cigarette pack from his pocket. "I need to stop these arseholes before they do any real damage. You two just need to stay out of the way."

"Sure." Mockler shook his head. "You're in great shape to take them all on."

"We have even more urgent problems, kiddies," Gantry huffed, tossing the crumpled pack onto the table. "I'm out of ciggies."

CHAPTER 28

THE HOUSE SUDDENLY felt too stuffy, too claustrophobic and she needed some air. Standing under the bare porch light, Billie gazed out across the yard to the houses on the far side of the street. Two of the homes had Christmas lights strung under the eaves, twinkling away in their warm colours. It hadn't even snowed yet, she thought. The air was cold, so she zipped up her coat against the chill. Maybe tonight would be the first snowfall. The first one was always kind of magical.

Magic, she thought. Black magic, the supernatural, the occult, witchcraft. The term 'magical' had lost all of its former innocuous meanings for her. How had it come to this? How could she have thought that she could block it all out?

A simple phone call had brought it all home. Kyle, of all people. While Mockler and Gantry argued over what to do next, her cell had gone off. Stepping into the kitchen to answer it, she was surprised to see the name of Kaitlin's boyfriend in the display. She didn't think Kyle even had her number.

"Kyle?" she said, answering it and imagining the worst. "What is it? Is Kaitlin okay?"

"No," Kyle said over the line. "Kaitlin is not okay."

Keep calm, Billie told herself. "Where is she?"

"I don't have a fucking clue where she is, Billie." His voice sounded odd, his words slow. "I hope you're happy."

He sounded drunk. Billie spoke slowly. "What happened, Kyle?"

"Can't you guess? She dumped me. Was that your plan all along, Billie? Huh? To manipulate her? Well, it worked. Now, you can have her all to yourself."

Billie hazarded a guess as to what transpired. "You two had a fight. I'm sure she didn't mean it, Kyle. People say things when they're mad."

"Not this time. I just cleared my stuff out of the condo. She wasn't mad or acting crazy. She just wanted me gone. So, I thought I'd call and say thanks a lot, you freak."

She wasn't in the mood for abuse. "Maybe we should talk when you're sober, Kyle. Goodnight."

"Wait!" he bellowed down the line. "Wait. Look, I didn't even call about that. Why would I call about that? I don't like you, Billie. Never did."

"I'm hanging up now."

"Wait! Shit." He panted, as if he'd just returned from a jog. "You have to help her, Billie. Kaitlin's all messed up and I fully blame you for putting all that stupid shit in her head, but you have to help her. She won't listen to anyone else."

There was another pause. Billie asked if he was still there.

"I'm here," he slurred. "I'm not asking you to help me change her mind, but she hasn't been the same since she got into this voodoo bullshit. She needs help, but, when she turned to you, you said you'd quit the whole thing. That's not good enough. Kaitlin's got her head all twisted up in this stuff. You need to help her with it now. You can't just drop her like a hot potato."

"I didn't drop her," she protested. "I—"

"Yes, you did! But no more. Go talk to her. Help her through this now, whatever it is." There was a pause. His exhale sounded down the line, and when he spoke again, his voice cracked. "Listen, I'm not asking you to get Kaitlin to take me back. That's finished. I just need you to help her because you're the only one she'll listen to. Please."

The raw sincerity broke through the slur and it snapped something inside her. "I will. I'll go see her right now."

She heard a sigh that she took as relief and then the line went cold as he hung up. Billie scrolled through the numbers on her phone until Kaitlin's name appeared. No, she thought. Don't call to tell Kaitlin you're on your way. Just show up. Kaitlin's place was up on Stinson, ten blocks from Mockler's house. At a brisk pace, she could walk it in 20 minutes.

The screen door creaked open. Mockler stepped out onto the porch. "I was wondering where you had disappeared to."

"I needed some air."

He came alongside her. "You okay?"

"I should have my head examined," she said. The cold wind tussled her hair and she brushed it back behind her ear. "The stupid things I do."

He waited a moment, thinking she had more to say, but Billie went quiet. "You have a bad habit of blaming yourself for everything. Why is that?"

"I am to blame. I screwed up again." She folded her arms, feeling the cold settle in. "I thought I could shut off my abilities for good. To just be normal. How stupid of me."

Mockler listened. He had seen her do this before, taking it inward. Sometimes dangerously so. In his experience, people fell into two camps when it came to accepting blame. Those who took it all on their shoulders and those who refused any part of it, shifting the blame to everyone but themselves. The woman beside him was in the former camp. "It's not stupid, Billie. No one in their right mind would want that ability."

"It was selfish of me, and other people paid the price for it."

"Like who?"

"Kaitlin. I shut her out when she needed help. Gantry, too. If I hadn't closed off when I did, I would have found him sooner." The words spilt out of her, tripping faster as she listed them off. "Or these nutjobs who killed Justin. I would have picked up on them, too—"

"Stop." He took her by the arms and turned her to face him.

"You didn't cause those things to happen. So, don't play Monday morning quarterback about how it should have gone. All we can do is deal with what we have."

Billie pressed her brow into his chest and let the words sink in. When she looked up, she said, "I need to see Kaitlin."

"Okay. I'll come with you."

"You don't have to."

"It's not safe going alone," he said. "Not with that weirdo assault team out there."

"What about Gantry? Do you trust him alone in your house?"

"My house, no. He'd burn it to the ground just to amuse himself. But, if I tell him it's gonna be *our* place, he'll mind his manners because of you."

She nodded. He was right, but the idea sat uneasily in her gut. Another unchecked box on her to-do list. "About that," she said, inching closer to him. As if proximity would ease the bad news. "Ray, I can't live here with you. I'm sorry."

The shock played and vanished in his eyes. "Why not? We can change it around however you like, to make it more of yours. We can renovate."

"It's not that." She slid her hands under his jacket and up his back. "It's Christina. It's her house. I know her stuff is all gone, but she's still here. You two had a life in this house and nothing will change that. There's echoes of her everywhere. I can't live with her ghost."

The light in his eyes snuffed out and, when he looked away, it almost broke her. "Hey," she said. "Look at me. I want to be with you. Don't misunderstand that. It's just this house. It could never be home no matter how badly I wanted it to be. Tell me you understand that."

"I get it," he said. His gaze refocused on her. "Honest, I do. I'll admit, I'd hoped you'd say yes, but I understand."

"I'm sorry. I know you love this place."

"It's just a house." He leaned in to kiss her. "I'm glad you were honest about it. That's what matters."

The screen door banged open and Gantry marched across the porch and down the steps.

"Whoa," Mockler said. "Where are you going?"

Gantry turned, a sour look on his face. "Here I thought one of you nice people was running down the shop for me fags, but no, you're out here getting all lovey-dovey while I'm suffering a nic fit. I'll get 'em meself, thank you very much!" He stormed off, flapping his coat.

"Come straight back and stay put," Mockler hollered after him. "We're going out."

"Out?" the Englishman sputtered. "What the hell am I supposed to do?"

"Sit quiet and don't wreck anything."

"Sod that," Gantry bellowed as he stomped past the hedge to the street. "I'm helping myself to your booze and ordering some porn on the telly!"

Billie laughed. "You sure you don't want to stay behind to

babysit?"

"How much damage can he do?"

~

"Do you mind waiting here?" Billie asked as they pulled into the parking lot of Kaitlin's building. "I need to talk to Kaitlin alone."

"Okay." Mockler scanned the street around them, east and west, as if looking for anything unusual. "But keep your phone handy."

She darted inside and waved to the concierge on duty, whom she knew well. "Hey, Anton. I'm gonna surprise Kaitlin, okay?"

He waved her through and she took the grand staircase, running through what she was going to say to her friend. Approaching the door, she was about to knock when it flung open. Kaitlin stood there. "Hi," she said.

"Did Anton buzz you?" Billie asked, confused.

"No, I just knew it was you. Come in."

Kaitlin closed the door behind them and Billie quickly surveyed the loft space. It was usually spotless, but the tangle of blankets on the sofa and the mess on the coffee table had all the earmarks of a break-up. The wine glass, three big tea mugs, the empty ice cream container and the standard issue tissue box.

"Pretty cliché, huh?" Kaitlin shrugged at the mess.

"I heard. I'm sorry." Billie turned to her friend. "How are you feeling?"

"I'll be fine." Kaitlin waved her forward and they both sunk into the sofa. "It's for the best."

"Is it really over? You two have been together since forever."

"Too long," Kaitlin said. "It probably should have happened a while ago, but I don't think either of us wanted to face it. You know?"

"Sure." Billie took a second look at the place. "Has Kyle moved out?"

"Not yet. He's crashing at a friend's house."

"Friend? You don't mean..."

"No," Kaitlin said. "His buddy, Josh. You met him." Kaitlin sighed, her eyes heavy. "I almost wish it was a 'friend.' That would almost make it easier to deal with."

"I don't think it would. It would just hurt in a different way."

"I guess," Kaitlin conceded. She gripped Billie's wrist. "I'm glad you came."

Billie chewed her lip. "I wanted to apologize for being a selfish bitch to you."

"Selfish?" Kaitlin laughed. "That adjective doesn't really apply to you."

"I shoved you away when you needed help, Kaitlin. You can't get much more selfish than that."

"You had to. I know that now."

"I shouldn't have," Billie said. "I'm sorry."

"Water under the bridge," Kaitlin replied. "Do you want

something? I just opened this wine."

The wine was poured. Billie settled back, watching her friend's slow movements and drooping eyes. "Last time, you said you weren't sleeping well. Bad dreams?"

"They never stop," Kaitlin muttered, dejected and consigned. "Every night."

"Your nightmares...are they about the Bourdain woman?"

Kaitlin nodded. "Her. Or being in that house. What it was like to feel her inside me, controlling me. It's awful."

"I still dream about her, too," Billie conceded.

"You do?"

"Yeah. It's trauma. There's going to be fallout from it. You can't go through something like that without coming out damaged in some way." Billie put her hand on Kaitlin's knee. "But it can get better if you deal with it. Talk it through. We can do that together. You and me."

Kaitlin smiled. "I thought you wanted to forget all of this."

"I can't, and there's no sense in hiding from it. Monsters only thrive in the dark. Let's drag it out into the light." Billie sipped her wine. "We can talk it through, figure it out. It's not like we have anyone else to talk to about this." She raised her glass and they clinked them together in a toast.

The chime from the glass faded away and Billie's face darkened as she thought back to the men who had stormed her apartment. Kaitlin knew nothing of that, but she was reluctant to go into it now. Her friend had enough to deal with at the moment.

"What is it?" Kaitlin asked. Billie demurred, but Kaitlin nudged her in the ribs. "Come on. We just agreed to work through this stuff, didn't we? Out with it."

"I have bad news," Billie sighed. "Do you remember your ghost-hunter friend, Justin? He was murdered 10 days ago."

Kaitlin went white. "What? How?"

"In some kind of occult ritual, in the woods near Crooks Hollow." She saw the fear flaring hard in Kaitlin's eyes. "It wasn't the Bourdain woman. She's gone. Someone else killed Justin."

Kaitlin went silent, taking it in. When she spoke, her voice was hushed. "I felt it happen."

"I thought you felt Owen in pain."

"I did, but I felt Justin, too. Almost two weeks ago, I had a weird flash of him in pain. It was late at night. I thought it was just another nightmare."

"What did you see?" Billie asked. "Or feel?"

"Pain and fear. Not just fear, terror. It was dark, but there were trees and it was cold. My hands were tied together." Kaitlin shuddered, as if the memory chilled her. "That's all I remember. Like I said, at the time, I thought it was another bad dream."

Billie tucked her legs under her, mulling over Kaitlin's account. "It wasn't a nightmare. You're an empath."

"I thought that, too," Kaitlin said. "But why those two? Why did I get an empathic flash from them? We were barely friends, and then they got possessed by Bourdain and tried to kill me."

"I don't know. Maybe it was just the danger they were in. The pain. It was severe enough for you to sense it." Billie set her glass down. "You've sensed when I was in trouble before."

"That's different. I care about you."

"I can't explain it. None of this stuff follows any logic. It's all intuitive." Billie shrugged. Then she smiled at her friend. "But, you were right all along. You do have abilities. Welcome to the club."

"How lame," Kaitlin grumbled. "Feeling other people's pain. What a crummy psychic power to have. Why couldn't it be something cooler, like reading someone's mind or seeing the future?"

"I don't think you get to choose," Billie replied. "It's not lame to be an empath."

"It kinda is," Kaitlin disagreed. "It's like being in the Super Friends but you're not Batman or Wonder Woman, you're, like, Aquaman."

"Aquaman is cool."

"What can he do?" Kaitlin asked. "Breathe under water? Big whoop."

"He rides a big seahorse?" Billie offered. It was a stretch. Laughter trickled out and faded away. Kaitlin finished her wine and reached for the bottle. "Refill?"

Billie waved her off. "No, I need to keep my head clear right now." She chewed her lip again, turning a thought over in her mind. "Kaitlin, do you think you could sense Owen now? If you tried?"

"I don't know. I sensed his pain when he was hurt, but I don't think it works the other way."

"But it might," Billie said. "If you try."

Kaitlin shrugged. "Maybe, but do I want to feel his pain again? His terror? No, thanks."

"What if it saved him from the people who want to hurt him?" Billie asked. "I need to find him, Kaitlin. The people who took him are planning to kill him the same way they killed Justin."

Kaitlin's posture fell, like she had already given up. "I don't think I can do it, Billie. I'm not that strong."

Billie reached for her friend's hand. A tiny frisson in the contact. Then, Billie looked up, her eyes bright. "I have an idea."

CHAPTER 29

THE FLOOR IN Mockler's bathroom was porcelain tile and cold. Small mercies, Gantry thought as his head lay against it, the chill of the floor cooling his feverish brow. He may have pushed it a little too soon this time, but how was he to bloody know? It's not like there was a field guide to clawing your way back from death.

Returning to the empty house on Bristol Street, he had pilfered the only bottle he could find in Mockler's cupboards, an Irish whiskey of passable repute. Pouring a lethal length of it into a glass, he lit a cigarette from the fresh pack and settled into a chair in the living room to think, to plan. The rich vibe of an old Lee Hazelwood song spun out of the Hi-Fi cabinet.

Then, his guts revolted on him, sending him racing for the bog before he lost his lunch. Retching into the toilet, he crumpled to the cold floor and stayed very, very still. With his forehead cooling against the tile, he wondered if the lit cigarette he had dropped was burning a hole through the detective's sofa. He grinned at the thought, but even that tiny effort was agony.

He pushed himself up and leaned back against the wall, wheezing from the exertion. He touched his brow, hot with fever. It was like a nasty flu and a vicious hangover mixed and shaken together. Maybe he should have stayed dead.

It took a full 10 minutes to simply get down the stairs, but, when he reached the first floor, he felt better. Or, at least, not so absolutely wretched. His skin felt cooler and he wondered if the fever was breaking only to realize that the temperature in the house was dropping. As if a door had been left open to let the cold wind whistle through the house. Were the happy couple home already?

Something clattered in the kitchen. Followed by a scraping noise from the back of the house. Gantry felt his heartbeat ratchet up. Had the bizarro assault team found them? If they had, then he was a goner, barely able to stay upright, let alone run for the hills. The cold spell should have twigged him to who it was.

He never thought that he would be relieved to see the legless ghastly little boy, but he whistled in gratitude that it wasn't the assault troop with their guns and stun grenades. The Half-Boy crawled over the lintel of the doorway, pulled himself along on his hands to the centre of the ceiling and stared down at the sickly-looking man below. The look on his face was not friendly.

Gantry backed up. He was in no shape to tussle with the ghostly amputee. His hands went up like a white flag. "Hold on, son. I don't wanna scrap."

The boy crept forward in his eerie imitation of some outsized gekko toward the man below.

"If you're looking for Billie, she's not here." Gantry backed up against the wall. The front door was another 30 paces through the hall. Useless. There's no way he could outrun the ghost, not even a legless one who walked on his hands. The gruesome Half-Boy would thrash him senseless. Think fast. "What is it with you and Billie anyway? What's your secret?"

The boy slowed his advance, his head tilting like a dog hearing a strange sound.

"You're a nasty piece of work," Gantry went on. "But, she's got a soft spot for that ghastly mug of yours. God knows why."

The Half-Boy skittered down the wall to the floor.

Keep talking, Gantry thought. *Distract the little bastard.* "You know she's trying to find out who you were. Your name. How you died. Why would she bother?"

The boy hunkered down, not unlike a cat lowering itself onto its haunches, like he wanted to hear more.

"She said you were part of a séance act put on by some charlatan. Is that true?"

There was no reply, of course, but the mute phantom flinched at his words all the same and Gantry studied the child crouched there. How dreadful was that existence? His own brief experience with death had humbled him to his core and the wily mage wondered how awful it must be for this ghost child, alone and lost in the cold netherworld of the unmourned dead, unable to communicate, visible only to those individuals with gifts like Billie. Was it any wonder that the boy clung to the bird who could see him?

"Why don't you help her?" Gantry asked. "I know you can't speak, but give the girl a clue, yeah? Scratch out your name with a piece of chalk at least."

He watched the boy closely, scrutinizing how the legless child shrank from his question like he'd been stung. Gantry grinned. It was obvious, really. It even made sense. "You don't want her to know, do you? You're ashamed of it. Scared she'll think less of you."

Now, it was the ghost who backed away, pushing his truncated form toward the shadows. A wary child retreating from the fist of a wrathful father.

Gantry pressed the issue, inching closer. "She won't judge you," he said. "It's not her nature. You should know that by now. Tell her who you are. She'll understand." He lashed out, quick as a rattlesnake. The ghost hissed and slapped his hands away, scuttling away to a dark corner.

Gantry took hold of the lamp and tilted it until the circular pool of light hit the dark corner where the phantom had retreated. There was nothing. Just the dusty baseboard. The boy had vanished. Gantry opened his hand and, looking down at the small object in his palm, smiled.

~

"I can't do it," Kaitlin said. "It doesn't work that way."

"Yes, you can. You just need to try."

Kaitlin clenched her jaw, reluctant to even contemplate the idea. "When I sensed Owen before, it was out of the blue. I had no control over it. I wasn't even thinking about him when it happened."

"I know," Billie said. "But it's still a two-way street."

"You want me to reach out somehow and find him? I don't even know how." Kaitlin dug in her heels. "He was in pain last time. Why would I want to feel that again?"

"If there's a chance you could help him, shouldn't you at least try?" Billie asked.

The hard set to Kaitlin's eyes retreated. "How?"

"You need to open up that part of you," Billie said. "Close your eyes and take a deep breath."

"Sounds like yoga."

"Whatever works," Billie suggested.

"I hate yoga."

"Think of it like meditation. Just calm your breathing and clear your head." Billie watched her friend close her eyes and become still. "Then, think about Owen. You told me once that he wasn't such a bad guy. Think about the good parts of him. What was nice about him?"

"He was considerate," Kaitlin said, her eyes still closed. "He went out of his way to make me feel included in their crew."

"Good. Focus on that and only that. Keep Owen in your mind and breathe slowly." Billie moved closer on the couch and then slid her hand into Kaitlin's fist.

Nothing happened. Kaitlin continued to breathe. Billie scowled, disappointed her plan didn't work. She hoped that her ability to strengthen a ghost would work in this case, too, boosting Kaitlin's empathic abilities so that she could sense Owen again. She was disappointed when no eerie spark emitted from Kaitlin's touch. Maybe it only worked on the dead.

"Ouch," Kaitlin winced in pain and pulled her hand away.

Billie gripped her hand tighter, not wanting to break the connection. "What is it?"

"It hurts."

"Is it him?"

"I don't know. There's just this awful pain on my back and down my chest. Jesus, this hurts, Billie."

"Hold on," Billie urged. "Try to look around. See what he sees."

"It's dark," Kaitlin whispered. "There's someone else here. They're hurting me. I mean Owen. They have a knife. A small one, like a scalpel. Oh God, they're cutting me."

Kaitlin flinched and recoiled, trying to get away from the pain. She tugged her hand away again. Billie squeezed harder. "Hold on, Kay. Stay with him a little longer."

"I can't. It hurts too much. God, there's blood everywhere."

"Are they trying to kill him?"

Kaitlin shook her head. She was panting hard for breath. "No, they're just cutting his skin in weird ways. It's like they're carving something into him. Why are they doing that to him?"

"Look around. Find something that you can identify, something that could locate him."

"It's too dark and this hurts too much. Billie, I don't want to do this anymore."

"Open your eyes, Kaitlin. Now."

Her eyes opened, terror flushed hard in them. Kaitlin reared back and scrabbling away.

"Tell me what you see," Billie demanded.

Kaitlin's eyes darted around. "I'm underground...in a basement or something. There's windows, but they're painted black."

"What else? Look harder."

"There are two men in the room, but I can't see their faces. They're coming back. They have knives. Oh God—"

Kaitlin gritted her teeth in agony, growling through the pain. Billie watched in horror as blood appeared on her friend's neck, just above the collar bone. A thin line of it, as if she was being cut by a blade.

Billie released her. "Kaitlin, let go." The naked terror remained in the woman's eyes, still caught in the bond with the suffering man. Billie shook her, smacking Kaitlin's cheek to make her untether from Owen. "Let him go! It's over."

The break was instant. Kaitlin collapsed into Billie like a house of cards coming down and her shoulders heaved as she gasped for breath. Billie wrapped her arms around the woman and held her tight, whispering to her that it was all over.

~

The car was getting cold. Mockler started the engine and turned up the heat. He jumped when the door flung open.

"We need to get back," Billie said, dropping into the passenger seat.

Mockler turned around as Kaitlin climbed into the back. "What happened?"

"I'll explain on the way. We need to talk to Gantry."

The detective spun the car out of the parking space and roared back onto Ontario Street. He glanced at the woman next to him and the pale wash of panic in her face made him stomp the accelerator.

A groan issued from the backseat. Billie turned around. "Kaitlin? What's wrong?"

"My head is killing me." Kaitlin sat hunched over with her head in her hands. "Is this what a migraine feels like?"

"Keep your head down and breathe through it," Billie said. "It'll pass in a while."

"Does this always happen?"

"Yes," Billie confirmed. "It hurts to open up. I'm sorry."

Charging a yellow traffic signal, Mockler laid on the horn as a warning as he cut through the red light. The honking protests faded behind them. "Almost there," he said.

~

"What do you mean they're going to kill Owen?" Gantry shouted over the loud music, incredulous. "How do you know?"

The three of them burst into the house to find John Gantry sitting cross-legged on the floor before the stereo cabinet. The volume was cranked all the way and the stand-up ashtray next to him was full of crushed cigarette butts, the air poisoned with second-hand smoke.

"For Christ's sakes, Gantry," Mockler barked as he lowered the volume. "Smoke outside, not in my house."

"It's cold outside," Gantry said. "Cut me some slack, mate. I just returned from the dead, remember."

"Shove it," Mockler replied. He took away the ashtray and marched to the kitchen. "You don't get to play the sympathy card anymore."

"Crabby tonight, are we?" Gantry scoffed and then shifted gears as he smiled up at the new arrival. "Hullo, Kaitlin. How have you been, luv?"

"I've felt better," Kaitlin said, sinking into a chair.

"You look a little green, girl." Gantry looked at Billie. "What have you done to her?"

"She found Owen," Billie answered. "She sensed him being carved up. Just like the other one. I think they're preparing him for the ritual now."

Gantry shook his head. "Can't be. The next full moon isn't for a week from now." He turned back to Kaitlin. "Are you sure of what you saw?"

Kaitlin nodded. "Positive."

Mockler lifted the window sash to air the place out. "So, these people have moved up the timeline. That means Owen will die soon if we don't find him. What else?"

"It means that they don't need the full moon," Billie said. "What changed?"

"I don't know," Gantry said. "It's a moot point though. They're summoning Old Scratch now. We can't let them do that."

Kaitlin looked at Billie. "Old Scratch?"

"It's a demon, luv," Gantry said. "A nasty one."

Kaitlin's jaw dropped as she looked from the Englishman to the psychic. "Demon?"

"It's a long story," Billie shrugged.

"For the record," Mockler said, speaking to Kaitlin, "I can't swallow the demon business either, but it doesn't matter. If these people are performing this voodoo trick now, then that means they're going to kill Owen. We need to find them before that happens."

"That's the tricky part," Gantry grumbled. He looked to

Billie. "Did you two pick up on anything about where he's being held?"

"Kaitlin sensed a basement," Billie said. "With the windows painted black."

Mockler stirred. "Black?"

"It was a church," Kaitlin interjected.

Billie turned to her. "Are you sure?"

"Yes, I didn't realize it until now, but it was definitely a church."

The two men slapped their foreheads at almost the same instant.

"The church of the black windows," Mockler uttered. He looked to the Englishman on the floor.

"Szandor," Gantry snarled. "That worthless sack of shite."

Billie and Kaitlin exchanged glances before turning to the men. "Who?"

"Szandor LaVey," Gantry said. "The deacon of our local Church of Satan.

Mockler spoke up. "I questioned him. The son of a bitch acted as innocent as a lamb."

"You met him once," Gantry said to Billie. "Remember the bald prat with the face like a nun's arse? That's him."

Billie shot to her feet. "Mystery solved. Let's go get Owen."

"Hold on," Mockler warned. "We need to think this through."

Billie turned on him. "What's there to think about? Owen is at that weirdo church. We need to go get him."

"He's right," Gantry said. "We can't just waltz in there and take him. We need a plan."

Kaitlin chewed a fingernail. She looked at the police detective. "Can't you just call in more cops and storm the place?"

"Not without a warrant," Mockler said. "Or putting all of us into trouble. No cops. Just us." He hated seeing eye-to-eye with Gantry on any detail, but this point was crystal clear. "We need a plan."

"Then, we'll figure one out on the way." Billie gripped her man's arm and tugged him toward the door. "Let's go."

Mockler scowled at the idea. "Give me a second," he said and marched into the kitchen. The cupboard next to the refrigerator was still bare except for a large bowl on the top shelf. He reached into it and pulled down his service weapon. He placed it here every night when he came home from work, a habit he had developed from living with someone who suffered numbing bouts of depression. Depressing the release lever with his thumb, he slid the magazine from the handle. A full deck. He knew for a fact that there was no round in the chamber, but he racked the slide just to be sure. The magazine slid back into place and the Glock went back into its holster.

Billie entered the room and saw the detective bring up a baseball bat, the same one that Christina had almost brained her with.

"Gantry," Mockler said, brandishing the bat, "you ever use

one of these?"

Gantry stood at the sink, filling a glass of water. "Not my sport, mate."

"Take it."

"Give it to Billie," Gantry said, opening a pill bottle. He tossed a handful in his mouth and washed it down. "I don't need it," he mumbled through a full mouth.

"What is that?" Billie asked.

"Painkillers," Gantry garbled. "I found 'em in the medicine cabinet."

The scowl on the detective's face deepened. "Maybe you should stay here."

"You need me, sonny."

"You can barely stand up. God knows what we're walking into."

Gantry waved him away. "I'll nap on the way over. Let's crack on."

Mockler didn't move, rooted to the spot with the baseball bat in his hand. Kaitlin stepped up and took the bat from him. "I'll take this. We'd better go."

Kaitlin led the way and Mockler followed. Billie and Gantry stepped out onto the porch together. "Your friend popped in earlier," he said.

"Friend?"

"The one without legs."

"He was here?" Billie asked. "What did he want?"

"He didn't say, did he? I guess he was looking for you."

Billie gripped his arm. "You two didn't fight, did you?"

"I conceded this round," Gantry said as they reached the car. "We'll rematch later. I tried to talk some sense into him, but he's a stubborn little prick that one."

Billie opened the passenger door. "What did you say?"

"He doesn't want you to know the truth about him. He's ashamed of it." Gantry said, flinging into the backseat and closing the door after him.

Billie went still, propping the door open. "Ashamed?"

CHAPTER 30

IT BEGAN TO SNOW.

Light and tentative at first, pixie dust swirling under the cones of light from the streetlamps and, then, fuller and brighter, swarming in the headlights. When they pulled up before the church with the blackened windows, the night was alive with twinkling snowfall, the first of the season and the thoughts of all inside the car turned momentarily to Christmas.

Climbing out, Billie looked up at the sky to let the snowflakes fall onto her face. Then, the moment passed and everyone regarded the dark church before them.

The detective signaled the women. "You two stay here. Gantry, you're with me."

"We're not staying behind," Billie protested.

"It's not safe," Mockler said.

"You're not leaving us here to play hero, Ray. Safety in numbers." Billie brushed past him toward the front steps. "How do we do this?"

"We pair up," Gantry said. He nodded at Mockler and Billie. "You two take the front door. Kaitlin and I will go around back."

Kaitlin lingered near the car, the baseball bat dangling from her hand. She gulped.

"That's a stupid plan," Mockler said. "We stick together, everyone stays behind me, so you don't accidentally get shot."

Gantry scorned the idea and Billie rolled her eyes. They didn't have time to bicker now.

"He's not here," Kaitlin said.

The bickering stopped. "Are you sure?" Billie asked.

"Come here." Kaitlin reached out and took Billie's hand. She closed her eyes for a moment. "Owen's not inside."

"Shite," cursed Gantry. "So much for the plan."

"Can you see where he is?" Billie asked.

Kaitlin shook her head. "I can't sense anything."

"Sod this. We're already here." Gantry took the steps two at a time, flung open the tall door and slipped inside.

"Goddamnit, Gantry." The detective rushed after him.

Billie tugged Kaitlin. "I guess we're going in." They raced up the stairs and entered the dark church.

~

The interior of the church was darker than the night outside. Holding hands, Billie and Kaitlin bumped into a pew and groped their way along.

"I can't see anything," Kaitlin whispered.

"Everything's painted black," Billie said. "Ray? Where are you?"

A flashlight popped on, its beam playing over the pews as Mockler approached them.

Kaitlin looked over the nave of the church. The pews, floor, and walls were all painted flat black. The ceiling above and the tall windows were painted as well. "This is freaky."

"It looks empty," Mockler said.

"Where's Gantry?"

"I can't find him."

"That idiot," Billie seethed. Then, she hollered. "Gantry!"

Mockler snatched her arm. "Quiet."

A cry rose up from below. Obscenities hurled out and echoed into the rafters of the church. Gantry.

It took a moment to locate the basement door in that flat black interior. Mockler flung it open and charged down, calling the Englishman's name. Unlike the nave, the church basement hadn't been repainted black. They filed out one-by-one into a large hall.

"Gantry?" Billie called.

"In here!" The voice rang out from a doorway to their left.

Gantry was bent over, wiping vomit from his chin. When Billie reached him, she saw the reason why and clutched a hand over her own mouth to keep from doing the same.

"Oh God," Kaitlin cried, retreating quickly from the room.

Something large lay on the floor, lit up in the throw of the flashlight. A twisted wrack of fur and bone. Blood was pooled across the floor and splattered against the wall. The stench was gamey and ripe. Flies rose from the carcass and boiled around and settled into the blood again.

"What is it?" Billie whispered.

"Hard to tell what kind of animal it is," Gantry said. "The head's gone."

Billie looked again. The butchered meat of the severed neck and bone stump made her look away.

"It's a deer carcass," Mockler said. "A whitetail."

"You can tell?" Gantry asked.

"I used to go deer hunting with my old man," the detective replied.

"Why would they do that?" Billie asked.

"Who knows," Gantry said as he staggered out of the room and back into the hall. "Szandor and his band of merry Satanists are all batshit crazy."

"What now?"

Mockler arced the flashlight over the hall. "Stay with him. I'm gonna sweep these rooms, then we're getting out of here."

Gantry leaned against the wall, his face slick with sweat. Billie scrounged her coat pockets and found a pack of tissues. She tore out a few and handed them to him.

"Ta." He spat onto the linoleum and wiped his mouth.

"Will you be all right?" Kaitlin asked.

"If we don't stumble across any more butchered carcasses, I should be fine."

Mockler returned a minute later to where the trio stood. "There's no one here."

Gantry's eyes dropped to something in the detective's hand. "What'd you find?"

"Flashbangs." Mockler held up two of the cylindrical weapons in his palm. "Maybe we can give 'em a taste of their own medicine."

"Lovely," Gantry smiled, fumbling for another cigarette with trembling hands. A few fell to the floor. "But we still need to find these arseholes first."

Kneeling down, Kaitlin retrieved the fallen cancer sticks from the floor. She straightened up to find the eyes of the others locked on her. She took a step back. "No, I don't want to do that again."

"We have to locate them, luv."

"Please," Kaitlin pleaded. "That pain was awful."

Gantry's gaze swung back to Billie. "Can you find them?"

"Not the way Kaitlin can. I don't have her ability." Billie brushed the dust from her hands. "I can ask the dead. Sometimes, they can find people, but it will take a while."

"The boy might be dead by then," Mockler said.

"Okay, okay!" Kaitlin snapped. "I'll do it. Just give me a minute." She paced back and forth, taking deep breaths as she screwed up her courage. "Billie?"

Billie took her friend's hand. "All right. Just like before. Push everything out of your head and concentrate on him."

The detective stepped back, but Gantry leaned closer, studying them, eager to see how it played out. The air grew still and the only sound was Kaitlin's breathing. Mockler snuck a peek at his watch as the minutes ticked by.

Kaitlin flinched and her knees buckled. Billie caught her and propped her up. Mockler rushed in to help, but Billie shook her head at him to stay back. "Kaitlin," she said softly. "Is it him?"

"Everything hurts," Kaitlin gasped. "What did they do to him?"

"Can you see where you are? Can you hear anything?"

"It's loud. A roaring noise all around. It's constant."

"What else?" Billie asked.

"Trees. It's cold. I'm outside."

Mockler stepped closer, glancing between the woman with her eyes closed and the woman holding her up. "What else, Kaitlin? Anything you see or hear. Any detail at all."

"I'm being dragged through the woods. The ground is uneven. There's big loose rocks everywhere. I can hear water."

"Water?" Billie asked. "Do you mean the lake?"

"No. Running water. Like a creek. I can barely hear it over the roaring noise."

"What kind of noise? Like an engine or a train?"

"No, it's big, and it echoes. It never stops."

Kaitlin faltered and Billie struggled to keep her upright. She waved the detective off again, afraid the psychic bond would snap if Mockler touched the woman. "Look around, Kaitlin. Tell us what you see."

"There's a bonfire. People passing before it. Trees and rocks. Water." Kaitlin spasmed, as if hurt, and she struggled. "There's a cross."

"A cross?" Gantry asked, exchanging a glance with Billie.

"Way up high. It's all lit up." Kaitlin jerked again, her face twisting in pain. She slipped from Billie's grip and fell. Mockler scooped her up.

"It's gone," Billie said. The connection had severed the moment Mockler had touched her.

Gantry snapped open one of the folding chairs stacked against the wall and Kaitlin dropped into it, putting her head to her knees.

"Will she be okay?" Mockler asked.

"She'll be queasy for a while," Billie said, rubbing her friend's back. She looked up at the two men. "Do you know the place she saw?"

"It's not a lot to go on," Mockler said. "I don't know what the roaring noise would be."

"A highway?" Billie suggested.

Gantry shook his head. "The cross doesn't make any sense. These wankers are Satanists. Why would they be near a cross?"

"Maybe there's another church," Mockler said. "In a rural

spot, like with the other victim."

"Near running water," Billie added.

"It's not a church," Kaitlin wheezed.

All three turned to look at the woman in the chair. Kaitlin propped herself up on her elbows, her face looking drained. "It's the punchbowl."

Mockler snapped his fingers. "Of course!"

Gantry raised an eyebrow. "Punchbowl?"

"It's a ravine up the mountain," Billie answered. "Called the Devil's Punchbowl."

"The Devil's Punchbowl?" Gantry barked with laughter. "You've got to be kidding me."

His laughter died out when the grim set of their faces negated any chance of a joke.

~

"Come on," said Gantry. "Is it really called that?"

"It is," Kaitlin replied. "It's a huge waterfall carved out of the escarpment, like a bowl. It's a landmark."

Gantry just shook his head in wonder. "It all seems too convenient, doesn't it? A pack of empty-headed Satanists trying to conjure a demon at a place called the Devil's Punchbowl. Christ on a stick!"

"Wait till you see it," Billie said, turning to look at him in the backseat. "It's kinda majestic."

"Oh, I'm sure it is, luv." Gantry leaned his head back and closed his eyes. "Remind me to be awed when we get there."

They drove east, out of the city and into the outlying neighbourhood. Gantry and Kaitlin in the back, Billie in the passenger bucket. When they approached the parkway that would take them up the escarpment, Mockler drove straight through.

"Wait," Billie said, looking back at the intersection. "Aren't we going up the mountain?"

"Nope," Mockler answered. He tilted the rearview mirror to see Kaitlin. "You saw the cross above you, right?"

"Yeah. Up really high."

Mockler adjusted the mirror to its former position. "That means they're in the bottom of the gorge."

"Yes, but there's the footpath down to the bowl. You start at the cross and walk down."

"There's a quicker way to the bottom. Over the train tracks."

Seven blocks on, Mockler turned up Mountain Avenue to where the street ended and swung the car around the concrete barrier blocking the dead end. He killed the engine. "We're here."

A soft snoring rumbled from the backseat. The detective turned to Kaitlin and said, "Wake that bastard up, would you?"

The trunk lid popped open and bounced gently on its hinges. Mockler reached in and outfitted everyone with a heavy Maglite.

Retrieving the two flashbang grenades, he pocketed one and handed the other to Billie.

"I don't want it," she said. "I don't even know how to work it."

Mockler held the grenade up and tugged gently at the pin. "Hold it like this, pull the pin and throw. Just put it in your pocket for now."

Reaching back into the trunk, he lifted out the baseball bat that he had insisted they bring and handed it to her. Next, he slid the Glock from the holster on his belt. "Gantry, do you know how to use one of these?"

"Nope."

"Time to learn." The detective racked back the slide to ensure the chamber was empty and then offered it to the Englishman. "It's dead easy. Here."

"I hate guns," Gantry said. "Give it to Billie."

Billie threw up both hands in protest. "I don't want it."

"I'll take it," Kaitlin offered.

"You know how to use this?"

"Kyle took me to a firing range a couple times. Give me a quick refresher course."

Kaitlin handed the bat to Billie and Mockler walked her through how the gun worked. "Put it in your coat pocket," he said, "and keep it there until I tell you to draw it."

Billie looked at the detective, now unarmed. "What are you going to use? Your fists?"

Reaching back into the trunk, Mockler pulled out a shotgun, a big twelve-gauge in a matte black finish. Wide shot and maximum damage, standard issue for a police assault team. "I brought this." There was one last item among their gear; heavy bolt-cutters. He handed them to Gantry. "You carry this."

"Oh aye. Maybe I can snip the bastards to death."

They marched past the dead end of the street and into the wet brush until they came to a chain link fence. Gantry snipped the links from the ground up and bent back the wire to make an opening. The troop ducked through the breach and stepped onto the gravel expanse of the railway line.

Stepping over the tracks, Billie looked east down the line of rail, lit up in the hazy swirl of snowfall under the glow of lamps. It was eerily picturesque, she noted before quickening her pace to catch up to the others.

The roaring sound grew louder as they crept onto a dirt footpath through the foliage, flashlights pointed directly at the ground before them. Following the creek, they clambered over rocks and roots until a light glimmered up ahead through the dead tree branches. Gantry's mouth dropped open as he got his first look at the punchbowl, a circular gorge that rose 120 feet to the escarpment above. Water cascaded down the shale rock to a thunderous, constant crash at the basin. The light up above emanated from a 30 foot tall cross that glowed against the snowfall in the night sky. "Frig me," he uttered. "Lookit that."

Mockler hushed him and they pressed on slowly until the

detective stopped. Light up ahead flickered through the trunks of the trees. Not as elegant as the cross on the cliff above them but closer and brighter. A bonfire crackling in the night, blotted now and then by figures passing before it.

"Kill the lights," Mockler hissed as he crouched among the thicket.

Gantry came alongside him. "How many are there?"

"Did you learn to whisper in a barn?"

"They can't hear us over that racket, mate." Gantry peered out at the fire in the distance, trying to discern the congregants gathered, but all were clad in black. "Doesn't look like too many. A handful of tossers. Do you see the lad?"

Mockler shook his head. The two women crept closer and Kaitlin pointed at something. "There. Just to the left of the fire."

The fire sawed eastward as the wind pushed it and a figure flared up in the shifting light. Pale and scrawny, the prisoner lay stretched over a fallen log, his naked flesh muddied with blood and dirt and dead leaves.

"I can't tell if he's still alive," Billie said.

"He's alive," Kaitlin said. "How do we get him out of there?"

Mockler stood the butt end of the shotgun on a slab of rock, the barrel at the sky. "We shock them first. Toss in a flashbang and then charge in with a warning shot from the rifle. They'll scatter for cover, and we grab Owen. Anyone who puts up a fight gets a round of buckshot to the chest."

"That's the plan?" Gantry sneered. "And what happens when

they don't scatter."

Mockler spit into the dead leaves. "I suppose you have a better one?"

"Give me one of the grenades. Stick with your plan. I'm just gonna soften them up first."

"What does that mean?" Mockler groused, handing over one of the flashbangs.

The Englishman turned the metal cylinder in his hand, muttering something strange as he did so. Then, he put the weapon to his lips like a devotee kissing a saint's relic and rose to his feet.

"Wait!" Mockler hissed, but it was too late.

Gantry stomped toward the fire making no attempt to be silent, but there was no need with the roar of the waterfall drowning out his approach. The black clad figures, caught up in their chanting, did not see the Englishman until he stepped into the light of the bonfire and hollered at them.

"Oy! Which one of you retards brought the marshmallows!"

The cult members spun around. Two of them held long knives, but a third produced a gun from the folds of his robes and aimed it squarely at the intruder's torso.

"Don't even bother with popgun, mate." Gantry ignored the weapon, searching the hooded faces of the group. "Szandy! Show your ugly face."

One man had kept his back to the Brit, but he turned around now. Szandor LaVey, high priest of the Church of Satan, leered at the newcomer with eyes so bloodshot that Gantry wondered with what he had juiced his veins. His lips gibbered wetly as he smiled. He held something big tucked under his arm and when he turned fully, Gantry saw the severed head of the deer. Its eyes reflected the fire and gore dripped from the neck stump.

"Gantry," was all the priest said. His smile broadened even wider, as if he couldn't be more pleased to see the man.

"Santa's not gonna be too happy with what you did to poor Rudolph there," Gantry said, nodding at the gruesome thing. "That'll put you on the naughty list for sure."

A fifth figure loomed in the smoky haze of the bonfire, hovering over the limp form of the prisoner. Clutched in both hands was an enormous battle-axe, deadly on both ends. He watched the priest like a hawk, awaiting his cue.

Szandor LaVey's eyes bulged from their sockets, his pupils dilated in a fever. He staggered to his left, teeth chattering as he forced out just a few words. "Just. Fucking. Kill. Him."

Gantry looked at the cult member with the gun. "I wouldn't do that if I were you, son."

The man pulled the trigger. The gun blew up in his hand. He dropped to his knees, cradling the bloodied catastrophe of his gun-hand against his chest.

"Told ya," Gantry said.

The rector of the group was shaking hard, seizing in some type of fit. He seemed unaware of the misfired weapon, as if caught up in some delusion only he could see.

The cult charged. Gantry pulled the pin and tossed the flashbang into the fire.

~

Billie ducked when she heard the first pop, unaware that it was a misfire. The second explosion was louder. The bonfire blew, erupting flames 30 feet into the snowy night. Mockler shot to his feet and brought the shotgun to bear. "Get Owen," he barked. "I'll take care of the others."

They ran into the clearing, their footing unsteady as they hit the loose slabs of shale. The detective fired a warning shot over the heads of the dark figures and two of them bolted into the darkness. Smaller fires blazed over the basin from where the flaming shrapnel had landed and smoke was everywhere. A figure charged out of the smoke at a dead run and tackled the detective to the rocky ground. The shotgun went off, its bark echoing up the canyon walls.

"Ray!" Billie called out. The smoke was impenetrable and she had lost sight of him. Only the glow of the bonfire shone through the hazy fog, a compass point from which to navigate.

Kaitlin tugged her arm. "Come on," she urged.

Hanging onto one another, they scrambled into the fog, their shoes tripping on the loose shale and icy rocks. Billie fell hard on one knee, cursed and pushed on.

"Oh God," said Kaitlin.

"What's wrong?" Billie gripped her friend tight, afraid to lose her in the smoke. Then, Kaitlin gave out a sharp cry of pain and fell back against her. The momentum brought both of them down. Billie struggled to get up, pinned under Kaitlin's dead weight.

"Kaitlin!" She shook the woman, but Kaitlin remained limp, her eyes closed.

A horrid sound shrieked through the smoky air, a pitch so foul it was like nothing Billie had ever heard. Then, something came tumbling down the shale incline and rolled against Billie's knee.

Owen Rinalto's dead eyes looked up at her, his mouth twisted in a rictus of pain. Billie screamed and kicked the severed head away from her.

~

Szandor LaVey ate dirt, his face pushed down into the slime by Gantry, but the cult leader didn't seem to care. He kept repeating a phrase over and over through chattering teeth.

"It is done. It is done."

"Shut up, you stupid bastard!" Gantry pushed his face further into the muck, hoping to drown the bald-headed git. He'd clearly lost his marbles somewhere between the church and the gulch of the punchbowl. How else could he explain cutting the head off of an animal with a chainsaw? He snapped his eyes right and left, wondering where the antlered head had fallen.

When the unearthly sound shrieked through the gorge, Gantry's blood went cold. He'd heard that sound before. Spinning round, he finally understood what Szandor had been blathering about.

It was done. The bastard had succeeded.

The body of the naked boy on the rock was now upright, descending the stony berm, but something was all wrong from the neck up. Where Owen's face should have been, there was now the grisly head of the buck with its rack of antlers rising majestically above. The hide of the beast was sutured into the flesh of the man in some obscene fusion and a foul, dark blood dribbled from the flared nostrils. The great antlers swung about as it turned in Gantry's direction.

Then, it came on, the sharp rocks cutting the naked soles of his feet.

CHAPTER 31

"SZANDOR, YOU USELESS twat!" Gantry roared, rolling up onto his knees. "What have you done?"

The monstrosity that was once Owen Rinalto shambled forward, its great antlered head dipping low. Its nostrils flared hot with steam like a toro about to charge. Gantry pushed himself up, his knees wobbly and his footing uneven on the broken shale. The little strength he possessed had been spent tackling the demented church leader. There was nothing left in his limbs to face the perverse creature before him.

Szandor LaVey was a different story. He sprang up and chittered like an ape, his eyes mad with glee at what he had accomplished. The man's wits were dashed, his words garbled into a rambling prattle of gibberish.

"Knock it down, Szandor." Gantry seized the church leader by the collar, shaking him. "Whatever trick you pulled to make the damn thing, undo it!"

The glassy eyes of the deer head shone in the firelight as the thing picked up steam. Old Scratch had found a new vessel and John Gantry wondered if he should have stayed dead back in that sterile morgue. On his best day, he was no match for the demon. As sick and weak as he was, he posed as much of a threat as a blind kitten. Game over.

The malignant thing charged, the ten point rack rushing in fast at the Englishman. Self-preservation kicked in. Gantry yanked the Satanic priest hard and pushed him into the path of the charging monster. The impact knocked LaVey and Gantry both across the stony ground. Gantry crashed into the fire and Szandor LaVey sprawled atop him, his lung punctured by the antler's strike.

Detective Mockler was seeing stars as his breath was choked from his windpipe. The robed figure was on top of him, his hands locked around the detective's throat, crushing the life from him. His attacker was grunting like an animal, but, over the man's animal noises, Mockler heard Billie's voice cry out for help. His groping hand found the barrel of the shotgun and he swung it hard against the man's skull.

The figure tumbled sideways and Mockler rolled up fast. Gripping the barrel in both hands he swung again and heard a loud crack as it connected with the man's temple.

Scrambling up the loose rock, he couldn't see Billie in the

miasma of smoke, but something else rose up near the fire. Mockler blinked, trying to decipher what he was seeing. A man in a mask? The smoke cleared for a moment and he saw the naked form of the man they had come to rescue, but his head was gone. In its place rose the antlered head of the buck.

A mask, he thought. A trick of the light. Then, the monstrous deer-headed man bolted forward, antlers down. It slammed into LaVey and Gantry, hurtling them both into the fire.

Mockler charged, racking the slide of the shotgun and levelling the barrel at the monstrosity. The stock seated into his shoulders as he aimed and when the grotesque thing swung about to face him, he fired.

The blast of a 12-gauge Mossberg was enough to flatten anyone, especially at this range. The thing with the antlers stayed on its feet even as its flesh was flayed with buckshot. Mockler pumped the slide again, spinning the spent shell from the chamber. The thing charged at him.

The shotgun clattered lengthwise against the sharp antlers, saving him from being gored in the face. Landing hard on his back, he gasped as the wind was knocked out of him and panic bit deep when he couldn't breathe.

Get up, he snarled in his own head. *Move.*

Black blood dribbled from the beast's snout, splattering hot on the detective's face. He rolled away when the antlers hammered down, but he wasn't fast enough and something sharp pierced his ribs. The pain was blinding, but he snatched the horns in a tight grip and held on, keeping the monster's head down. The idea flashing hot in his head was simple, if ridiculous. If he kept the antlers down long enough, maybe Billie, wherever she was in the hazy smoke, would have enough time to get away. He wasn't strong enough. Slick with blood, the horns slipped from his hands and he felt cold air rush into the puncture wound in his side.

The sickly stench of burnt hair roiled in Gantry's nose, the scorching pain of fire clawing his sanity. He rolled out of the flames to the cold shale, his coat smoldering and his hands blistering badly. His ears registered the report of the shotgun as it echoed through the gorge and he looked up in time to see the abomination take Mockler down, goring him with its antlers. His eyesight blurred from the smoke, but, even through the haze, he knew the demon was turning toward him.

Digging into a pocket, he found the short nub of chalk hidden there. No ordinary chalk, this piece had been cured with the dusty bones of a forgotten saint that Gantry had ground into powder himself. Scraping the chalk over the large stones and slabs of shale, he drew a protective seal around himself, muttering the incantation that would trigger its power. The language was foreign and he prayed that the pronunciation was correct. The thing with the horns lumbered closer. He felt something hot on his ankle and spun about to see Szandor LaVey breaching the circle…or, what was once Szandor. His flesh was charred and sizzling. The only part of him that wasn't burnt black were the whites of his eyeballs. The rector of the diabolical church clawed at him, snarling through his agony. Gantry scrabbled to his feet and kicked the man back into the flames. Szandor LaVey's hands clawed at the night sky and, then, he became still and thrashed no more.

When Gantry swung back around he was face-to-gruesome-face with the stitched together deer-man. Its nostrils blew hot and the rancid smell made him gag more than the smoke. The chalk was gone from his hands, lost among the stones. The protective circle unfinished.

He scrambled for something to say. If he was going to die, he'd go down swinging, even if all he had the strength for was a flip word. "Scratch," he spat. "You're a damned ugly sight. They should have sewn that thing's rump to your neck."

The creature raised one hand and Gantry steeled himself for the blow, but no strike came. Its finger stretched, pointing to the fire behind him.

The flames licked up in an unnatural way and shifted into a human form. Gantry's first thought was that it was LaVey but the man's remains lay at the base of the pyre, still and dark among the orange flames. The fire at the apex incandesced into the shape of a woman and, when it spoke, John Gantry staggered back.

John?

Gantry fell to his knees. "No," he whispered and shut his eyes against it.

What have you done, John?

He opened his eyes and she was still there, the woman in the fire. His voice cracked. "Ellie."

Was it worth it? asked the woman. *Did you get what you wanted?*

"Don't, Ellie. Please…"

Do you know what's it like, John? Down here in the fire.

"Stop!" He cupped his hands over his ears and began to rock back and forth like some troubled half-wit. The tears blurred his vision, so he shut his eyes. "I can't save you! I tried!"

Do you ever think of me? Or have you pushed it from your mind like every other sin that you committed?

Gantry coiled up tight, his brow pressed against a stone and his voice no more than a whisper. "Every day. Every bloody day."

A timber in the fire popped and the wood crumbled, sending embers up into the night and the woman in the fire dissipated in the sparks. The antlered thing tilted its head down to regard the whimpering man at its feet.

Billie reeled from the horror around her. Everyone was down, leaving her the last one standing. Kaitlin was unconscious, Gantry coiled into his own personal hell and Mockler was collapsed on the shale clutching a hand over his ribs. The detestable thing with the antlers turned to her. It seemed to gloat over its fallen enemies, to challenge this last woman standing on the rocky slope.

Billie held no weapon in her hand, not a gun or a blade or even a rock from the ground. She had nothing.

The creature did not speak, but she sensed it communicating something to her. A challenge.

Come. Try me.

"I won't fight you," she said.

It shambled closer, raising its arms wide as if demanding she look in awe at what it could do.

"I'm not impressed," Billie spat. "You are nothing. Just hatred and violence. You are less than nothing."

Its nostrils blew hot, its chest puffed out. She couldn't tell if it was angered or simply winding up before striking.

"I used to wonder what Hell was," she said. "Looking at you, now I know. It's a garbage heap, where everything useless in this world is tossed."

The thing blew hotter, rage building toward the unarmed woman. It lowered its antlers to charge, but then it faltered, hesitating.

Billie understood why when she felt a chill pressing in from her left. Owen Rinalto stood there, looking on in horror at what had been done to his earthly remains. He turned to Billie and asked why but she had no answer for him.

355

The hybrid creature shook its head to dispel the hesitation. Its footing was unsteady but still it prepared to charge. Then, the shotgun went off and flesh stripped away from its torso, causing the monster to stumble sideways.

Mockler was on his knees, the barrel of the gun smoking. He pumped the action again, priming another round, and hollered at Billie to get back. The second blast brought it down, the antlers rattling heavy against the stones. It thrashed, struggling to rise.

Another voice went up in the night, stringing together a thread of obscenities. There was a glint of light as the broad axe swung down hard. It sunk deep into the buck hide and a pitiful cry gurgled from its maw. Shoving a boot onto its neck, Gantry yanked the axe free and swung it back like some mad lumberjack. The second blow docked the head from the body. Both parts of the thing flopped lazily and didn't move.

Gantry let the axe drop and fell back onto his rear on the stones. He sat wheezing at the gore before him. A figure shambled past him and he watched Billie climb the loose shale to where the deer head lay. Gripping it by the horns, she hurled it into the fire.

~

"Any word?"

"Not yet," Billie said.

"Bloody doctors," Gantry said. He dropped into the chair

beside Billie. The waiting room was quiet, the two of them the only occupants at this hour. A page rang out over the hospital's PA system. "Where did Kaitlin scamper to?"

"She went for a walk," Billie said. "Hospitals make her uneasy now."

"Can't blame her. Wretched places these are, like sterile abattoirs." The gallows humour was crude and unneeded at a time like this. He realized that when he saw her turn away to hide her tears. "I'm sorry. My mouth runs on like a bad faucet. He's going to be alright, Billie. I promise."

"Are you psychic now?"

"He's a tough bloke. It'll take more than a goring to take him down." He patted her hand to reassure her, careful not to touch the bandage over her scraped knuckles. "If anything, I'd be more worried about what he's going to tell his bosses back at the copper station."

Billie turned to look at him. A detail she hadn't had a chance to consider yet. "He can't tell them what happened. They'd think he's crazy."

"I know, but Mockler's a bit of a straight arrow, isn't he? He'll feel compelled to explain something. You should convince him otherwise."

"I don't think there will be anything to report," Billie said. "Did you see that fire when we left?"

"Aye."

They had all seen it, an inferno ripping through the basin of the gorge. The four of them had limped down the shale slope like a troop of battered soldiers. Mockler had to be propped up part of the way, Gantry huffing hard to keep him from collapsing. Crossing back over the train tracks, a crackling roar ripped open the night air and they turned to see the fire blaze up above the treeline. They sallied on like drunken sailors until they reached the car.

"There won't be much, but a few crispy bones by the time the authorities tromp through the ashes," Gantry said as he leaned his head back against the seat. "So it's best for your boyfriend there if it remains unsolved."

Billie wiped her palms together. She had scrubbed her hands thrice since arriving at the hospital, but they still felt grimy. A nurse marched past them at a brisk pace and moved on, then, the waiting room was quiet again.

"Can I ask you something?" she said.

He grinned. "You can ask anything you like, but I can't promise I'll answer."

Billie considered her phrasing. "That woman who appeared in the fire. That was your wife, wasn't it?"

Silence. All he did was close his eyes.

"I want you to tell me about her," she said. "Not now, but when you're ready."

Gantry puffed out his cheeks and exhaled slowly. "Okay." He wagged his head to shake it off and then launched out of the chair. "Time to run."

"Now? Don't you want to see if Mockler's okay?"

"He's fine," Gantry scoffed. He already had a cigarette in his fingers, impatient to leave. "There's too many eyes here for me."

Billie surveyed the empty waiting room. A ghost town. "There's no one here."

"There's always someone. According to official records, I'm dead. I'd like to keep it that way for now." He turned to leave. "Toodles."

"Wait. Are you going back to Mockler's place or mine?"

"Neither," he called out, limping toward the stairwell door. He disappeared.

Billie fumed, but her indignation didn't last long. A doctor appeared before her, looking down over the rim of his glasses. "Are you Billie?"

"Yes. He asked to see you." The doctor pushed his glasses back up his nose. "Do you want to hear the details and confusing jargon or do you want to just go see him?"

Billie was already halfway down the corridor.

Gantry had said that he was a tough bloke but the detective didn't look so tough in the hospital bed. He was pale and his eyes were bloodshot. The shroud of gauze bandaged over his ribs was stained with a few bloody smears, but he smiled when she burst into the room.

"Hey," he rasped in a low voice. "You waited for me."

"Of course, you goof." She swatted at him and then smoothed her palm over his brow. "You scared the hell out of me."

He saw the gauze on her hand and the raw cut on her chin. "You got hurt?"

"Just a few scrapes." Her eyes went to the dressing on his torso. "How bad is it?"

"It looks worse than it is. The puncture didn't go too deep. I didn't even break a rib. What about Kaitlin and Gantry?"

"Kaitlin's a little shaken up, but she's not hurt. Gantry left."

"Of course he did."

"Don't worry about him. Just rest up and heal." Billie touched his cheek and a smile bloomed over her face. "This is like how we met. In a hospital room."

"When I almost killed you?" he grinned. "You're not gonna let me forget that one, are you?"

"Nope," she smiled wider. "Not ever."

CHAPTER 32

MOCKLER WENT WITH the lie that the injury to his ribs was caused by an accident at home. He told the staff sergeant and his partner that he had fallen from a ladder while repairing a light fixture in the garage. It wasn't a complete fabrication, as he was currently in the process of fixing up the house. Odinbeck had called him a klutz, advising his younger partner to hire a contractor next time.

Over the following days, he paid close attention to the investigation into the fire at the Devil's Punchbowl. Detectives Agostino and Mortimer were acting as primaries on the case and both were currently frustrated trying to piece together what had caused the fire in the bottom of the gorge. The remains of three individuals had been recovered in the ash and, given the charred state of the bones, any hope of identifying the victims looked doubtful. One of those individuals remained a mystery to Mockler, as he had only witnessed the fates of Owen Rinalto and

Szandor LaVey. He didn't know who the third person was, one of LaVey's nameless acolytes was his best guess.

Curiously, there had been no mention in the incident report of any animal remains among the ashes. No deer skull, no antlers. Had it immolated completely?

It was excruciating to hold his tongue around Agostino and Mortimer as they puzzled over an arson involving three deaths. He hated to see them struggle, but revealing the truth wouldn't help anyone. There was no way to corroborate the details. Despite the fact that he was supposed to be home recuperating, he had gone back to the church with the blackened windows. The door was unlocked and the place cleaned out. The big inverted cross over the altar was gone, along with every artifact within the sacristy. The carcass in the basement had been carted away and the floor scrubbed. They had been thorough, erasing any detail that could back up any claim he could make.

The only nagging point was the demise of the kid, Owen. He was still listed as missing and his parents would cling to a delusional hope that he might return some day. Discussing the arson case with Agostino, Mockler mentioned that he still had a missing person case on his desk. Maybe one of the remains found on the scene could be him. Agostino took the information from him and called the medical examiner about comparing them. It would take a while, but, at least, the boy's parents would know the truth.

Four days after the incident at the gorge, Detective Mockler stepped onto his porch to find a blanket of snow covering the yard and hatched in the boughs of the trees. An SUV had pulled into the driveway and he waved at the driver climbing out. "Morning."

"I hope this isn't too early," said Cynthia Trucillo. "It was the only time I had to stop by."

"Busy day?" Mockler asked as he crossed the driveway.

"I have three showings today. I don't know how I'm going to manage it." Cynthia opened the back of her vehicle. "Do you mind giving me a hand with this thing?"

"Sure." Mindful of his injury, they lifted the sign out of the back and slotted the post into the base. Mockler nodded to the picture of the woman on the sign. "That's a nice photo of you."

"Thanks. I just had it redone. My old headshot was looking dated." Cynthia took a step back, plodding through the snow in her expensive boots and took in the sign against the backdrop of the house. "There. That's just a start. It'll have your neighbours talking."

"Thanks for dropping it off," he said, regarding the sign with an uneasy eye.

"Nervous?"

"It's just weird," he said, "finally doing this."

"It's for the best," Cynthia said, climbing back into her vehicle. "A new chapter, detective. Ciao."

Mockler waved as she backed out of the driveway and then he turned back to the post planted in his snowy yard. A colourful realtor sign with a swinging shingle underneath that read: Home For Sale.

He still felt queasy about it, but tried his best to shrug it off. Going back up the porch steps, his phone rang. He smiled when he saw the caller display.

~

Billie was teetering on a wooden ladder, draping a wire over a nail, when she heard the door open. "Hi," she said.

"Whoa." Mockler dropped the heavy bag near the door and crossed the room, taking hold of the ladder to stop it from wobbling. "You should have someone hold the ladder when you do that."

"You're here now," Billie smiled, threading out the wire along the top of the wall. "Did you bring the tools?"

"Yup. What are you doing up there?"

"Putting up some lights. I wanted something festive." Billie descended the ladder, kissed him in greeting and then knelt down near the outlet in the baseboard. "Here goes."

She plugged in the cord and the run of faerie lights twinkled across the top of one wall and down another. Billie turned off the overhead light and the atmosphere changed instantly, the twinkle of lights bathing the apartment in a warm glow. "What do you think?"

"I like it," he said, nodding in approval. "Warms the place up.

Are you getting into the holiday spirit?"

"I just wanted something different. Plus, it hides the damage."

Mockler looked down to the patch of floor at which she was pointing. A black scorch mark was left on the floor from the flashbang grenade. "It won't wash off?"

"It's burnt into the wood."

With the overhead light off, the string of ambient lights masked the ugly blemish on the floor. "It does hide it." Mockler looked over the apartment. "Did you get the glass?"

"Near the window. I managed to get it home without breaking it."

"Let's get it fixed."

The broken window had been patched over with a length of plywood, cut to size and tacked into place to block the wind. Billie popped the overhead back on and Mockler fetched the bag he had brought. "Here," he said, handing her a package. "Knead this."

It looked like white clay in a sealed bag. "What is it?"

"The glaze. Work it until it's pliable." Mockler took the piece of glass that Billie had bought from the hardware store and unwrapped the craft paper from it. Getting his cordless drill from the bag, he withdrew the few screws holding the plywood patch in place. "We'll try to do this quickly, so that we don't let in too much cold air."

Wind blasted through the breach when the plywood came

away. The temperature had dropped to below zero and the wind carried a frosty sting to it. The replacement pane was fitted into place and Billie held it still while Mockler pushed in the steel tips to secure it. "These old-style windows aren't very efficient. The whole thing ought to be replaced."

"The landlord won't do that," Billie said. "If he replaces one, he's gotta do them all."

"We shouldn't even be fixing this," Mockler said, sliding in the last of the glazier's points. "Your landlord ought to take care of it."

"That would violate our unstated agreement."

He looked at her. "Which is?"

"I don't ask for anything and he doesn't raise the rent."

"I see—" Mockler winced as he straightened up, a hand shooting to his ribs.

"Does it still hurt?" she asked. "Maybe you're pushing it too much."

He waved it away. "It's fine. Cut open that package and we'll put the glaze on." Once she ripped the packaging away, he tore off a piece of the dun putty and worked it in his hands. "Smooth it into a tube, and then press into the corner."

She watched him apply the glaze along the vertical run and then scrape it smooth with a putty knife. With the material warm and pliable in her hands, she gave it a try on the opposite run. "Gantry's coming over," she said.

His hand slipped, smearing putty down the sash. "You talked

to him?"

"He called earlier and said he'd stop in. He wanted both of us here."

"That doesn't bode well," Mockler said. As usual, the Englishman had vanished when the smoke cleared. "I went back to that flat of his."

"Was he there?"

Mockler shook his head. "The whole place had been cleaned out. Needless to say, there was no forwarding address."

"Did you expect one?" said a new voice.

Billie snapped her eyes to the front door, as did Mockler. Neither of them should have been startled by John Gantry's habit of popping out of thin air, but both were.

"Do you have to do that?" Billie huffed. "You could knock first, like a normal person."

"What, and spoil the fun?" Gantry stood at the door with a paper bag in his hand and snow dusted on his shoulders. Scanning the apartment, he nodded in approval at the string of Christmas lights. "I like what you've done with the place. I expected worse after those arseholes firebombed it."

"It hides the mess," Billie said. "What's in the bag?"

"Champagne." Gantry pulled a bottle from the bag and took a closer look at the label on the bottle. "Or a close approximation thereof. I brought some lagers too, in case the bubbly is shite."

Mockler got to his feet, a slight sneer to his features. "Are we celebrating?"

"What's there to celebrate? I just felt like something festive, given the season and all."

"We'll toast to Owen's memory." Billie ushered her guest inside and took the bottle from him. "This is posh stuff. I wish I had flutes for it."

"Screw the flutes," Gantry said, perching on the arm of the sofa. "Bubbly is best served in a dirty glass."

Crossing into the kitchen, Billie said, "I have a trick to show you."

With the host gone, the tension ratcheted up between the two men left in the room. Detective Mockler studied the man he had spent almost two years tracking down. The Englishman seemed diluted somehow, a paler shade of his usual self. His guts balked at any compassion for the man, but he blurted out his question anyway. "You look a little green around the gills, Gantry."

"Being dead will do that to you."

The tension thickened as the silence crept across the room. Billie returned from the kitchen, dispelling the air of bad blood immediately. She held three mismatched glasses in one hand and a bizarrely large knife in the other. "Check this out," she said.

"What's with the machete?" Mockler asked, his eyes on the big blade.

"It's called sabering. My old boss showed me how to do this," she said, snatching up the champagne bottle. "He was French." Holding the bottle horizontally, Billie laid the flat of the blade against the neck and tested it against the lip. With one stroke, the top of the bottle fired across the room, cork and all, and champagne spumed from the broken neck. She filled the glasses and handed them around. "To Owen," she said, raising her glass. "Even though we failed him."

The toast was sombre. Mockler watched the bubbles trickle up in his glass. "At least we put down that thing."

"That's nothing to celebrate," Gantry warned.

Billie looked up at him. "Why not? We stopped it, didn't we?"

"But we didn't send it back to where it belongs." Gantry nodded at the newly repaired window and the cold night beyond the glass. "It's still out there."

Billie lowered her champagne. "It's still a threat?"

"Always," Gantry said. "But, it's gone for the time being."

Mockler went back to work on the window, finishing up the glaze. "Is that what you wanted to talk to us about?"

"No, that's my problem." Gantry settled into the armchair and stretched out his legs. "It's about your nasty little pet."

That snagged Billie's attention. "The boy?"

"Aye." Gantry looked over the apartment. "Is the little sod here?"

"He was here earlier," Billie replied. As usual, the Half-Boy had appeared at sundown, but remained oddly quiet the rest of the evening. Coiled up in a corner, he simply watched her string up the lights with an aloof air. He vanished when Mockler walked through the door. "What about him?"

Gantry sipped his drink. "I did a little digging. The lad had a sister."

The glass almost fell from Billie's hand. "How do you know that?" A slight rise prickled her nerves. Had the boy chosen to communicate with Gantry instead of her? How could that be? He hated the Englishman.

"Last time we tussled, I came away with this." Gantry held something small in his hand, pinched between a thumb and forefinger. "It remained solid when it came off him, which is odd."

"What is it?"

He handed it across and Billie turned it over, examining it. The button was nothing special. A worn brass disk, green with patina. She felt nothing handling it, no eerie sense of its owner. She wondered if he was having her on. "You found out that he has a sister from this?"

"Sometimes, it's the small clues that reveal the biggest secrets." Gantry got up from the chair and scanned the apartment again. "Do you have a mirror? A big one."

"In the bedroom," Billie said. "Why?"

Gantry smiled. "So we can conjure the sister."

"Hold on," Mockler interjected. "No more of that stuff. It almost killed all of us."

"Not your call, mate." The Englishman turned to Billie. "Do you want to find out who he is?"

Doubtful, Billie chewed her lip. "Can we really conjure his

sister?"

"We fished your old man out of the darkness, didn't we? Same thing." Gantry reached down to the clutter on the coffee table and swept the magazines, remote control and bottles of nail polish to the floor. "Fetch the mirror, yeah? I need a bowl of water, too. A metal one."

The detective frowned at the mess swept from the table, but Billie raced to the bedroom without another word. He looked at Gantry. "The last time you pulled this trick, it went ka-blooey."

"It's not a science, Mockler. Things go tits-up all the time." Retrieving the paper bag he'd brought, Gantry placed five thick candles on the coffee table and snapped open his lighter. "Get the lights."

The overhead light was extinguished and the twinkle from the Christmas bulbs warmed the room with a cheery gaiety that ran counter to the proposed task. The metal bowl, filled with water, was placed carefully in the centre of the five lit candles. Billie had hesitated over using her good metal mixing bowl, the one she used for baking. She doubted it would be safe for mixing cookie dough once Gantry got through with it. She shrugged. A small sacrifice.

"Where does this go?" Mockler asked, holding the framed mirror. Another flea market find of Billie's.

Gantry took the wooden chair from Billie's makeshift work table and squared it on the opposite side of the coffee table. He stood the mirror on it, angling it so it reflected the empty sofa.

"That's the best we can do. If we all squeeze onto the sofa, we should be able to see her. Have a seat."

Billie and Mockler settled onto the sofa. Gantry stepped in, waving the detective aside. "Scooch over."

"I don't want to sit next to you."

"I need to be in the middle, mate. Scooch."

Squeezing between them, Gantry produced a pearl-handled pocketknife and opened the blade.

"What's that for?" Billie asked.

"Everything requires a small offering. Blood works best." Hovering over the bowl, he carved the blade into the heel of his hand until it ran red. The blood fell into the water and diffused like coils of red smoke. "Do you have the button?"

She held it out to him. "Here."

"You have to hang onto it. When I say so, drop it in."

The expatriate mumbled something under his breath and Mockler exchanged a quick glance with Billie. The look of annoyance never left the detective's face.

"Drop it in, Billie."

The relic made a tiny bloop sound as it hit the water. Billie kept her eyes glued to it, not wanting to miss what might happen next. Gantry fished out a cigarette and sparked his lighter.

"Do you have to smoke now?" Mockler grumbled, his annoyance deepening.

"Part of the ritual, mate."

"Bullshit."

"Shh," Billie said. "It just got colder in here."

The candles guttered south, as if buffeted by a northernly breeze.

"Watch the mirror," Gantry said.

She was small. Billie pegged her age at 11 or 12 years. The girl appeared hazy in the mirror, standing in the darkness behind them. Her dark frock was coarse-looking, the lace trim at the neck frayed and grimy. Billie studied the girl's gaunt face for any family resemblance to the boy, but she found none. The hands poking out from their threadbare sleeves were spiky thin, her features wan and malnourished. Whatever kind of life she had lived, it had not been prosperous.

"You're the sister, yeah?" Gantry said.

Billie gripped his wrist to silence him. His tone was too gruff and the girl in the mirror was already taking a step back. Oftentimes, the dead were wary or frightened, needing to be coaxed forward with gentle words like shy ponies. "Don't go," she said in a quiet tone. "Please. We're happy you came."

The girl in the mirror stopped. Studying the girl's drab garments, Billie noted that the only speck of colour on her was a shabby ribbon tied in her hair. Red, like the one found in the Half-Boy's pockets. The girl returned Billie's stare, her lips pursed in silence. A horrid thought came to Billie as she witnessed the mute ghost. Had the sister had her tongue cut out like her sibling? "I wanted to ask you about your brother," Billie ventured. "I'm worried about him."

The girl loomed closer, her head tilted to one side as if to hear better.

Emboldened, Billie went out on a limb. "What's your name?"

"Katie," the girl whispered, her voice as thin as her wrists. "Katie Cleary. What's yours?"

"Sybil," Billie answered, uncharacteristically offering her given name. She had never liked it, but it seemed appropriate now if she wanted the ghostly sister to be open with her.

"That's a pretty name," the girl named Katie said. "It's not Irish, is it?"

"I don't think so. You're Irish?"

The girl glanced at the two men beside Billie. "I was born there. We came across when I was wee. The year of our Lord 1896, or so me mum said."

Billie crossed her fingers before launching the next question. "Was your brother born there, too?"

"Which brother?" the girl queried. "Blaine and Michael were born in Cork. Thomas, Arden and Cillian came after the crossing. They were born here, in this city."

"The brother who's here," Billie said. One of the names uttered by the girl had flared hot in her mind but she kept quiet, needing to be sure. "The one with me."

"Tom," she said. Her gaze dropped to the floor. "Poor Tom, as we called him."

Tom.

Billie closed her eyes as a warm flush of relief flooded her nerves. Poor Tom Cleary. Of course, it was Tom. "Why do you call him that, Poor Tom?"

"There was always something odd about Thomas. Even as a wee bairn he was odd, born too soon and sickly. It sent father into a rage sometimes. Our Tom would get these falling spells, you see. He'd freeze up, stiff as a board and stare at nothing for a time. You couldn't get him to crack out of it. Then, he'd collapse to the floor. It was frightening. Father said he was nipped by the devil with those spells, but mother never believed that. Not that she'd dare speak against the man."

Billie chanced a glance at Mockler. The detective looked uneasy, clearly not comfortable speaking to a ghost in a mirror. She regarded the girl again. "Did you live here, in this building?"

"I wish we had," replied the girl, looking around. "It's grand compared to the filthy shack we lived in. It wasn't far from here, in Corktown. Sometimes, it would flood when the spring thaw came trickling down the mountain."

"Were you the oldest among the kids?" Billie asked.

"Second eldest. Blaine was firstborn. Thomas was seventh. I tried to protect him from father when I could."

Mockler spoke up. "Why did you have to protect him?"

The girl named Katie flinched at the timbre of a male voice and took a step back. Her eyes cast to the floor, refusing to look at the detective.

"Katie," Billie said, addressing the girl in a gentle tone. "This is Ray and this is John. They're friends. They won't hurt you."

"Yes, ma'am."

The girl dipped by way of a small curtsy, but averted her eyes from the men present in the room. Billie studied the girl anew, wondering what her life had been like, one where any man was treated with deference and fear. "Katie, why did you have to protect Tom from your father?"

"It was the spells. They enraged our father. He tried to beat it out of Tom, but that didn't stop the spells from happening." Katie's hands clenched together and she tucked them under her chin as if in prayer. "And there were the queer things that Tom would say when he was in his spells. They frightened father. They frightened us all, to tell the truth."

"What things?"

"That someone would die. Or another's house would burn to the ground. A bad fortune befalling another. These things came true a day or two after the spells." The girl rubbed her hands together as if cold. "The neighbours were frightened of him then, too. They said he was in league with the devil. Some of them believed that he caused these misfortunes to happen. When they started to shun the family out of fear, father tried to beat the falling sickness out of Tom. Mother took him to the church and begged the priest to drive the wickedness out of him. It didn't work."

A shudder rippled down Billie's spine. Like herself, the boy had a gift, one that frightened his parents and everyone around him. Was that the connection that drew the Half-Boy to her?

Tom, she reminded herself. His name was Tom. Poor Tom. She looked at the sister again. "Katie, did your father kill Tom?"

"No. He came close, mind you, with the flogging he would lay on him, specially after I was gone. But no, father didn't kill Tom."

"After you were gone?" Billie asked. "After you passed on?"

The girl nodded her head. "I had the fever. I died on Saint Anne's day. After that, there was no one to shield Tom from our father. When he was in his cups, he would blame Tom for all of his bad fortune, claiming that the boy had cursed the family. It was heartbreaking. All I could do was watch."

"You watched over him?" Billie said. "After you were gone."

"I wanted to help Tom, but he couldn't see me. No one could." The girl's eyes rose to meet Billie's. "You're like Tom, aren't you? You see things."

"Yes." Holding the gaze of the little girl, Billie smiled warmly, but the smile wasn't returned. The grim angle of the girl's mouth hinted at a face that had never smiled. "Katie, can Tom see you now. Now that you're both passed?"

"He can't. Or he won't, I don't know which. His shame is too great to see me. I wish that he could. He's been alone for so long."

Something snapped deep in Billie's chest. She pictured the boy, legless, filthy and alone all this time. "What happened to him? You said your father didn't kill him."

"He came close one night. He took Tom to the saloon,

thinking the boy could foretell the turn of the cards. It didn't work that way and Thomas was bedridden for days after the flogging father laid on him. He sold Tom a fortnight later."

Billie startled, thinking she had misheard the girl. Gantry and Mockler did the same. "Sold?"

"To a man named Crump. A charlatan. He was a wicked man."

"How?" It was all Billie could say, trying to comprehend the idea. It was unthinkable.

"Archibald Crump was a clairvoyant in the area. A magician and a seer. He performed magic shows at the Palladium and held séances at a tearoom on Victoria. He had heard of Tom's spells and came round enquiring about him. He told father that if the boy's talents were real, he'd consider employing the boy. Instead, Father sold Tom to the clairvoyant and mother never saw him again. Not alive anyway." Katie plucked a stained handkerchief from her sleeve and wiped her nose. "Tom didn't cry when he was taken away. I think that he felt he deserved his treatment, that he truly was the cause of the family's misfortune and that, without him, they would finally prosper."

"Did they prosper?" Mockler asked, unable to bite his tongue.

Katie lowered her eyes again, as if scolded. "No, sir."

Again, Billie speculated on the kind of life that the girl had had. She was as frightened and skittish as a bird, even in the realm where no man could hurt her. Billie softened her tone even more. "So, Crump used Tom in his act?"

"When he wasn't working Tom like a slave, which I guess was what he was, having been sold and whatnot. Crump knew how to exploit Tom's talent for his paying clients. He sat there at the table between the clairvoyant and the person who wanted to know their future, but Tom's divinations were not what these people wanted to hear. He would tell these rich men and their stuffy wives when they were going to die. The day and the manner. He told one gentleman that his house would burn down the next day, and how it would take his entire family with it. A lady from Aberdeen wanted to know if she should marry the man who was courting her. Tom told her that her suitor would soon be driven mad with syphilis and she would follow suit soon thereafter. All of Tom's divinations came true and, like before, people began to fear him, claiming that he was causing the misfortunes to occur. They said he was bewitched."

"Crump beat poor Tom, much the way father had, demanding that he foretell only happy events and not tragedies. Tom said he could only see the tragic moments in someone's life, never the joyous ones. Then, he told Archibald Crump that he would die at the hands of an angry mob, his head split open on the cobblestones under their boots."

Billie felt Gantry stir beside her, but she nudged him to stay quiet. "Go on, Katie. Did Crump hurt Tom for saying that?"

"He took a knife and cut out Tom's tongue. My brother never spoke again. It only got worse after that. He stopped using Tom in his act, keeping him out of sight, but working him like a dog.

When he was mad with the drink, he would attack Tom and take him." Here, the girl lowered her head again and made the sign of the cross.

"What do you mean 'take him,' Katie?"

"Like the men of Sodom in the Bible. The ones who surrounded Lot's house and demanded he give up his angels to them. Like a man takes his wife. Tom cried out to me then, that first time, trying to call out my name with his ruined tongue, although I'd been dead for two years. I could do nothing."

Another thread snapped in Billie's heart and her belly churned in equal measure with rage and horror. She had wondered for so long who this little ghost was and, now, she almost regretted learning the truth. She didn't know if she could bear to hear anymore.

Katie Cleary went on. "Tom tried to escape. The city was in turmoil, men gathering in the streets, hurling stones at the constables. Crump had rushed out to see the chaos, leaving the door unlocked. Tom slipped out, but he was seen by a neighbour, who caught him up and returned him to that horrid man. Crump went into a rage at his running away. He took an axe and cut both of Tom's legs off. Then, he threw him into the root cellar and Tom died there three hours later, alone as always.

"I stayed with him the whole time, watching him turn grey as he bled out over the earthen floor. I was almost glad that his suffering was over. At least now, he would see me and we could be together, but it was not to be. Tom slipped free from his body and looked down at his wretched remains, but when he saw me kneeling there beside him, holding his dead hand, he burst into tears and ran. On his hands, the way he does now. He hid, never letting me get close, and he's been alone all this time." Katie looked up at Billie. "Until now. Until he found you. I don't know what you did, Sybil, but he came to you. He let you get near him. Bless you for that."

Billie wiped the tear crawling hot down her cheek, but her voice was too constricted to form words. Mockler spoke, his tone as gentle as he could manage. "Katie, how did Tom end up in the harbour?"

"Crump tried to cover up his sin. The next night, the rioting was even worse. He took Tom's body to the pier as the streets burned and tossed it in. It was found the next morning and someone in the crowd recognized Tom as the boy from the séances. The people in the streets were still worked up from fighting the police and a crowd of men stormed Archibald's house, dragging him out into the street. They stomped his head into gristle against the pavement, just as Tom had foretold.

"News of it carried to mother and father. They feared their own crime would be found out, so they fled Hamilton. They packed up that day and left when the sun went down, moving to a small village about a day's ride out. They changed their name and started a new life. After that, there were no Clearys here. And no family for Tom to turn to."

Billie buried her face in her hands and Mockler shifted

uncomfortably, even Gantry was clenching his jaw to keep his eyes dry. No one spoke and the candles burned on.

Katie turned to the window, the one newly repaired with a clean plate of glass. "He's coming. I have to go."

"Wait," Billie said. "Stay. Maybe he'll come to you this time. You could help him."

"I wish it was so, but he won't. If he sees me here, he may not come back to you, Sybil. Watch over him. He needs you now."

"Please." Billie shot to her feet and turned to face the little girl, but Katie Cleary was gone.

Gantry blew out the candles and launched off of the sofa. "I need a fucking drink after that story. Christ."

The window sash rattled in its frame and the boy slipped into the room. He looked up in surprise to see the men in the apartment. His mouth soured in disappointment and, then, he hobbled across the floor and leaped onto the work table. He crouched there like a cat, watching them.

"I'm glad you're back," Billie said to him. "Tom."

The boy flinched at hearing his name. He looked at Billie and then turned slowly to the two men watching him. He dropped from the table and hobbled back to the window to leave.

"Wait," she said. She knelt down and touched his cold hand. "Don't go. Stay with me. I want you to get to know my friends."

The boy wavered, looking askance at the two men as if they weren't to be trusted. Billie felt him pull away, but she held on.

"You're safe here. I promise."

He stayed, huddled next to Billie on the floor, but the glint of suspicion never left his eyes.

"I forgot to ask her something," she said.

"What's that?" asked Mockler.

"What name the family took after they left the city."

"Does it matter?"

Billie shrugged. "I'm just curious."

Smoke billowed under the Christmas lights. Gantry crossed the room and lifted something from the floor. "She wrote it down."

"What do you mean?"

Gantry waved the small chalkboard in his hand. A child's slate that Billie had brought home in hopes of teaching the boy how to read. Gantry shook his head at the scrawl of letters scratched onto the slate. "She wrote the name they adopted here."

"What is it?" Billie said, rising up from the floor.

"I'm not sure you want to know, Billie."

"Of course I do. Let me see it."

Mockler watched the two of them, wondering why the Brit was being so cagey. Gantry handed the slate to Billie and Billie became still. A blank look settled over her face and she sank slowly onto the sofa. The chalkboard clattered to the floor.

"What is it?" Mockler said. "What's the name?" He fetched up the slate from where it had fallen and read the name written there. His face fell and then he wiped his hand over the slate, erasing it.

With the gypsy girl overwhelmed and the men blind to him, poor Tom Cleary hobbled to the newly mended window and slipped out into the cold December night.

AFTERWORD

WELCOME BACK. IF you've made it this far with the series, I just wanted to say thank you for coming along for the ride. Book Five. Wow. I've never gone this far in a series before. The response to the Spookshow has been more than I could have hoped for and I've met some truly amazing people because of it. I'm looking forward to writing more of these stories in the coming year.

In the Afterword to the first book, I wrote briefly about my own, small experience with the paranormal and asked readers for their stories. Lots of people were kind enough to share their stories and their responses blew me away. Some of these experiences are similar to mine, small occurrences that could be coincidental, but others have been truly eye-opening. A few have been downright frightening. All of them fascinate me and I remain grateful for their openness in sharing them with me.

I have a small rider to my own tale. This past summer, my wife and I attended a wedding of a cousin on my Dad's side of the family. It was a beautiful event for a lovely, charming couple. I don't see much of my Dad's side of the family anymore and I'd almost forgotten what it was like to be back among the McGregor clan. Scotch-Irish and strong Catholics through and through. It was customary for at least one member of each generation to join the clergy. A quick gander at the old photo albums turns up a lot of priests and nuns and at least one Mother Superior. As a kid, I was constantly given rosaries, bibles and prayer beads and I feared that I was being groomed for the seminary, but that wasn't the case. As the eldest male with the family name in my generation, I was meant to be the keeper of the faith. That didn't turn out as expected, lapsed Catholic that I am. However, with the books, I discovered that I may be the keeper of a different kind of faith.

Throughout my Dad's family, there's always been a fair amount of eccentricity and endearing oddity. Certain patterns seem to recur, such as a keen interest in psychology, an abiding faith in the Roman Church, and a love for creepy stories. A lot of that history has crept into the Spookshow books, some of it consciously, some of it not.

Back to the wedding. I caught up with my cousin S__, the mother of the groom. S__, whom I've always adored and looked up to since I was a kid, shared some family business that left me reeling. "We're all psychic," she declared. According to S__, everyone in the family has some kind of sensitivity, great or small, and that is the reason behind many of the eccentricities in the family tree. Needless to say, I was floored. To be honest, I still don't know what to make of that claim but it does go a fair ways in how I always felt that the clan was different somehow. Here, I thought they were all just crazy. I need to explore that more and dig into the family history, but, to be honest, I'm also a little leery of doing so, wondering what types of skeletons will come tumbling out if I go scrabbling into closed closets. Do I believe it? I'm still unsure. What my cousin told me makes a lot of sense on an intuitive level, but, perhaps, that's because I simply want it to make sense. Like Agent Mulder in the *X-Files*, I want to believe. Now, step back while I fling open the closet door.

Happy holidays

Toronto
December 2015

Tim McGregor is an author and screenwriter. He lives in Toronto with his wife and children. Some days he believes in ghosts, other days not so much. Find out more at timmcgregorauthor.com

Natalia Deprina is an artist and photographer currently residing in Lipetsk, Russia. Her photograph, *Portrait of Doom*, graces the cover of this book. To see more of her work, search for Natalia Deprina on Deviantart.com

A special thank you to **Emily Heinlen** for her help editing this book. You can find Emily at emilyheinlen.com

34934107R00221

Made in the USA
San Bernardino, CA
10 June 2016